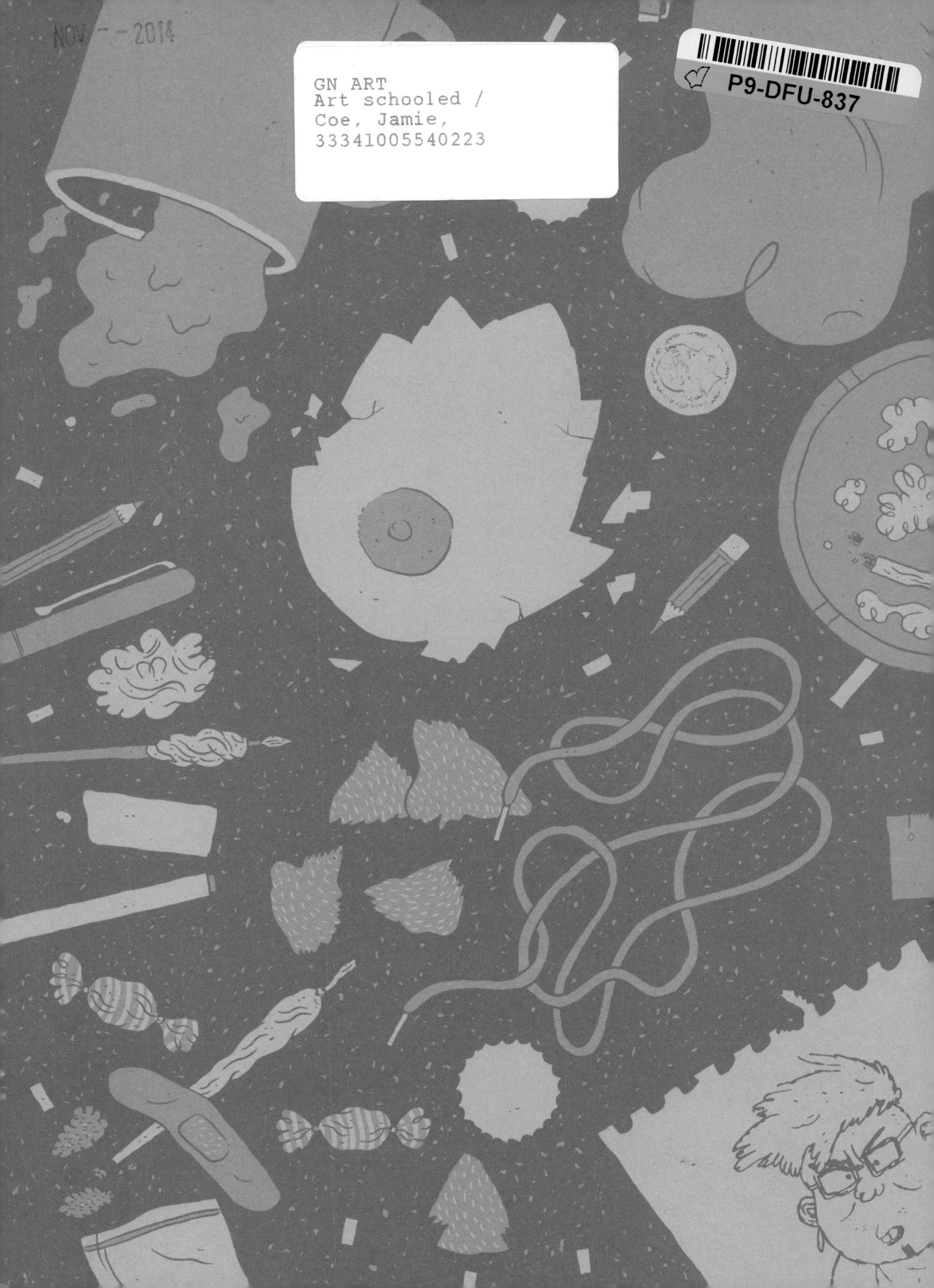

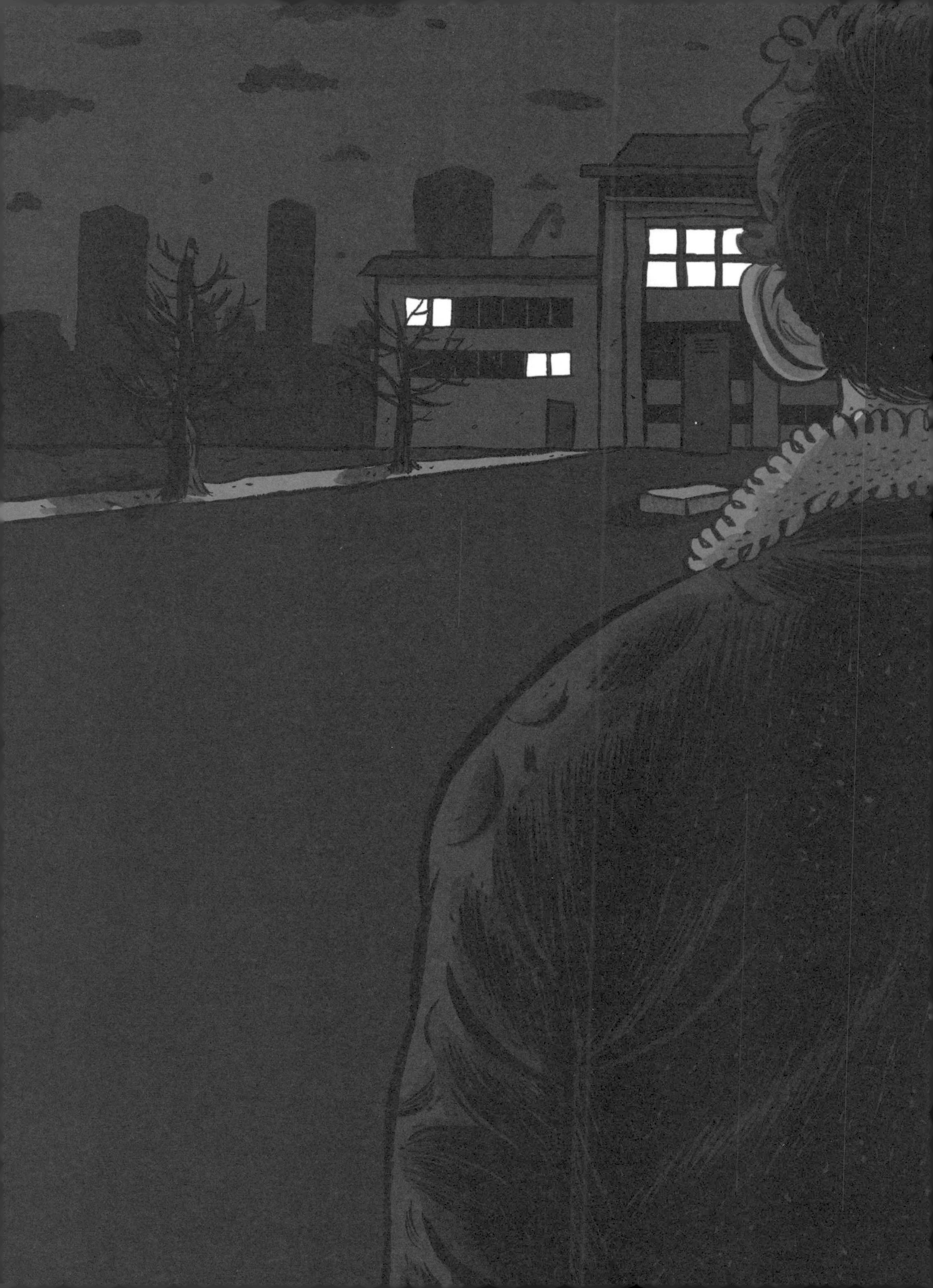

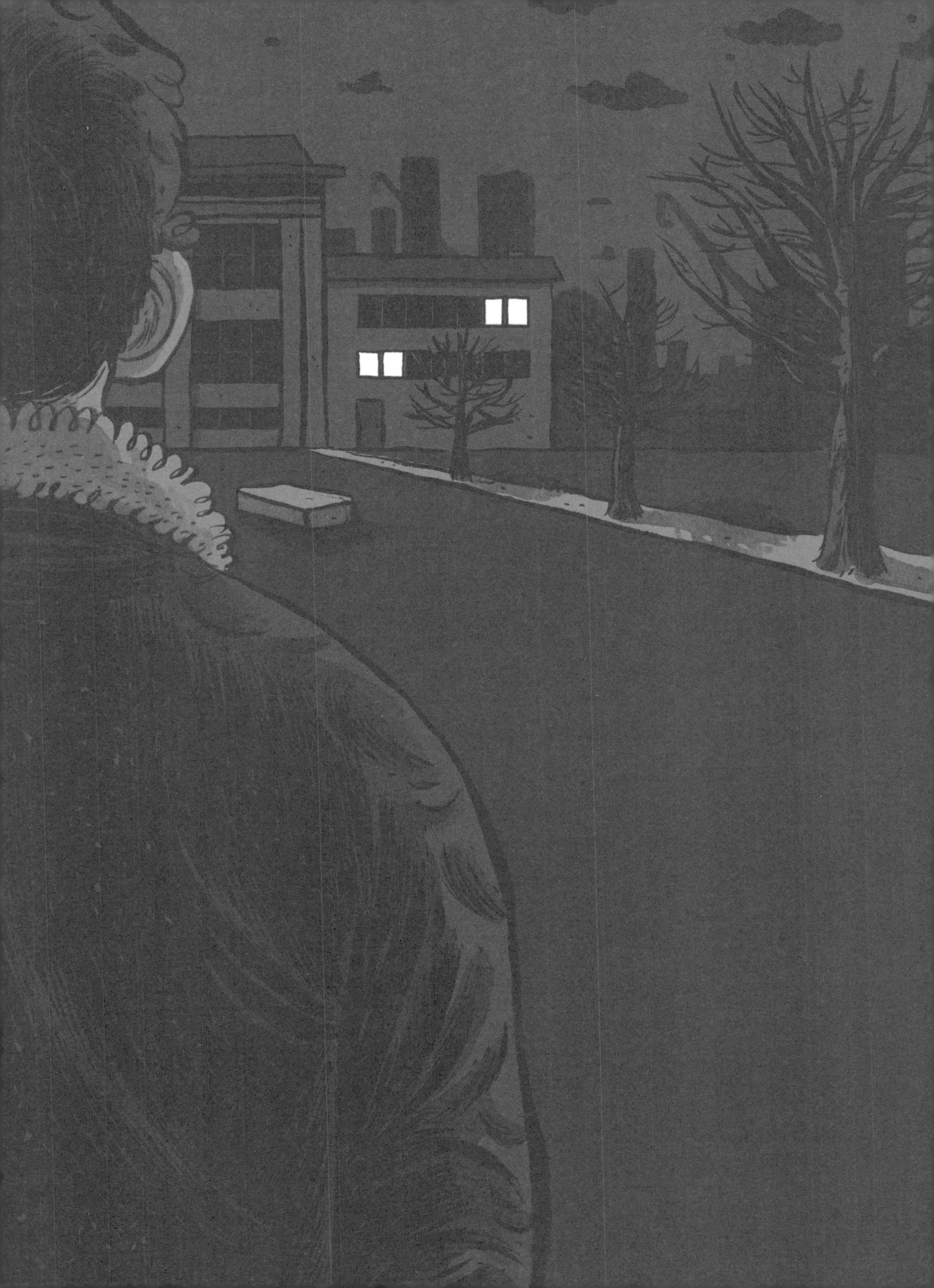

TO MY MUM AND DAD, NATALIA, YAYA AND POPS.

Art Schooled is © Nobrow 2014.

This is a first edition printed in 2014 by Nobrow Ltd. 62 Great Eastern Street, London, EC2A 3QR.

Text and illustrations © Jamie Coe 2014.
Jamie Coe has asserted his right under the Copyright, Designs and Patents Act, 1988, to be identified as the Author of this Work.

Edited by Alex Spiro.

Published in the US by Nobrow (US) Inc.

Printed in Poland on FSC assured paper.
ISBN: 978-1-907704-82-6

Order from www.nobrow.net

ART SCHOOLED

JAMIE COE

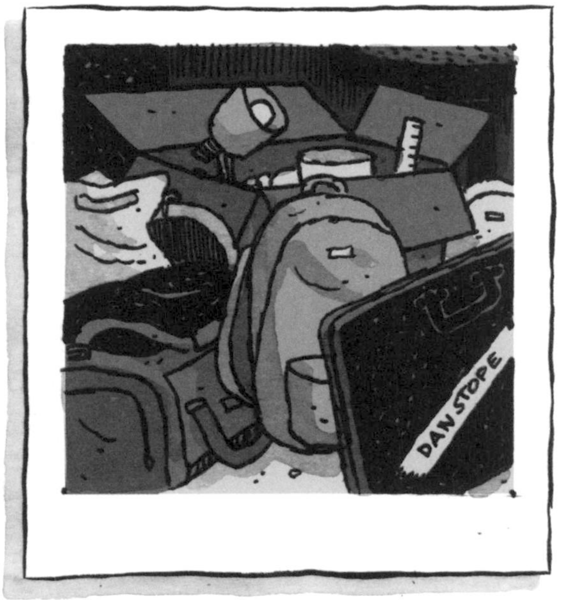
DAN STOPE

NOBROW PRESS

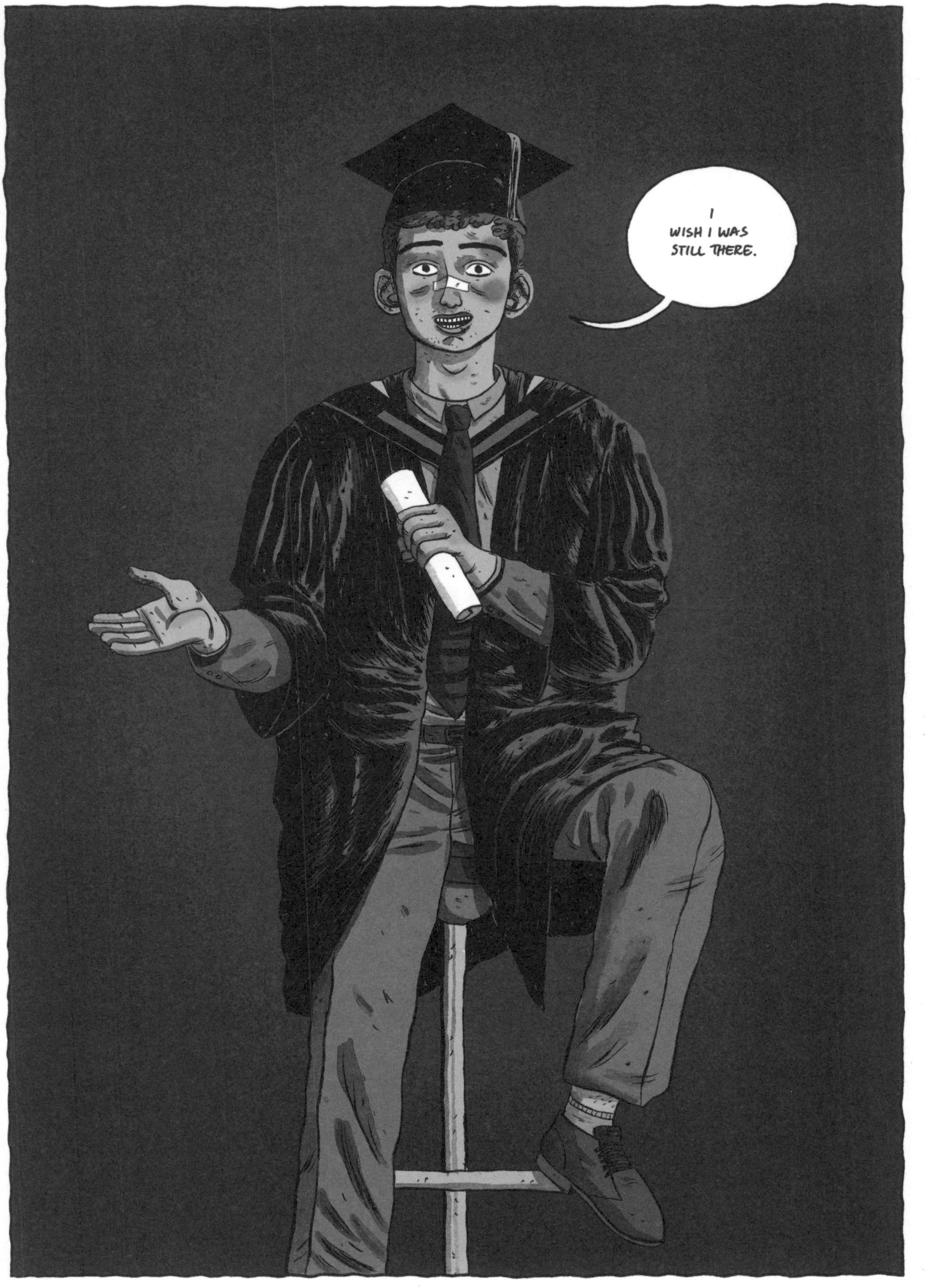
I WISH I WAS STILL THERE.

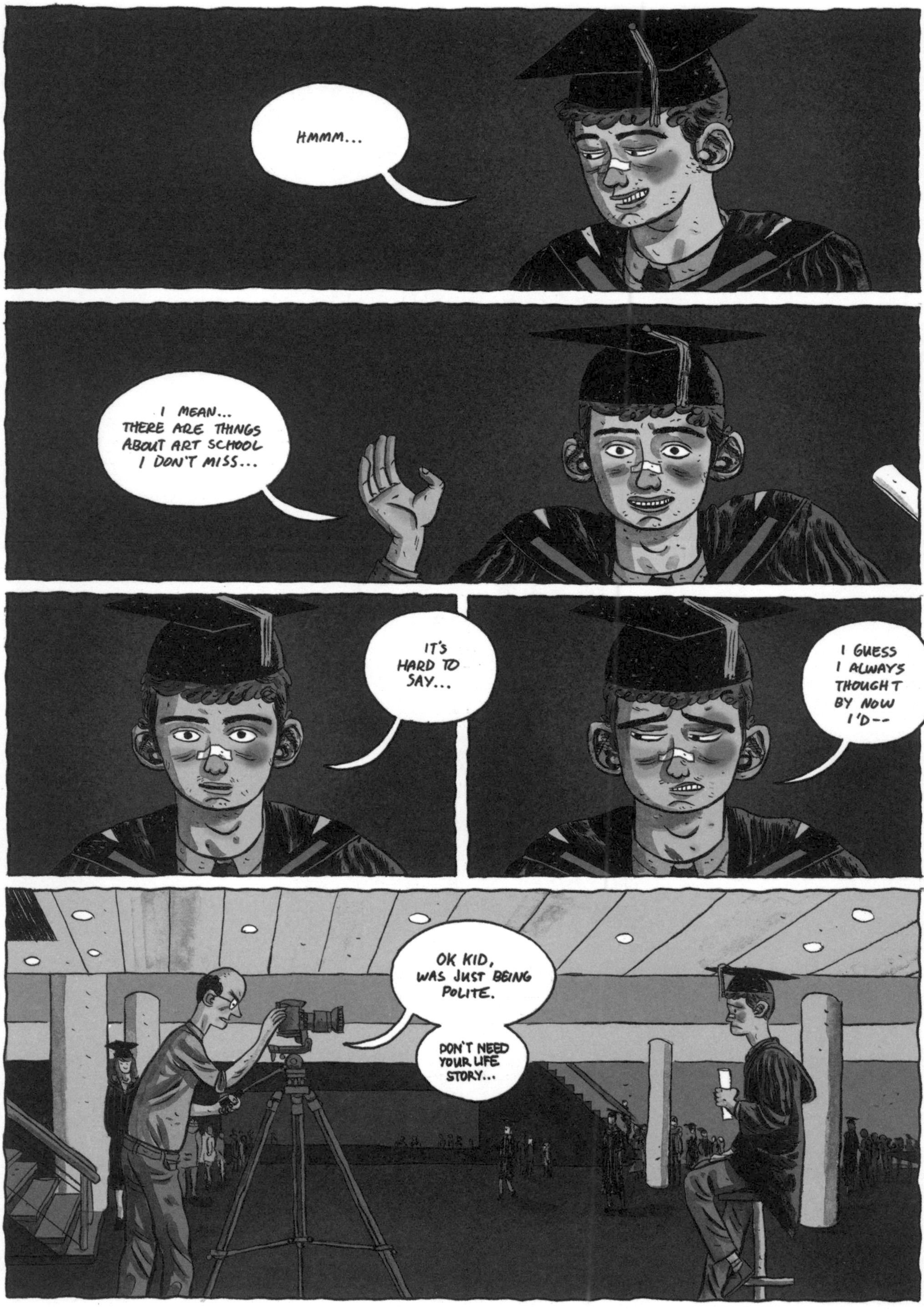
HMMM...
I MEAN... THERE ARE THINGS ABOUT ART SCHOOL I DON'T MISS...
IT'S HARD TO SAY...
I GUESS I ALWAYS THOUGHT BY NOW I'D--
OK KID, WAS JUST BEING POLITE.
DON'T NEED YOUR LIFE STORY...

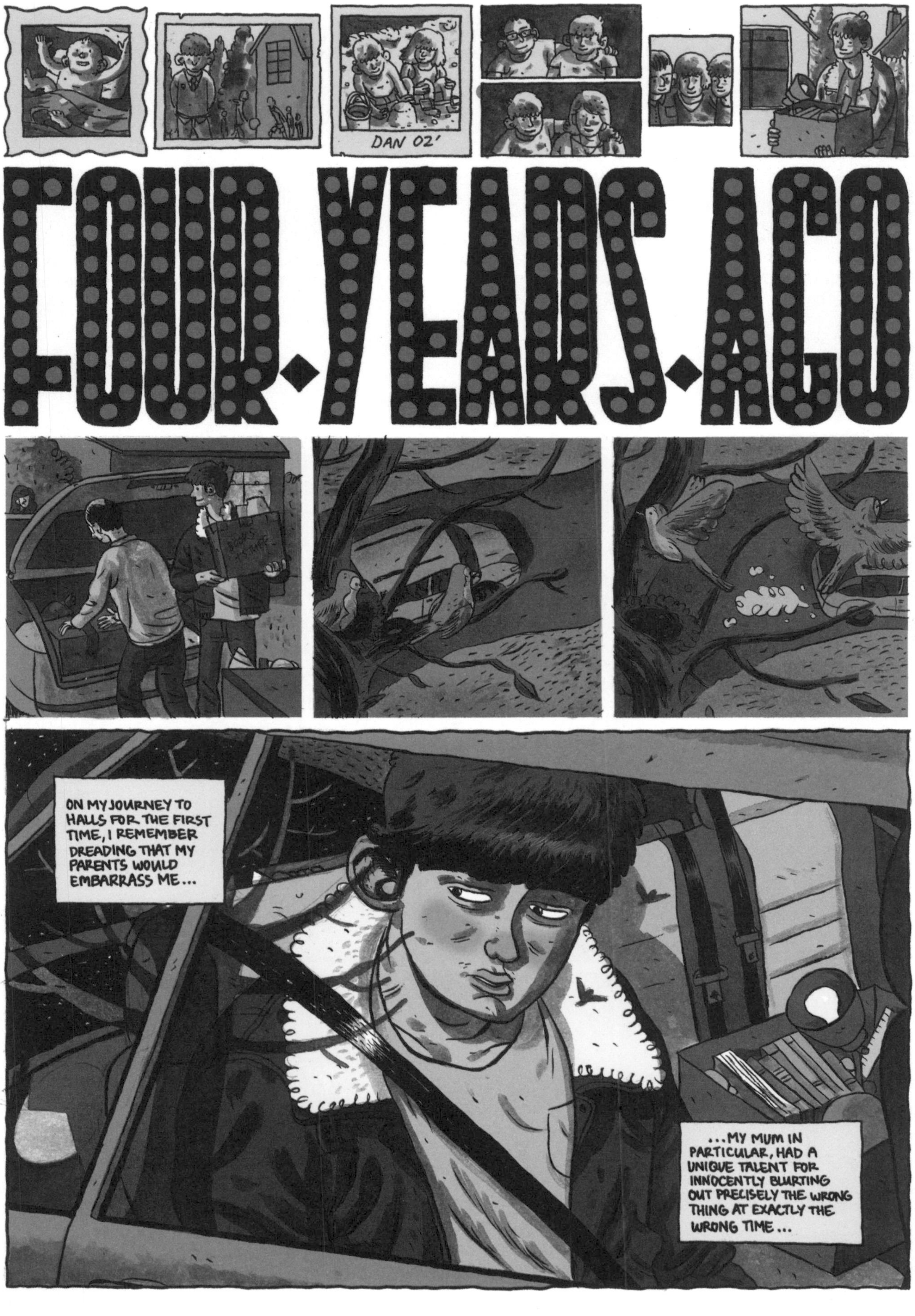
DAN 02'
FOUR·YEARS·AGO
ON MY JOURNEY TO HALLS FOR THE FIRST TIME, I REMEMBER DREADING THAT MY PARENTS WOULD EMBARRASS ME...
...MY MUM IN PARTICULAR, HAD A UNIQUE TALENT FOR INNOCENTLY BLURTING OUT PRECISELY THE WRONG THING AT EXACTLY THE WRONG TIME...

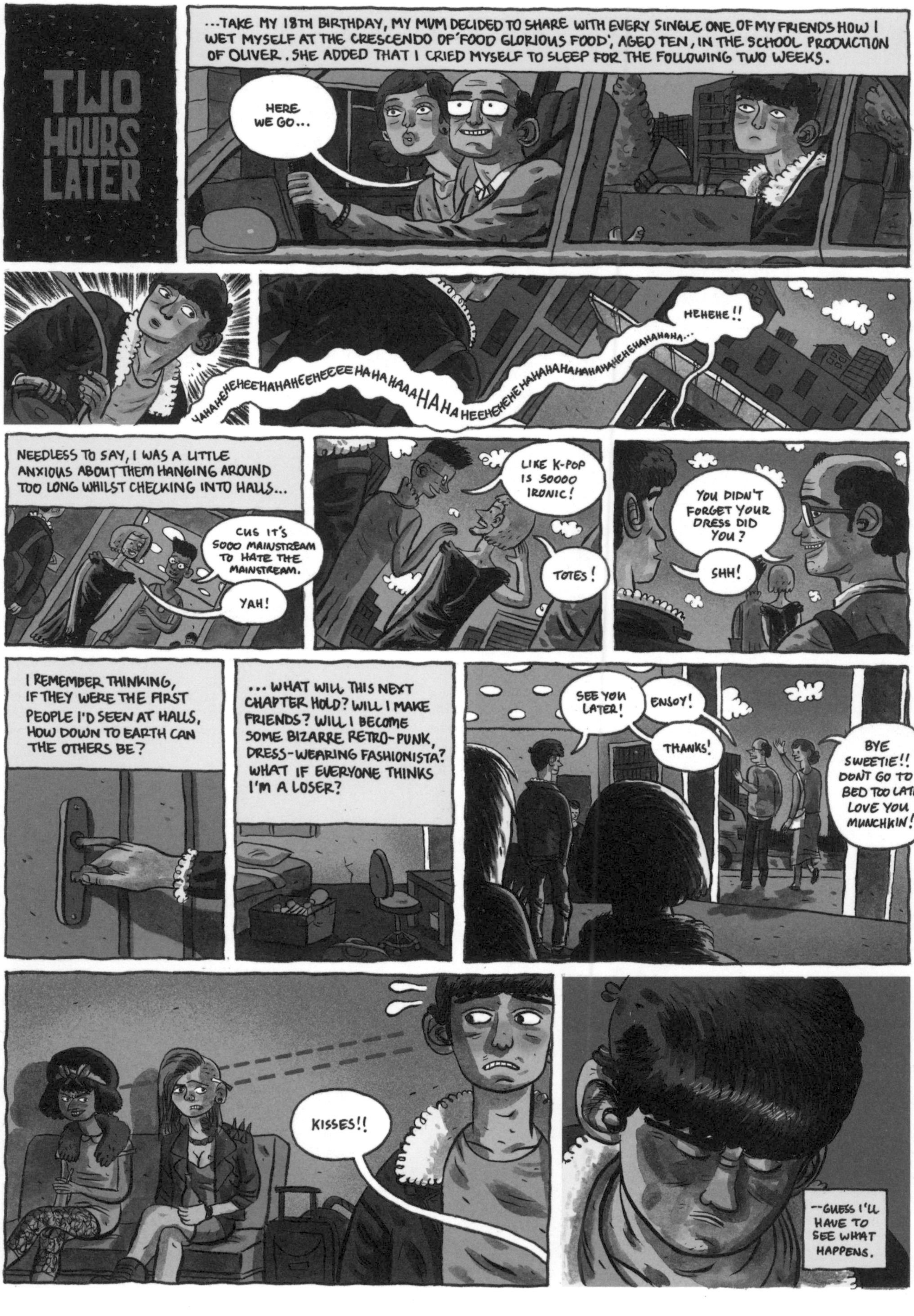
TWO HOURS LATER
...TAKE MY 18TH BIRTHDAY, MY MUM DECIDED TO SHARE WITH EVERY SINGLE ONE OF MY FRIENDS HOW I WET MYSELF AT THE CRESCENDO OF 'FOOD GLORIOUS FOOD', AGED TEN, IN THE SCHOOL PRODUCTION OF OLIVER. SHE ADDED THAT I CRIED MYSELF TO SLEEP FOR THE FOLLOWING TWO WEEKS.
HERE WE GO...
HEHEHE!!
HAHAHEHEHEEHAHAHAHEEHEEEEHAHAHAAAHAHAHEEHEHEHEHAHAHAHAHAHAHAHEHEHAHAHAHA...
NEEDLESS TO SAY, I WAS A LITTLE ANXIOUS ABOUT THEM HANGING AROUND TOO LONG WHILST CHECKING INTO HALLS...
CUS IT'S SOOO MAINSTREAM TO HATE THE MAINSTREAM.
YAH!
LIKE K-POP IS SOOOO IRONIC!
TOTES!
YOU DIDN'T FORGET YOUR DRESS DID YOU?
SHH!
I REMEMBER THINKING, IF THEY WERE THE FIRST PEOPLE I'D SEEN AT HALLS, HOW DOWN TO EARTH CAN THE OTHERS BE?
... WHAT WILL THIS NEXT CHAPTER HOLD? WILL I MAKE FRIENDS? WILL I BECOME SOME BIZARRE RETRO-PUNK, DRESS-WEARING FASHIONISTA? WHAT IF EVERYONE THINKS I'M A LOSER?
SEE YOU LATER!
ENJOY!
THANKS!
BYE SWEETIE!! DONT GO TO BED TOO LATE! LOVE YOU MUNCHKIN!
KISSES!!
--GUESS I'LL HAVE TO SEE WHAT HAPPENS.

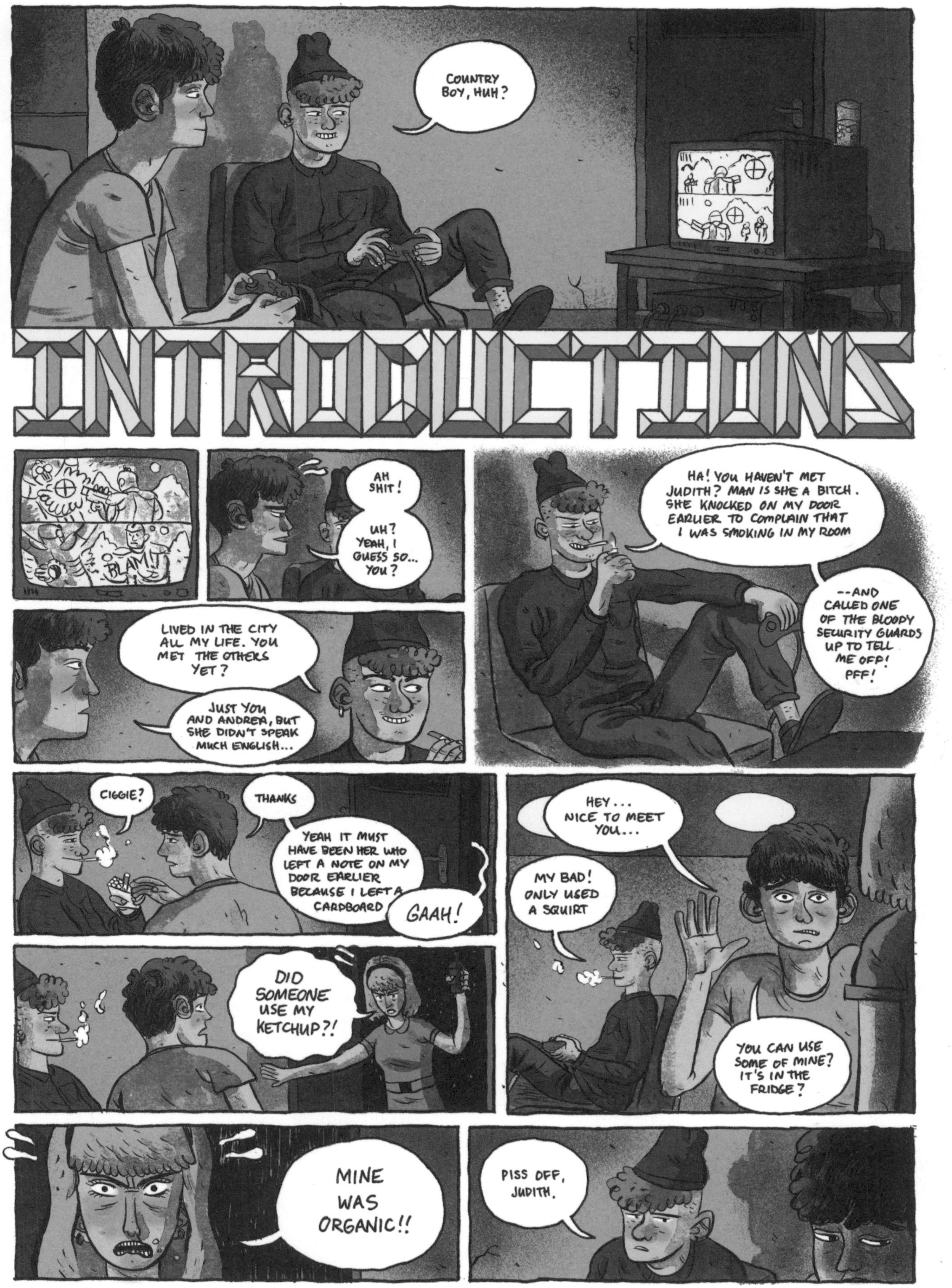
COUNTRY BOY, HUH?
INTRODUCTIONS
BLAM!!
AH SHIT!
UH? YEAH, I GUESS SO... YOU?
LIVED IN THE CITY ALL MY LIFE. YOU MET THE OTHERS YET?
JUST YOU AND ANDREA, BUT SHE DIDN'T SPEAK MUCH ENGLISH...
HA! YOU HAVEN'T MET JUDITH? MAN IS SHE A BITCH. SHE KNOCKED ON MY DOOR EARLIER TO COMPLAIN THAT I WAS SMOKING IN MY ROOM
--AND CALLED ONE OF THE BLOODY SECURITY GUARDS UP TO TELL ME OFF! PFF!
CIGGIE?
THANKS
YEAH IT MUST HAVE BEEN HER WHO LEFT A NOTE ON MY DOOR EARLIER BECAUSE I LEFT A CARDBOARD
GAAH!
DID SOMEONE USE MY KETCHUP?!
HEY... NICE TO MEET YOU...
MY BAD! ONLY USED A SQUIRT
YOU CAN USE SOME OF MINE? IT'S IN THE FRIDGE?
MINE WAS ORGANIC!!
PISS OFF, JUDITH.

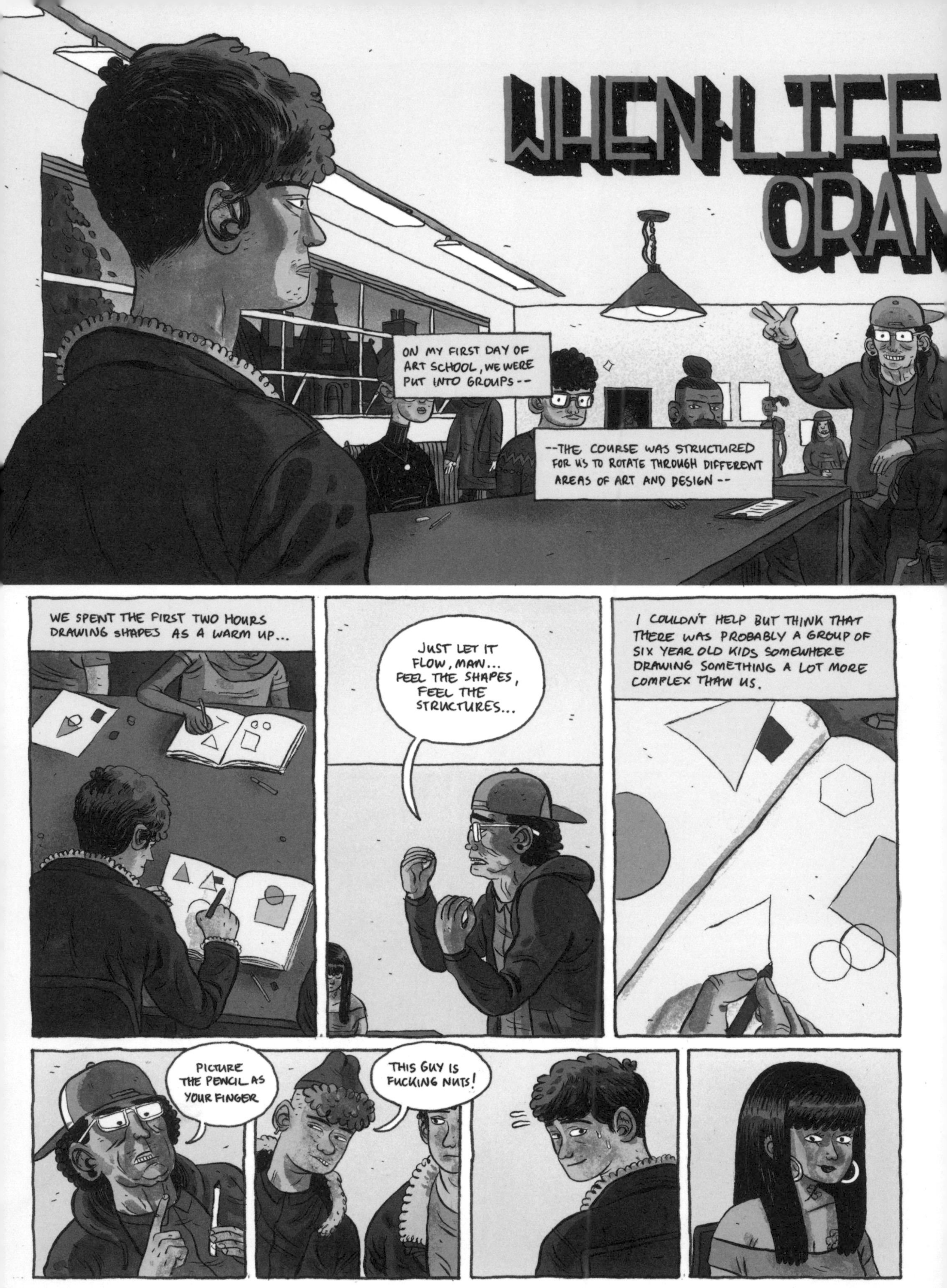
WHEN LIFE
ORAN
ON MY FIRST DAY OF ART SCHOOL, WE WERE PUT INTO GROUPS --
--THE COURSE WAS STRUCTURED FOR US TO ROTATE THROUGH DIFFERENT AREAS OF ART AND DESIGN --
WE SPENT THE FIRST TWO HOURS DRAWING SHAPES AS A WARM UP...
JUST LET IT FLOW, MAN... FEEL THE SHAPES, FEEL THE STRUCTURES...
I COULDN'T HELP BUT THINK THAT THERE WAS PROBABLY A GROUP OF SIX YEAR OLD KIDS SOMEWHERE DRAWING SOMETHING A LOT MORE COMPLEX THAN US.
PICTURE THE PENCIL AS YOUR FINGER
THIS GUY IS FUCKING NUTS!

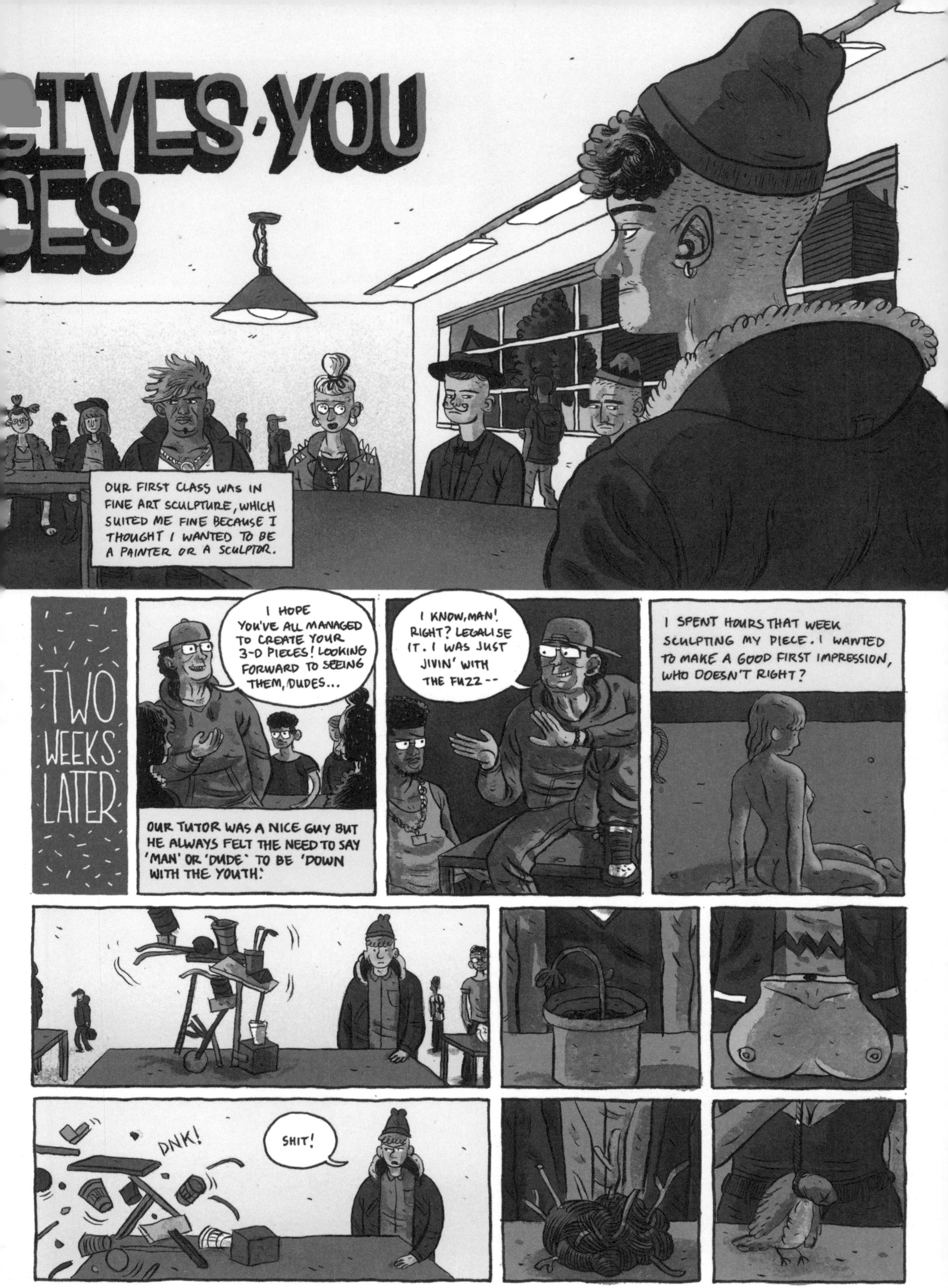
GIVES YOU
CES
OUR FIRST CLASS WAS IN FINE ART SCULPTURE, WHICH SUITED ME FINE BECAUSE I THOUGHT I WANTED TO BE A PAINTER OR A SCULPTOR.
TWO WEEKS LATER
I HOPE YOU'VE ALL MANAGED TO CREATE YOUR 3-D PIECES! LOOKING FORWARD TO SEEING THEM, DUDES...
OUR TUTOR WAS A NICE GUY BUT HE ALWAYS FELT THE NEED TO SAY 'MAN' OR 'DUDE' TO BE 'DOWN WITH THE YOUTH.'
I KNOW, MAN! RIGHT? LEGALISE IT. I WAS JUST JIVIN' WITH THE FUZZ--
I SPENT HOURS THAT WEEK SCULPTING MY PIECE. I WANTED TO MAKE A GOOD FIRST IMPRESSION, WHO DOESN'T RIGHT?
DNK!
SHIT!

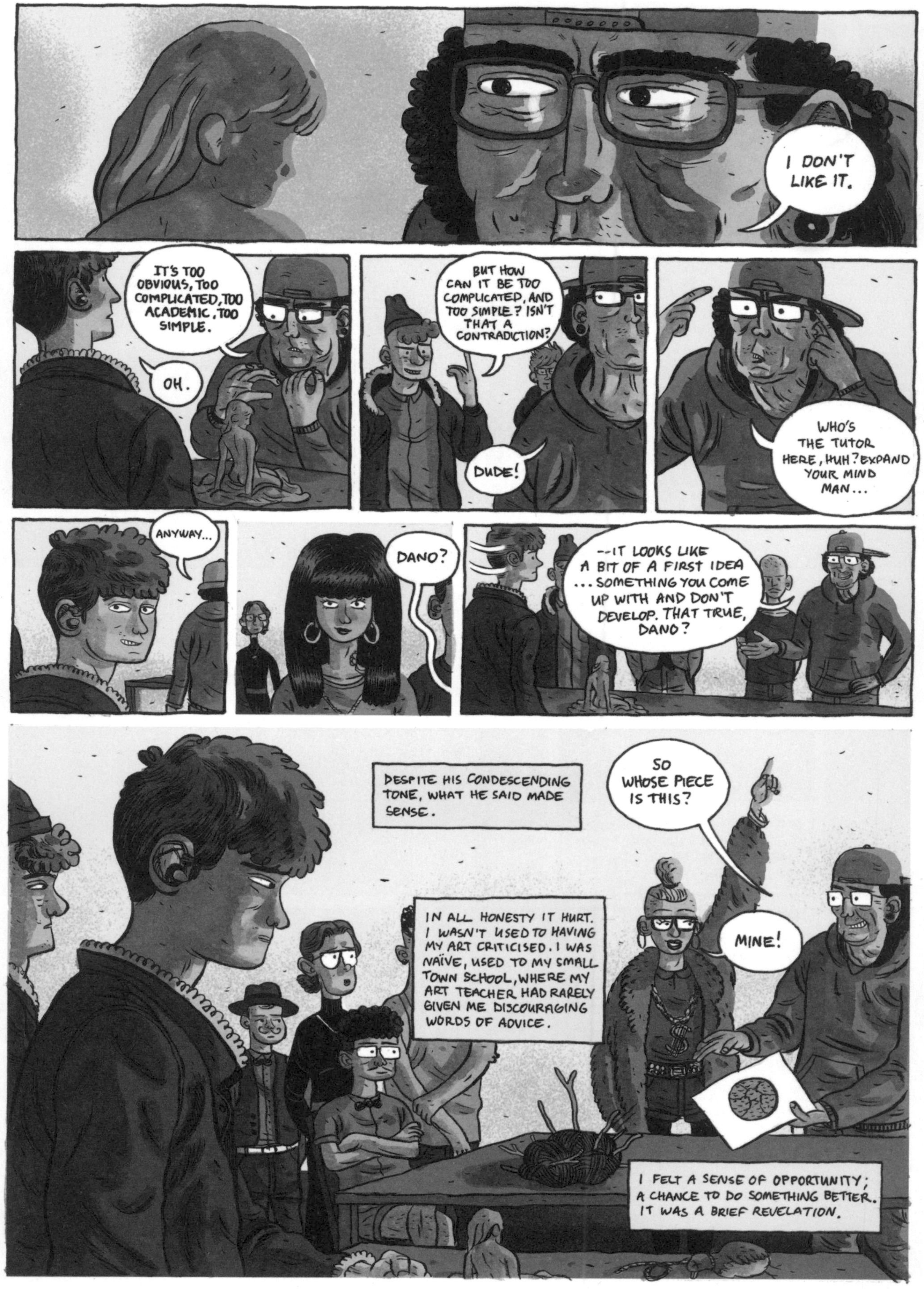
I DON'T LIKE IT.
IT'S TOO OBVIOUS, TOO COMPLICATED, TOO ACADEMIC, TOO SIMPLE.
OH.
BUT HOW CAN IT BE TOO COMPLICATED, AND TOO SIMPLE? ISN'T THAT A CONTRADICTION?
DUDE!
WHO'S THE TUTOR HERE, HUH? EXPAND YOUR MIND MAN...
ANYWAY...
DANO?
--IT LOOKS LIKE A BIT OF A FIRST IDEA ... SOMETHING YOU COME UP WITH AND DON'T DEVELOP. THAT TRUE, DANO?
DESPITE HIS CONDESCENDING TONE, WHAT HE SAID MADE SENSE.
SO WHOSE PIECE IS THIS?
IN ALL HONESTY IT HURT. I WASN'T USED TO HAVING MY ART CRITICISED. I WAS NAÏVE, USED TO MY SMALL TOWN SCHOOL, WHERE MY ART TEACHER HAD RARELY GIVEN ME DISCOURAGING WORDS OF ADVICE.
MINE!
I FELT A SENSE OF OPPORTUNITY; A CHANCE TO DO SOMETHING BETTER. IT WAS A BRIEF REVELATION.

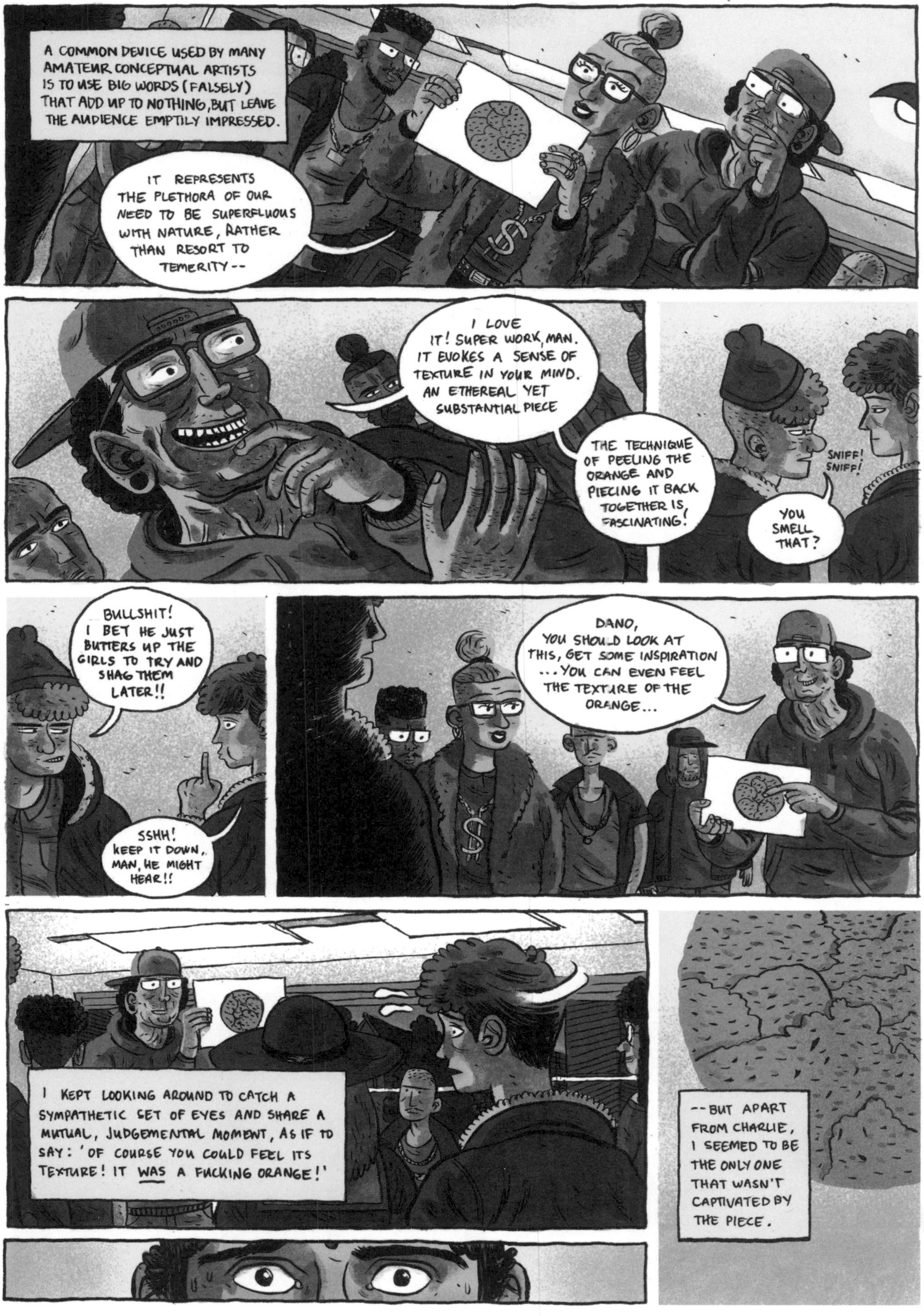
A COMMON DEVICE USED BY MANY AMATEUR CONCEPTUAL ARTISTS IS TO USE BIG WORDS (FALSELY) THAT ADD UP TO NOTHING, BUT LEAVE THE AUDIENCE EMPTILY IMPRESSED.
IT REPRESENTS THE PLETHORA OF OUR NEED TO BE SUPERFLUOUS WITH NATURE, RATHER THAN RESORT TO TEMERITY --
I LOVE IT! SUPER WORK, MAN. IT EVOKES A SENSE OF TEXTURE IN YOUR MIND. AN ETHEREAL YET SUBSTANTIAL PIECE
THE TECHNIQUE OF PEELING THE ORANGE AND PIECING IT BACK TOGETHER IS FASCINATING!
SNIFF! SNIFF!
YOU SMELL THAT?
BULLSHIT! I BET HE JUST BUTTERS UP THE GIRLS TO TRY AND SHAG THEM LATER!!
SSHH! KEEP IT DOWN, MAN, HE MIGHT HEAR!!
DANO, YOU SHOULD LOOK AT THIS, GET SOME INSPIRATION ... YOU CAN EVEN FEEL THE TEXTURE OF THE ORANGE...
I KEPT LOOKING AROUND TO CATCH A SYMPATHETIC SET OF EYES AND SHARE A MUTUAL, JUDGEMENTAL MOMENT, AS IF TO SAY: 'OF COURSE YOU COULD FEEL ITS TEXTURE! IT WAS A FUCKING ORANGE!'
-- BUT APART FROM CHARLIE, I SEEMED TO BE THE ONLY ONE THAT WASN'T CAPTIVATED BY THE PIECE.

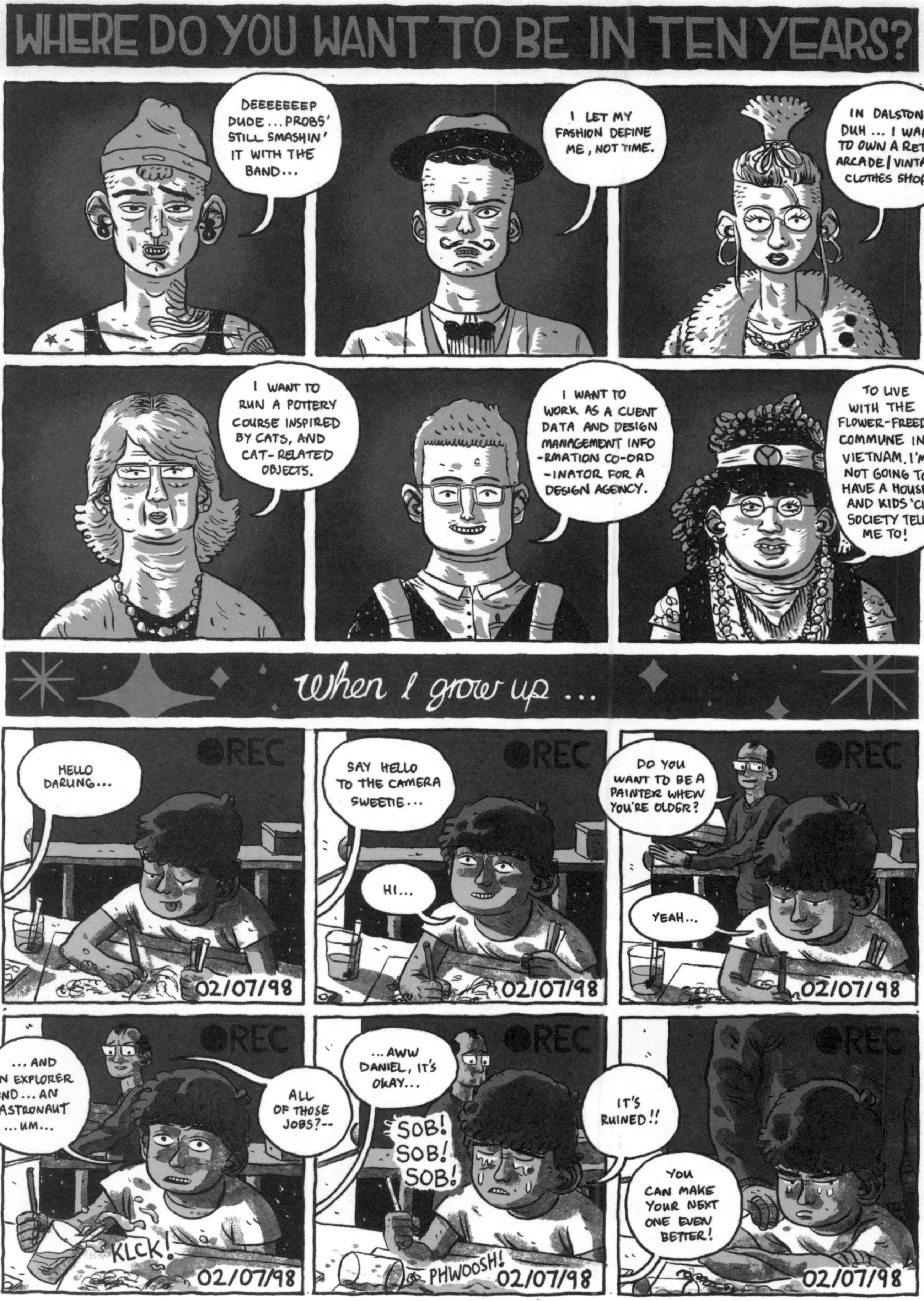
WHERE DO YOU WANT TO BE IN TEN YEARS?
DEEEEEEEP DUDE... PROBS' STILL SMASHIN' IT WITH THE BAND...
I LET MY FASHION DEFINE ME, NOT TIME.
IN DALSTON, DUH ... I WANT TO OWN A RETRO ARCADE / VINTAGE CLOTHES SHOP.
I WANT TO RUN A POTTERY COURSE INSPIRED BY CATS, AND CAT-RELATED OBJECTS.
I WANT TO WORK AS A CLIENT DATA AND DESIGN MANAGEMENT INFO-RMATION CO-ORD-INATOR FOR A DESIGN AGENCY.
TO LIVE WITH THE FLOWER-FREEDOM COMMUNE IN VIETNAM. I'M NOT GOING TO HAVE A HOUSE AND KIDS 'CUS SOCIETY TELLS ME TO!
When I grow up ...
REC
HELLO DARLING...
02/07/98
REC
SAY HELLO TO THE CAMERA SWEETIE...
HI...
02/07/98
REC
DO YOU WANT TO BE A PAINTER WHEN YOU'RE OLDER?
YEAH...
02/07/98
REC
... AND AN EXPLORER AND... AN ASTRONAUT ... UM...
ALL OF THOSE JOBS?--
KLCK!
02/07/98
REC
...AWW DANIEL, IT'S OKAY...
SOB! SOB! SOB!
IT'S RUINED!!
PHWOOSH!
02/07/98
REC
YOU CAN MAKE YOUR NEXT ONE EVEN BETTER!
02/07/98

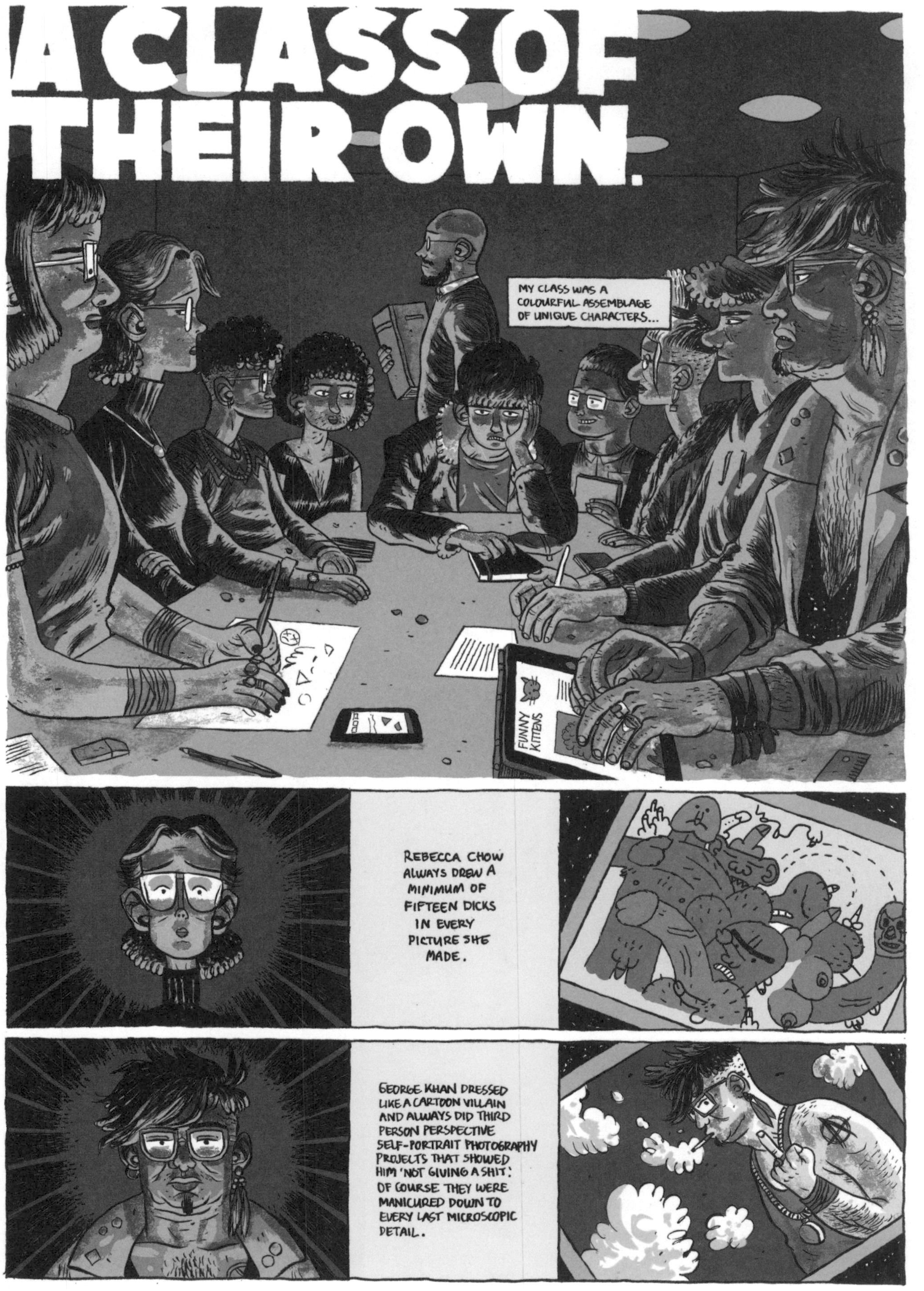
A CLASS OF THEIR OWN.
MY CLASS WAS A COLOURFUL ASSEMBLAGE OF UNIQUE CHARACTERS...
FUNNY KITTENS
REBECCA CHOW ALWAYS DREW A MINIMUM OF FIFTEEN DICKS IN EVERY PICTURE SHE MADE.
GEORGE KHAN DRESSED LIKE A CARTOON VILLAIN AND ALWAYS DID THIRD PERSON PERSPECTIVE SELF-PORTRAIT PHOTOGRAPHY PROJECTS THAT SHOWED HIM 'NOT GIVING A SHIT.' OF COURSE THEY WERE MANICURED DOWN TO EVERY LAST MICROSCOPIC DETAIL.

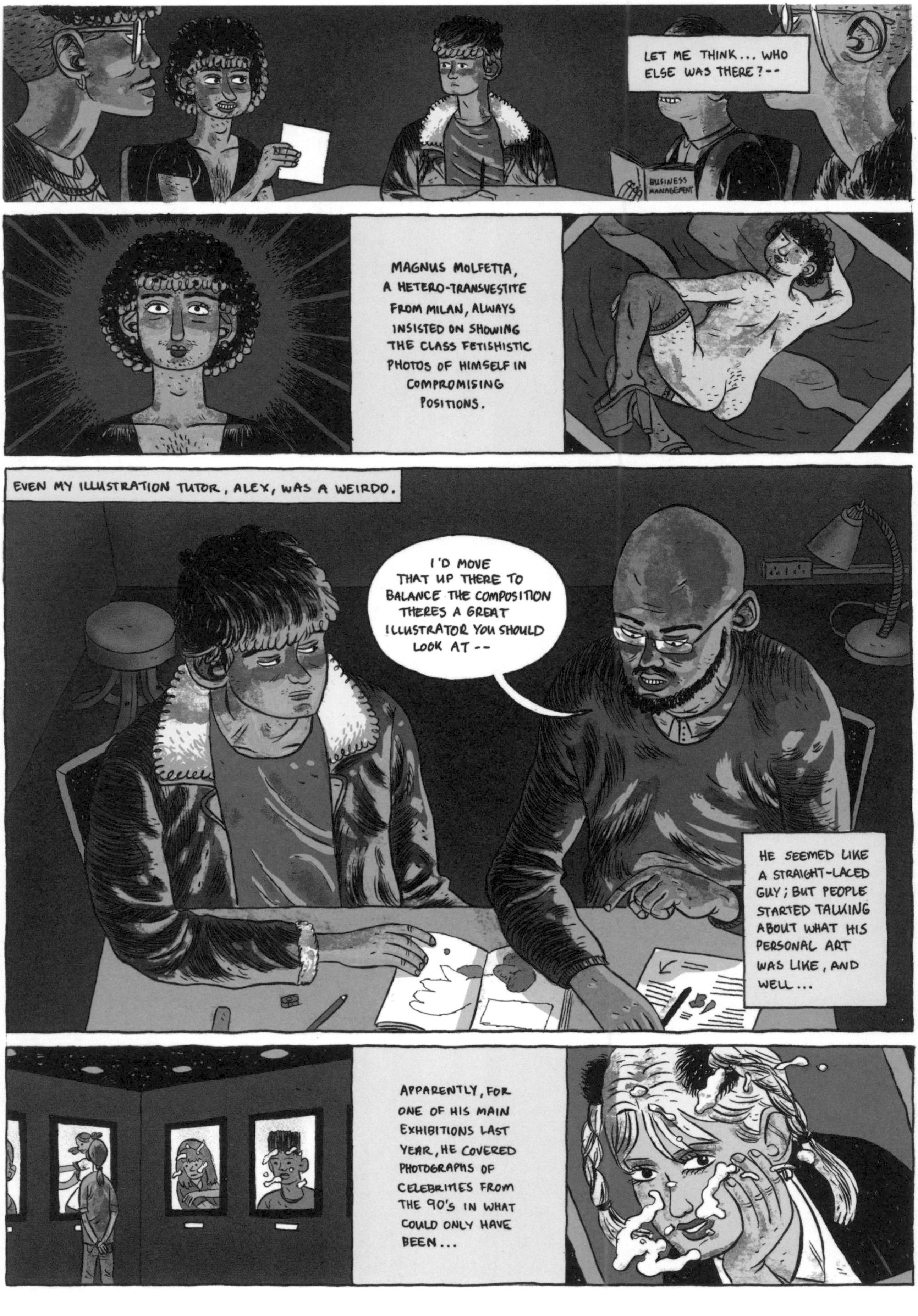
LET ME THINK... WHO ELSE WAS THERE?--
BUSINESS MANAGEMENT
MAGNUS MOLFETTA, A HETERO-TRANSVESTITE FROM MILAN, ALWAYS INSISTED ON SHOWING THE CLASS FETISHISTIC PHOTOS OF HIMSELF IN COMPROMISING POSITIONS.
EVEN MY ILLUSTRATION TUTOR, ALEX, WAS A WEIRDO.
I'D MOVE THAT UP THERE TO BALANCE THE COMPOSITION THERES A GREAT ILLUSTRATOR YOU SHOULD LOOK AT--
HE SEEMED LIKE A STRAIGHT-LACED GUY; BUT PEOPLE STARTED TALKING ABOUT WHAT HIS PERSONAL ART WAS LIKE, AND WELL...
APPARENTLY, FOR ONE OF HIS MAIN EXHIBITIONS LAST YEAR, HE COVERED PHOTOGRAPHS OF CELEBRITIES FROM THE 90'S IN WHAT COULD ONLY HAVE BEEN...

PIP LANG

PIP LANG WAS A DREAM GIRL...

SHE WAS INTERESTING, BEAUTIFUL...

...SHE WAS DARK, MYSTERIOUS...

...SHE WAS THE GIRL THAT NOBODY KNEW BUT EVERYBODY WANTED TO KNOW.

SHE ALWAYS KEPT A CIGGIE BEHIND HER EAR...

AT LUNCH I'D WATCH HER STEAL SANDWICHES FROM THE CAFETERIA...

I'D TRY TO WORK OUT WHAT HER TATTOOS MEANT...

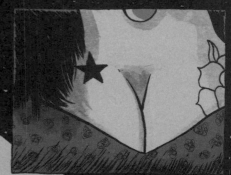

GULP!

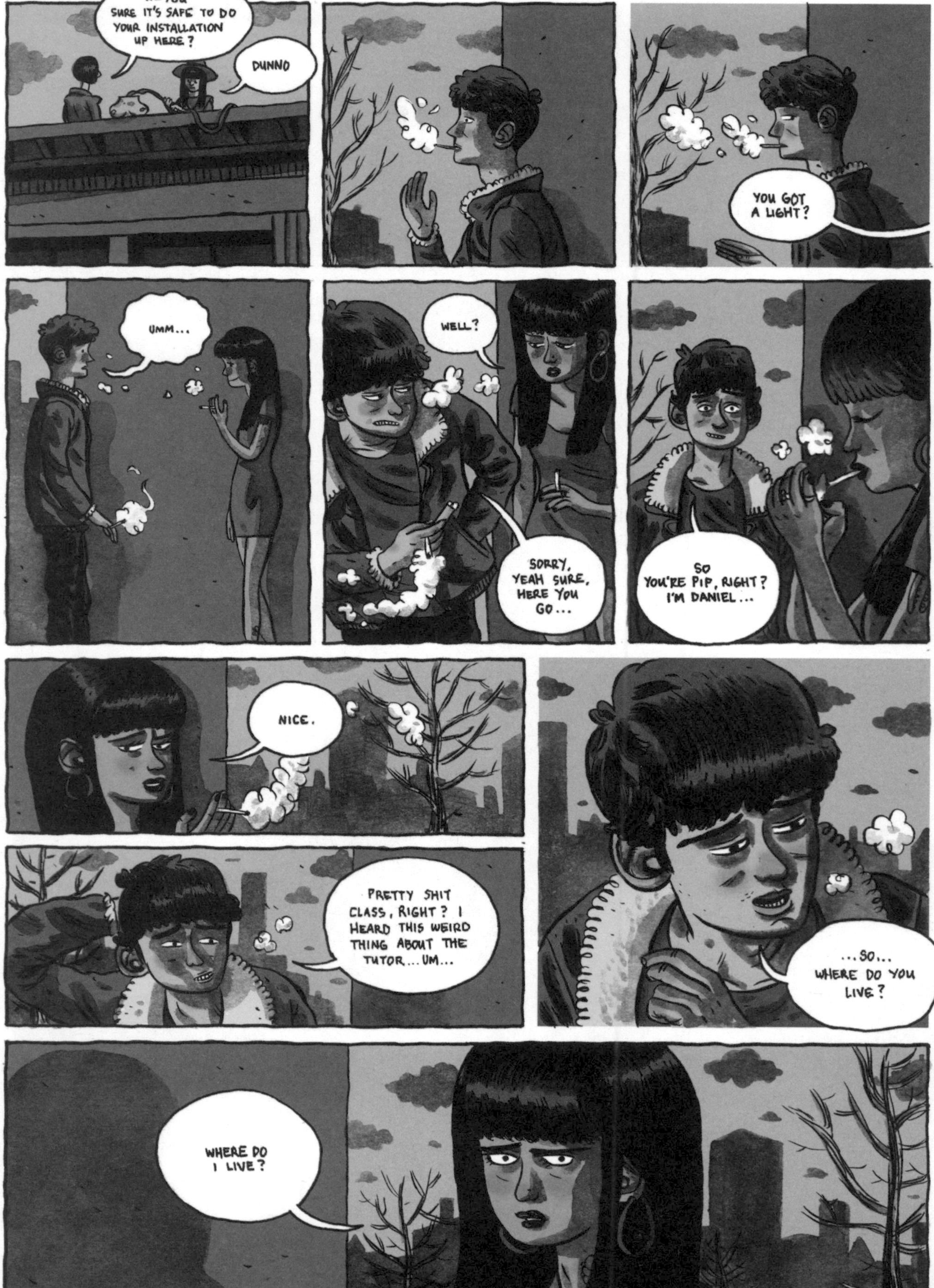
--YOU SURE IT'S SAFE TO DO YOUR INSTALLATION UP HERE?
DUNNO
YOU GOT A LIGHT?
UMM...
WELL?
SORRY, YEAH SURE, HERE YOU GO...
SO YOU'RE PIP, RIGHT? I'M DANIEL...
NICE.
PRETTY SHIT CLASS, RIGHT? I HEARD THIS WEIRD THING ABOUT THE TUTOR... UM...
...SO... WHERE DO YOU LIVE?
WHERE DO I LIVE?

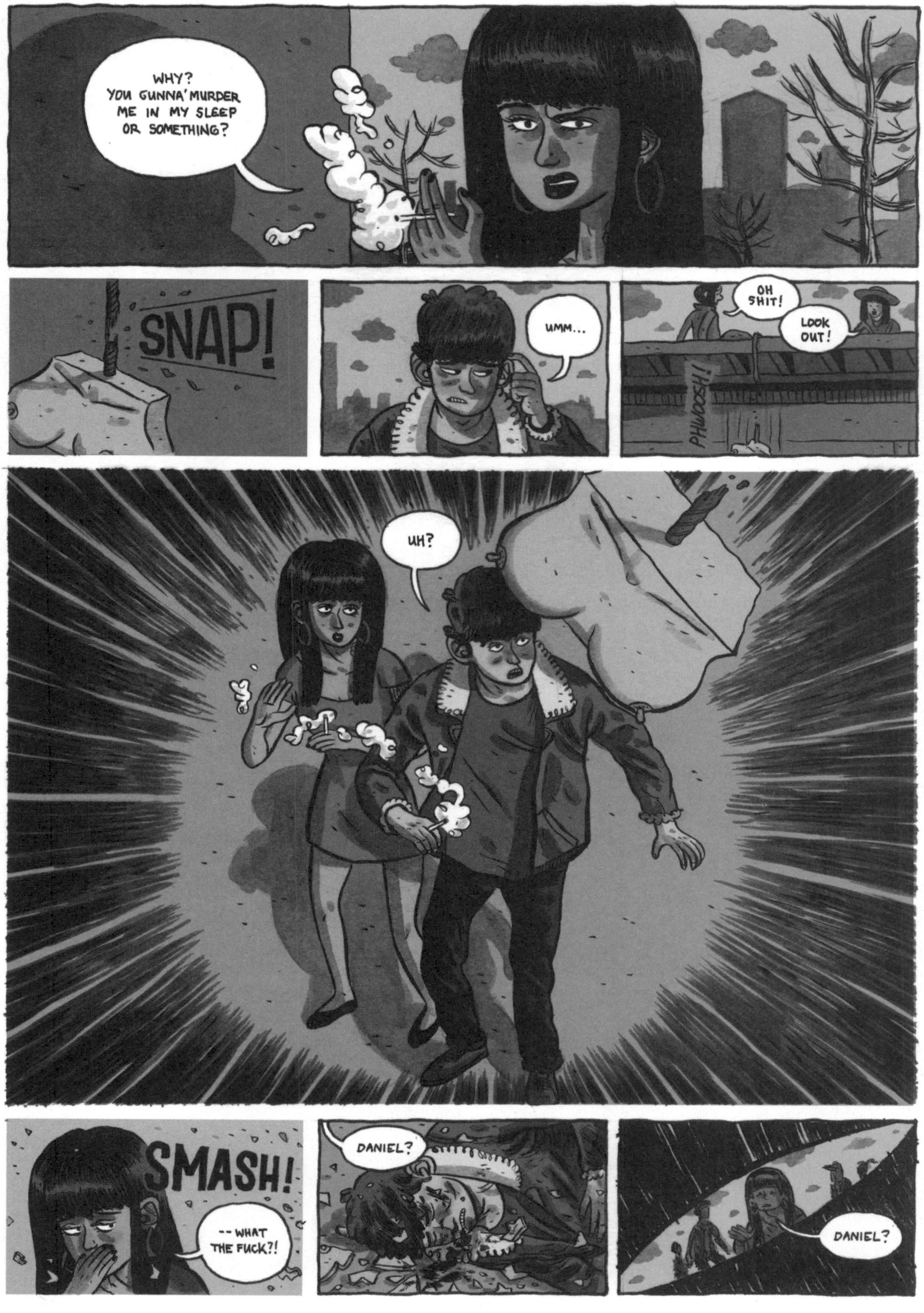
WHY? YOU GUNNA' MURDER ME IN MY SLEEP OR SOMETHING?
SNAP!
UMM...
OH SHIT!
LOOK OUT!
PHWOOSH!
UH?
SMASH!
-- WHAT THE FUCK?!
DANIEL?
DANIEL?

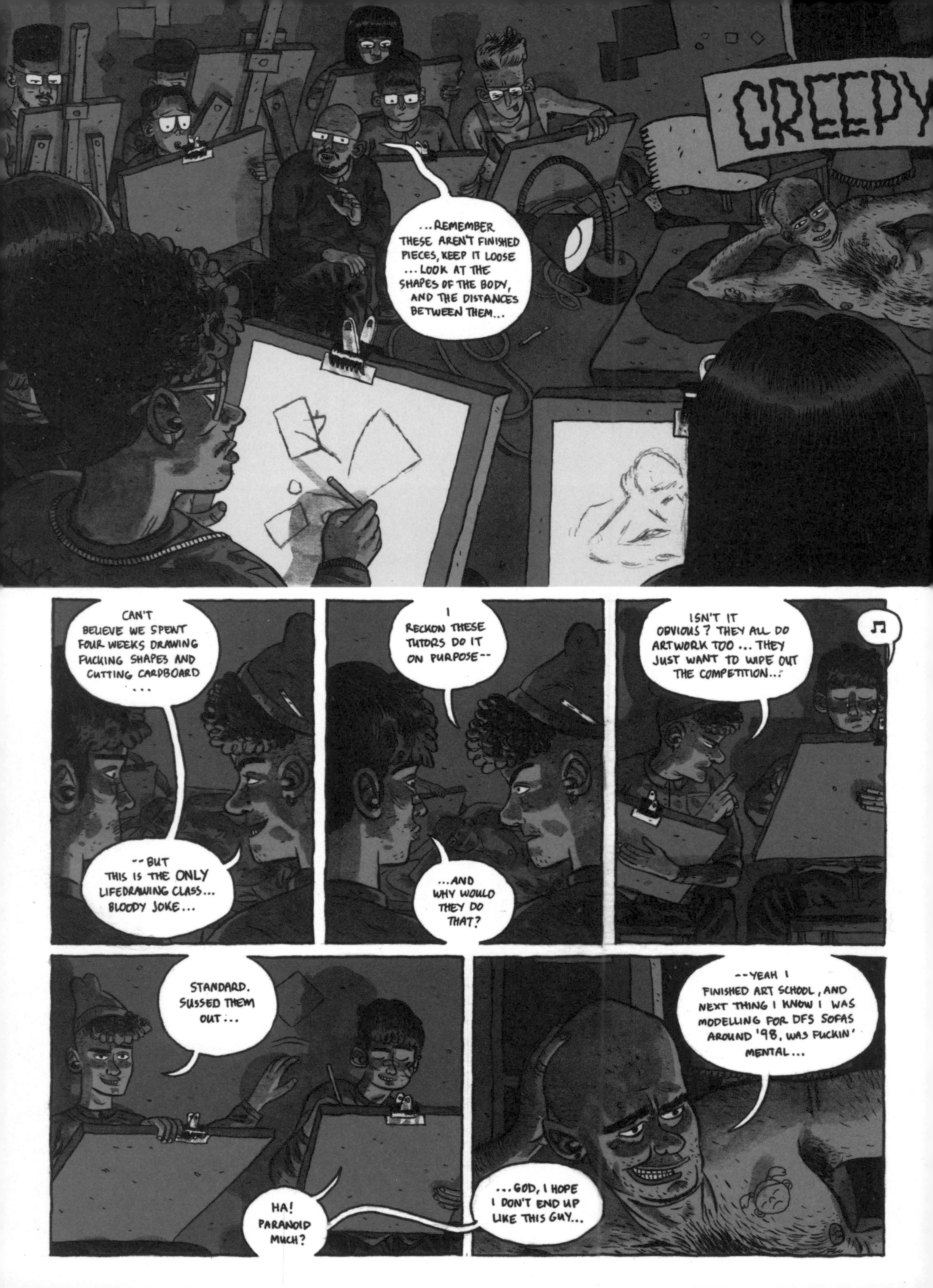
CREEPY
...REMEMBER THESE AREN'T FINISHED PIECES, KEEP IT LOOSE ...LOOK AT THE SHAPES OF THE BODY, AND THE DISTANCES BETWEEN THEM...
CAN'T BELIEVE WE SPENT FOUR WEEKS DRAWING FUCKING SHAPES AND CUTTING CARDBOARD ...
--BUT THIS IS THE ONLY LIFEDRAWING CLASS... BLOODY JOKE...
I RECKON THESE TUTORS DO IT ON PURPOSE--
...AND WHY WOULD THEY DO THAT?
ISN'T IT OBVIOUS? THEY ALL DO ARTWORK TOO... THEY JUST WANT TO WIPE OUT THE COMPETITION...
♫
STANDARD. SUSSED THEM OUT...
HA! PARANOID MUCH?
--YEAH I FINISHED ART SCHOOL, AND NEXT THING I KNOW I WAS MODELLING FOR DFS SOFAS AROUND '98, WAS FUCKIN' MENTAL...
...GOD, I HOPE I DON'T END UP LIKE THIS GUY...

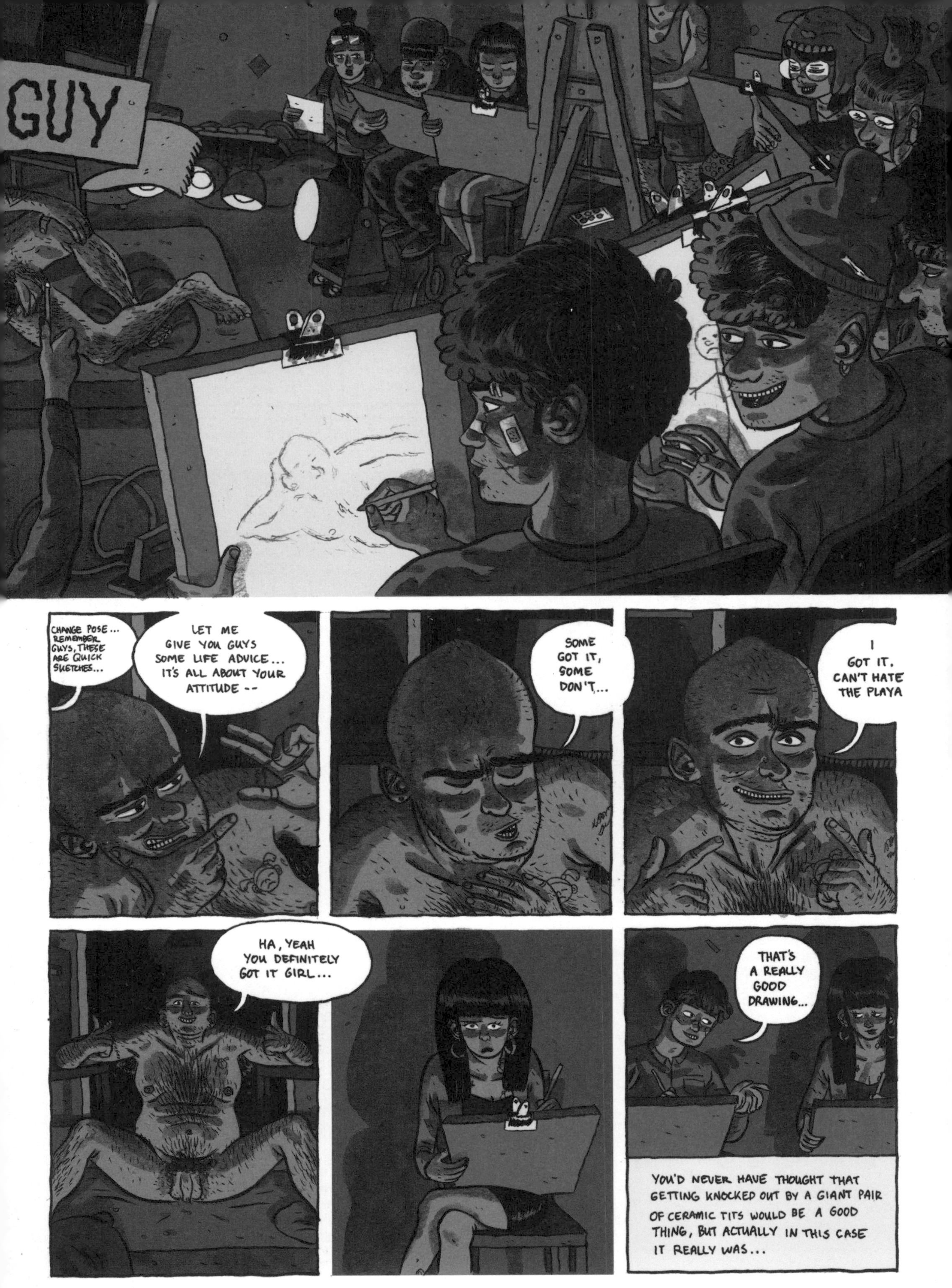
GUY
CHANGE POSE... REMEMBER GUYS, THESE ARE QUICK SKETCHES...
LET ME GIVE YOU GUYS SOME LIFE ADVICE... IT'S ALL ABOUT YOUR ATTITUDE --
SOME GOT IT, SOME DON'T...
I GOT IT. CAN'T HATE THE PLAYA
HA, YEAH YOU DEFINITELY GOT IT GIRL...
THAT'S A REALLY GOOD DRAWING...
YOU'D NEVER HAVE THOUGHT THAT GETTING KNOCKED OUT BY A GIANT PAIR OF CERAMIC TITS WOULD BE A GOOD THING, BUT ACTUALLY IN THIS CASE IT REALLY WAS...

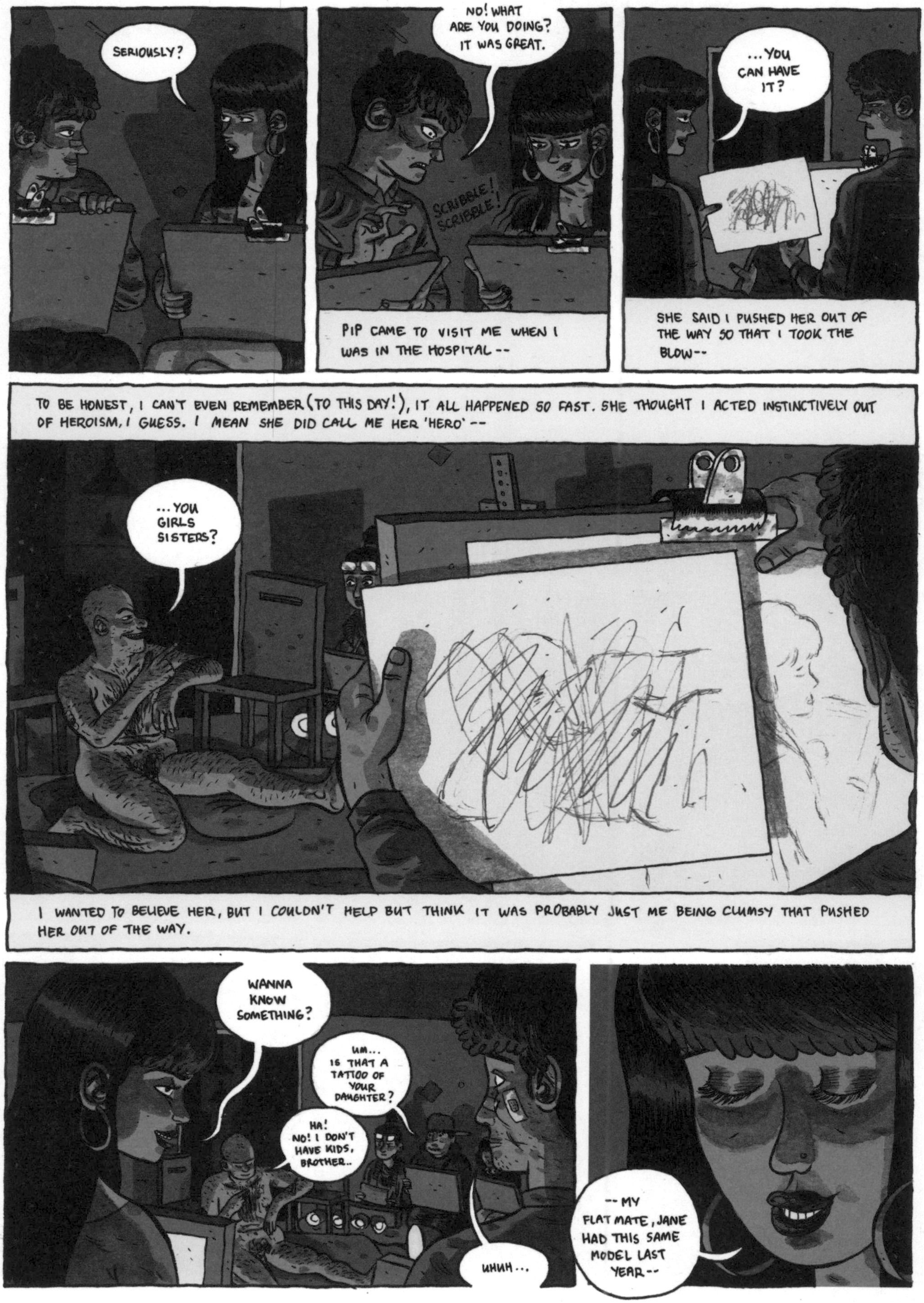
SERIOUSLY?
NO! WHAT ARE YOU DOING? IT WAS GREAT.
SCRIBBLE! SCRIBBLE!
PIP CAME TO VISIT ME WHEN I WAS IN THE HOSPITAL --
...YOU CAN HAVE IT?
SHE SAID I PUSHED HER OUT OF THE WAY SO THAT I TOOK THE BLOW--
TO BE HONEST, I CAN'T EVEN REMEMBER (TO THIS DAY!), IT ALL HAPPENED SO FAST. SHE THOUGHT I ACTED INSTINCTIVELY OUT OF HEROISM, I GUESS. I MEAN SHE DID CALL ME HER 'HERO' --
...YOU GIRLS SISTERS?
I WANTED TO BELIEVE HER, BUT I COULDN'T HELP BUT THINK IT WAS PROBABLY JUST ME BEING CLUMSY THAT PUSHED HER OUT OF THE WAY.
WANNA KNOW SOMETHING?
UM... IS THAT A TATTOO OF YOUR DAUGHTER?
HA! NO! I DON'T HAVE KIDS, BROTHER..
UHUH...
-- MY FLAT MATE, JANE HAD THIS SAME MODEL LAST YEAR --

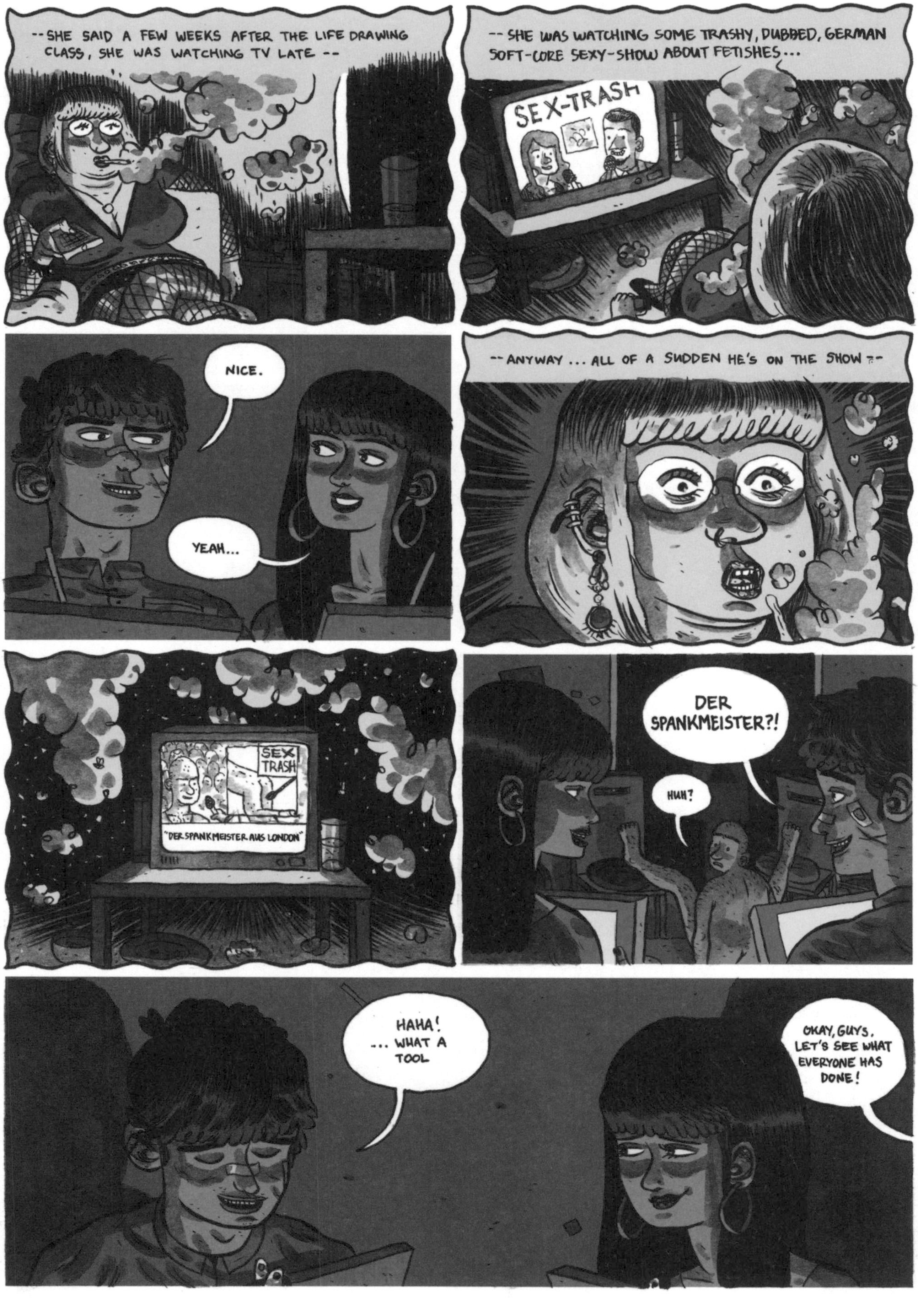
--SHE SAID A FEW WEEKS AFTER THE LIFE DRAWING CLASS, SHE WAS WATCHING TV LATE--
--SHE WAS WATCHING SOME TRASHY, DUBBED, GERMAN SOFT-CORE SEXY-SHOW ABOUT FETISHES...
SEX-TRASH
NICE.
YEAH...
--ANYWAY... ALL OF A SUDDEN HE'S ON THE SHOW--
SEX TRASH
"DER SPANKMEISTER AUS LONDON"
DER SPANKMEISTER?!
HUH?
HAHA! ... WHAT A TOOL
OKAY, GUYS, LET'S SEE WHAT EVERYONE HAS DONE!

ALICIA, NICE...VERY NICE...

YEP...TRY NOT TO DRAW DETAILS BEFORE YOU GET THE BASIC SHAPES, EMIL...

WHO DID THIS ONE?

HAHA! FUCK!!

SHH!

REBECCA CHOW, RIGHT?

mmhmm...

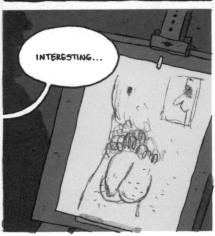

INTERESTING...

FROM THEN ON IT FELT LIKE I SAW PIP PRETTY MUCH EVERY OTHER DAY. WE JUST CLICKED. WE BOTH HAD THE SAME STUPID SENSE OF HUMOUR--

That WEEK

--WE LIKED SIMILAR THINGS (APART FROM HER QUESTIONABLE TASTE IN MUSIC)--

--WE COULD BE SILENT BUT STILL KNOW WHAT EACH OTHER WAS THINKING (OR AT LEAST, I FELT THAT WAY)--

--BUT EVERY TIME I'D TRY TO MAKE A MOVE, I COULD FEEL HER PULLING AWAY.

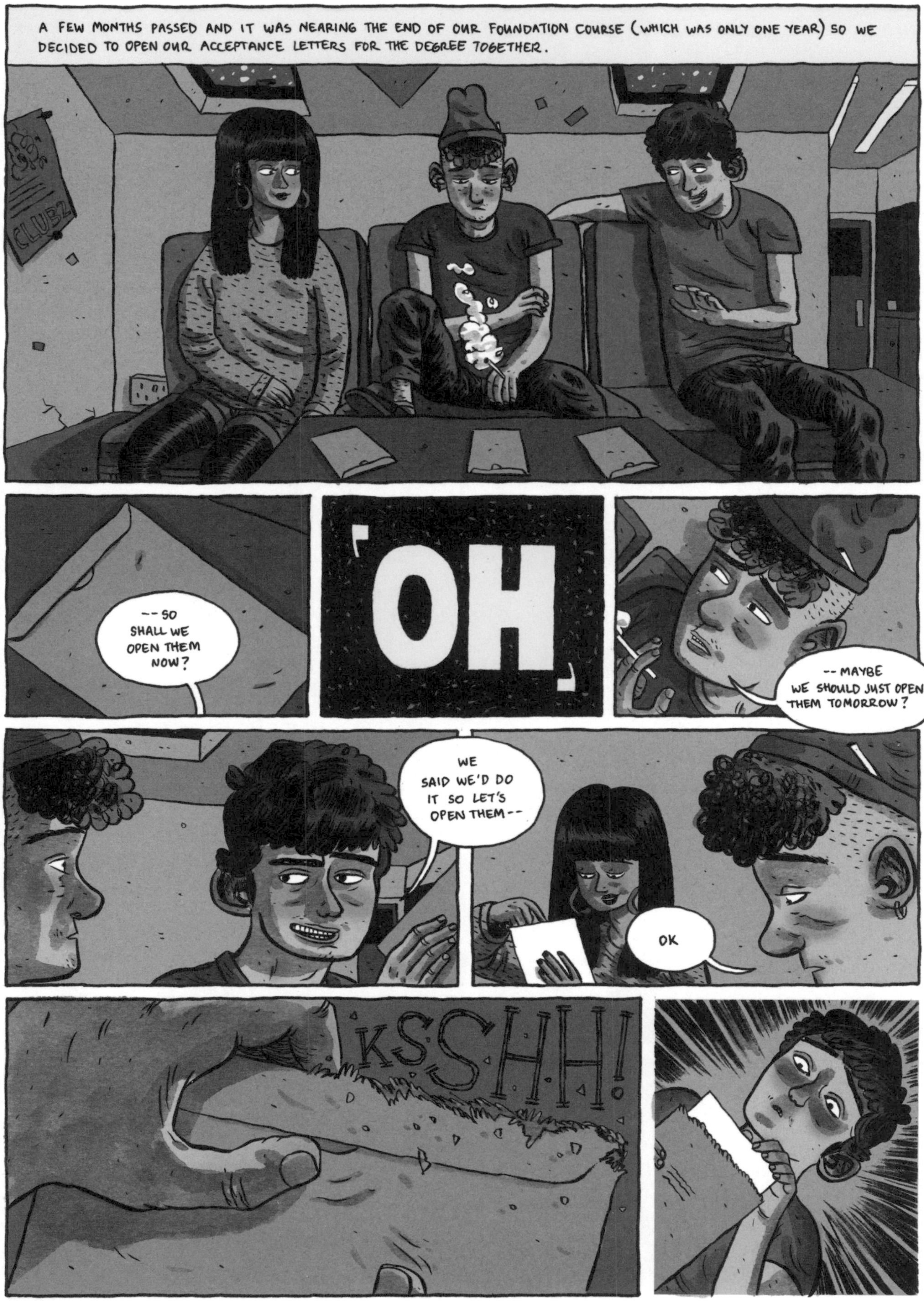
A FEW MONTHS PASSED AND IT WAS NEARING THE END OF OUR FOUNDATION COURSE (WHICH WAS ONLY ONE YEAR) SO WE DECIDED TO OPEN OUR ACCEPTANCE LETTERS FOR THE DEGREE TOGETHER.
CLUB2
--SO SHALL WE OPEN THEM NOW?
'OH'
--MAYBE WE SHOULD JUST OPEN THEM TOMORROW?
WE SAID WE'D DO IT SO LET'S OPEN THEM--
OK
KSSHH!

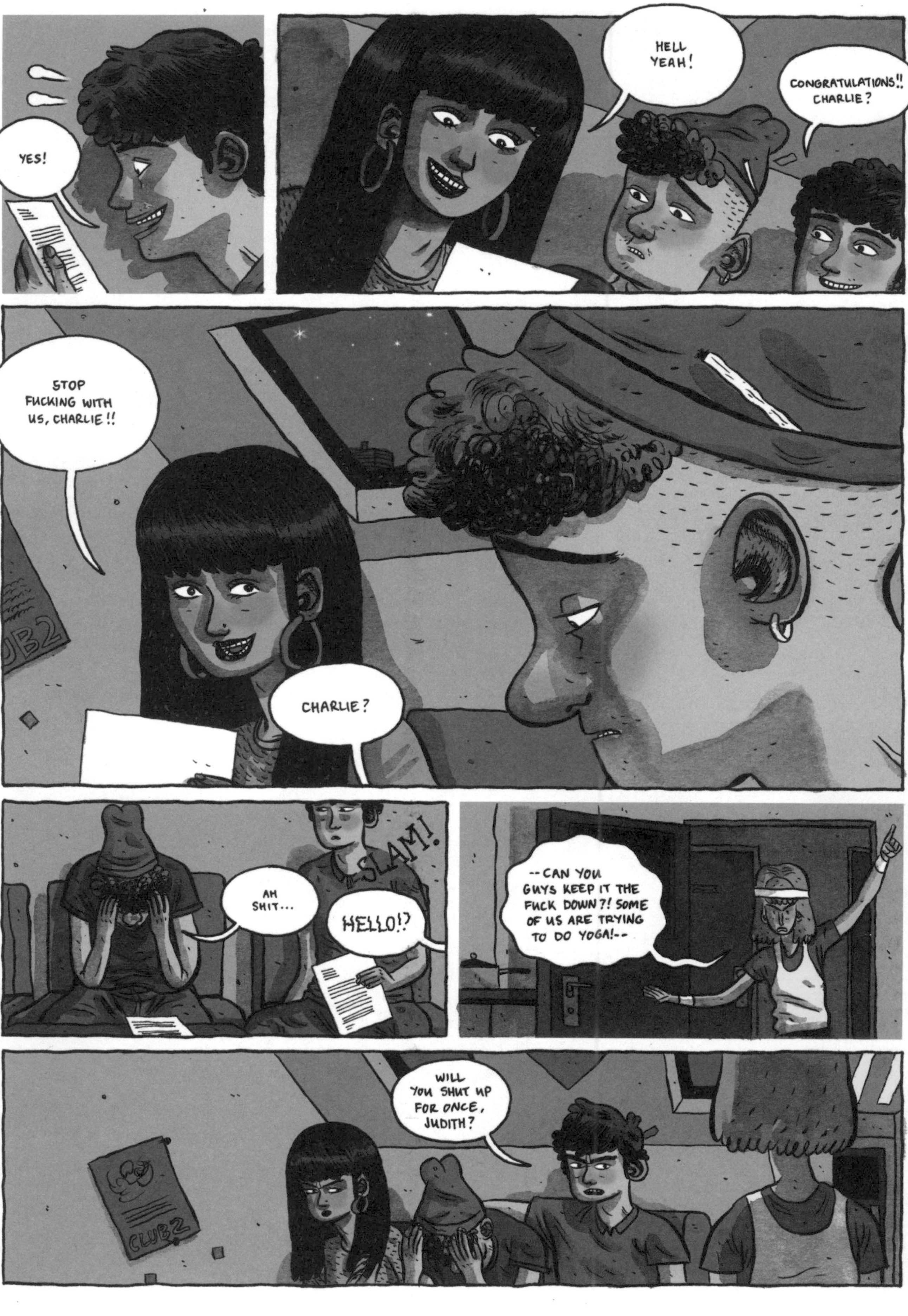
YES!
HELL YEAH!
CONGRATULATIONS!! CHARLIE?
STOP FUCKING WITH US, CHARLIE!!
CLUB2
CHARLIE?
AH SHIT...
SLAM!
HELLO!?
--CAN YOU GUYS KEEP IT THE FUCK DOWN?! SOME OF US ARE TRYING TO DO YOGA!--
WILL YOU SHUT UP FOR ONCE, JUDITH?
CLUB2

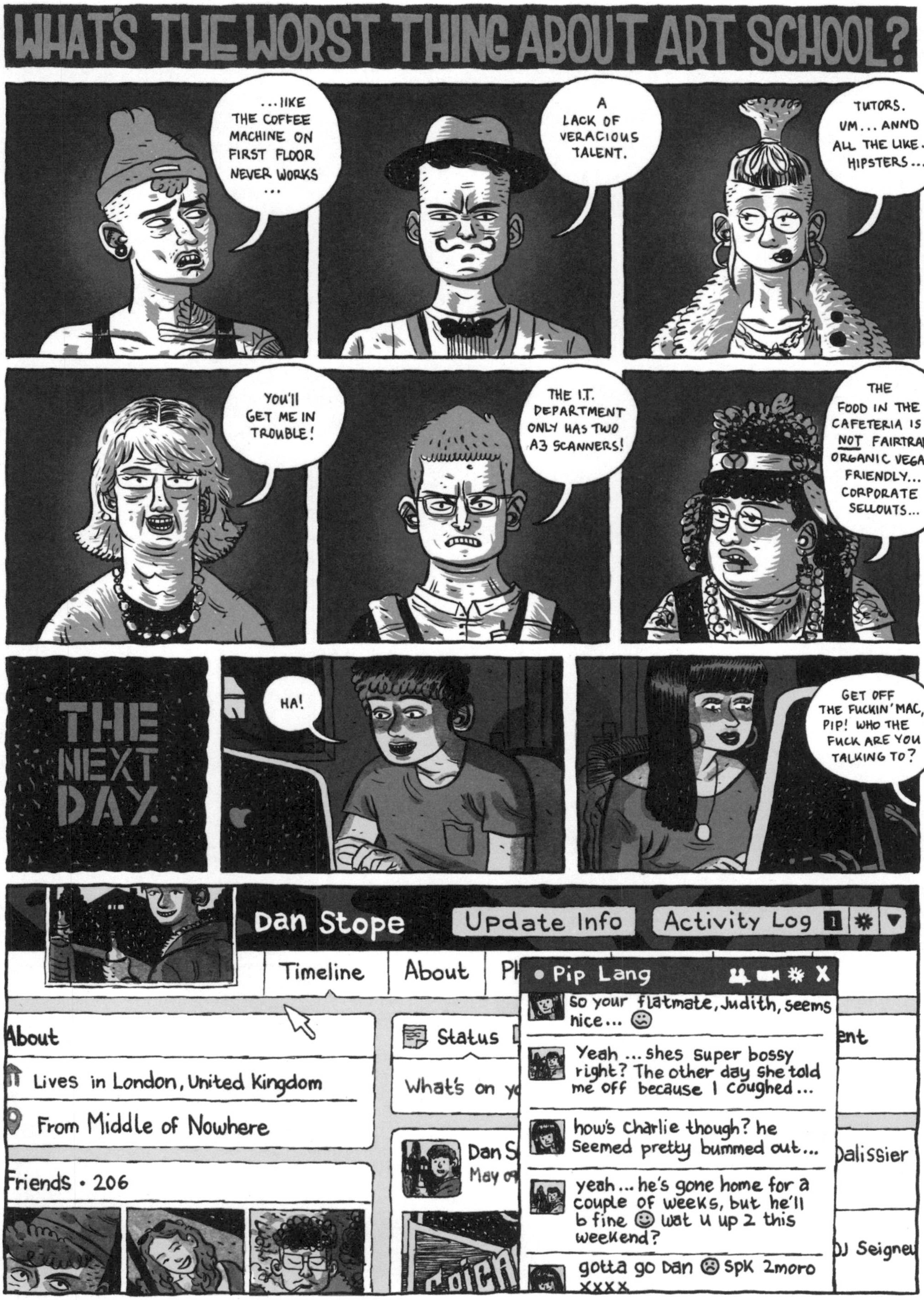
WHAT'S THE WORST THING ABOUT ART SCHOOL?
...LIKE THE COFFEE MACHINE ON FIRST FLOOR NEVER WORKS ...
A LACK OF VERACIOUS TALENT.
TUTORS. UM... ANND ALL THE LIKE... HIPSTERS...
YOU'LL GET ME IN TROUBLE!
THE I.T. DEPARTMENT ONLY HAS TWO A3 SCANNERS!
THE FOOD IN THE CAFETERIA IS NOT FAIRTRADE ORGANIC VEGAN FRIENDLY... CORPORATE SELLOUTS...
THE NEXT DAY.
HA!
GET OFF THE FUCKIN' MAC, PIP! WHO THE FUCK ARE YOU TALKING TO?
Dan Stope
Update Info
Activity Log
Timeline
About
Pip Lang
so your flatmate, Judith, seems nice...
Yeah ... shes super bossy right? The other day she told me off because I coughed...
how's Charlie though? he seemed pretty bummed out...
yeah... he's gone home for a couple of weeks, but he'll b fine wat u up 2 this weekend?
gotta go Dan spk 2moro xxxx
About
Lives in London, United Kingdom
From Middle of Nowhere
Friends • 206
Status
What's on

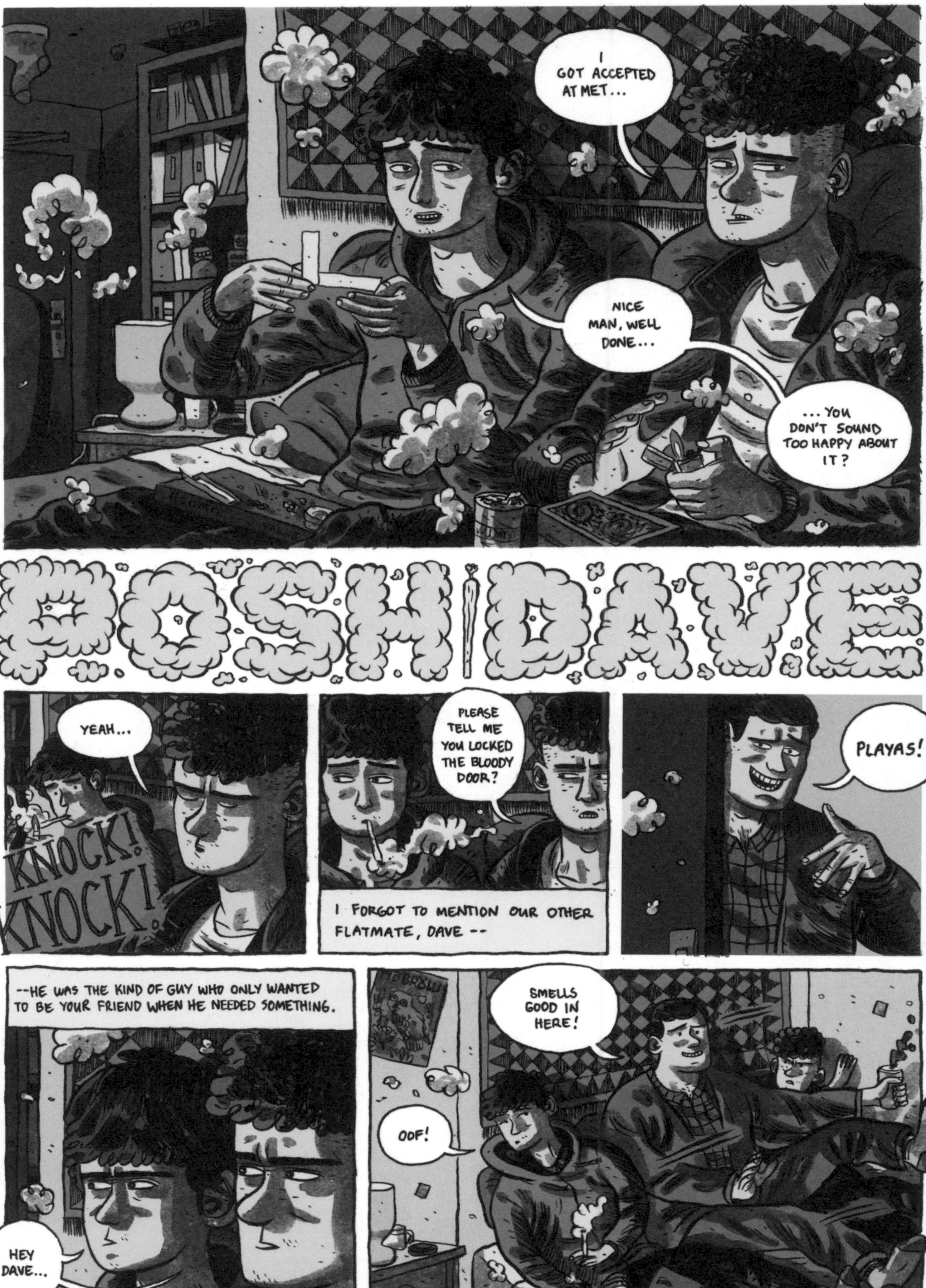
I GOT ACCEPTED AT MET...
NICE MAN, WELL DONE...
...YOU DON'T SOUND TOO HAPPY ABOUT IT?
POSH DAVE
YEAH...
KNOCK! KNOCK!
PLEASE TELL ME YOU LOCKED THE BLOODY DOOR?
I FORGOT TO MENTION OUR OTHER FLATMATE, DAVE --
PLAYAS!
--HE WAS THE KIND OF GUY WHO ONLY WANTED TO BE YOUR FRIEND WHEN HE NEEDED SOMETHING.
HEY DAVE...
SMELLS GOOD IN HERE!
OOF!

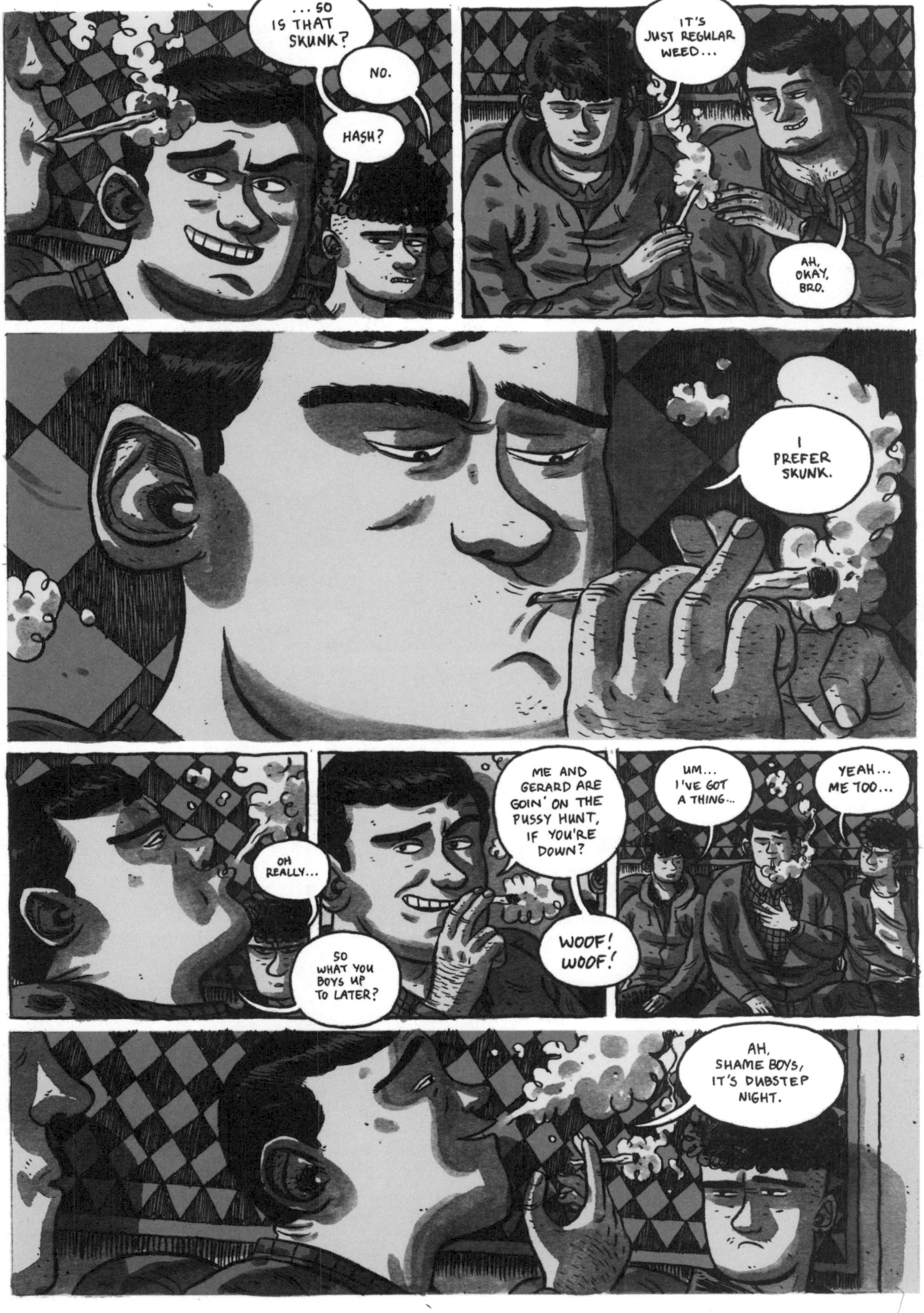

...SO IS THAT SKUNK?
NO.
HASH?
IT'S JUST REGULAR WEED...
AH, OKAY, BRO.
I PREFER SKUNK.
OH REALLY...
SO WHAT YOU BOYS UP TO LATER?
ME AND GERARD ARE GOIN' ON THE PUSSY HUNT, IF YOU'RE DOWN?
WOOF! WOOF!
UM... I'VE GOT A THING...
YEAH... ME TOO...
AH, SHAME BOYS, IT'S DUBSTEP NIGHT.

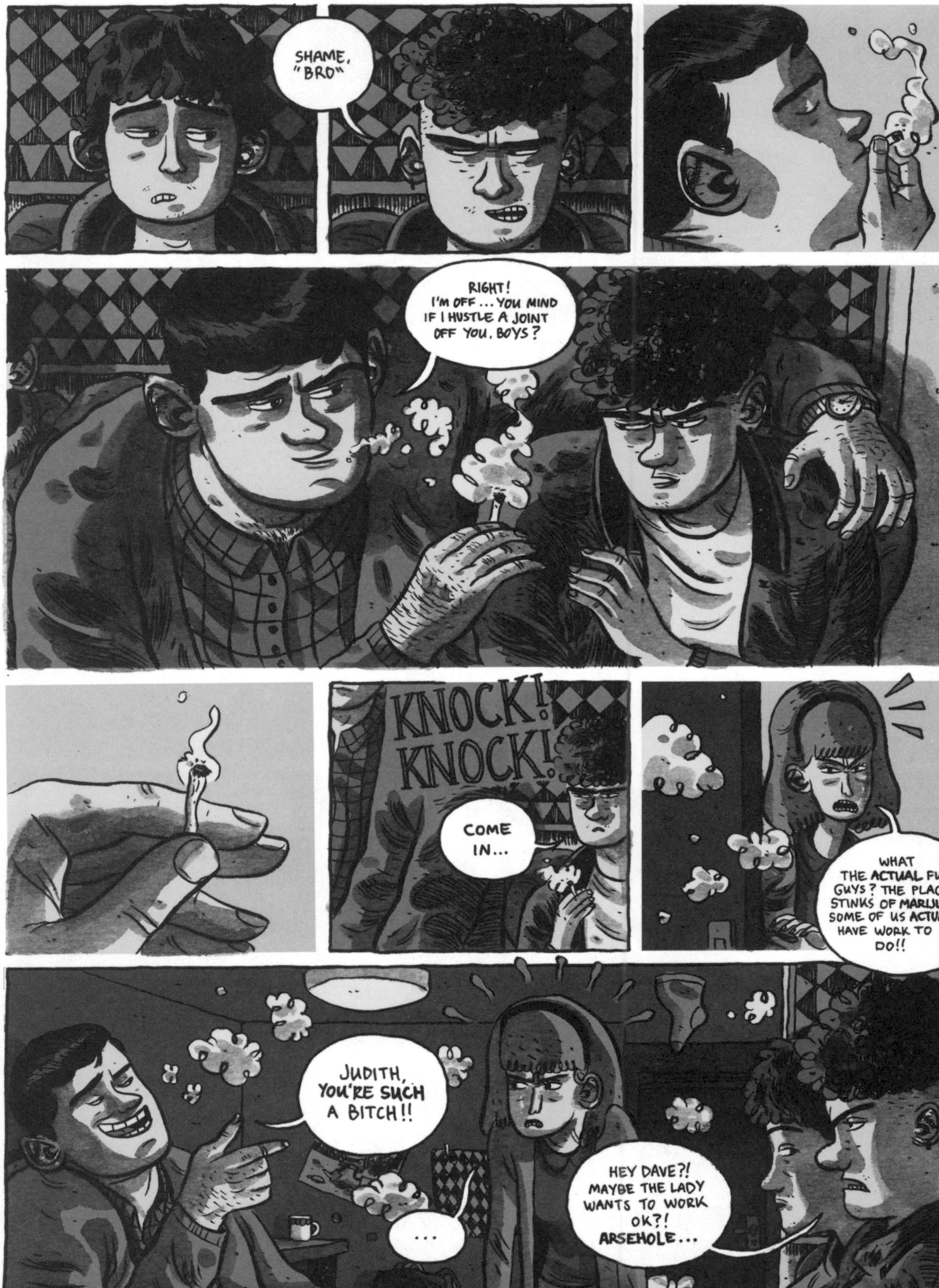
SHAME, "BRO"
RIGHT! I'M OFF... YOU MIND IF I HUSTLE A JOINT OFF YOU, BOYS?
KNOCK! KNOCK!
COME IN...
WHAT THE ACTUAL FUCK, GUYS? THE PLACE STINKS OF MARIJUANA! SOME OF US ACTUALLY HAVE WORK TO DO!!
JUDITH, YOU'RE SUCH A BITCH!!
...
HEY DAVE?! MAYBE THE LADY WANTS TO WORK OK?! ARSEHOLE...

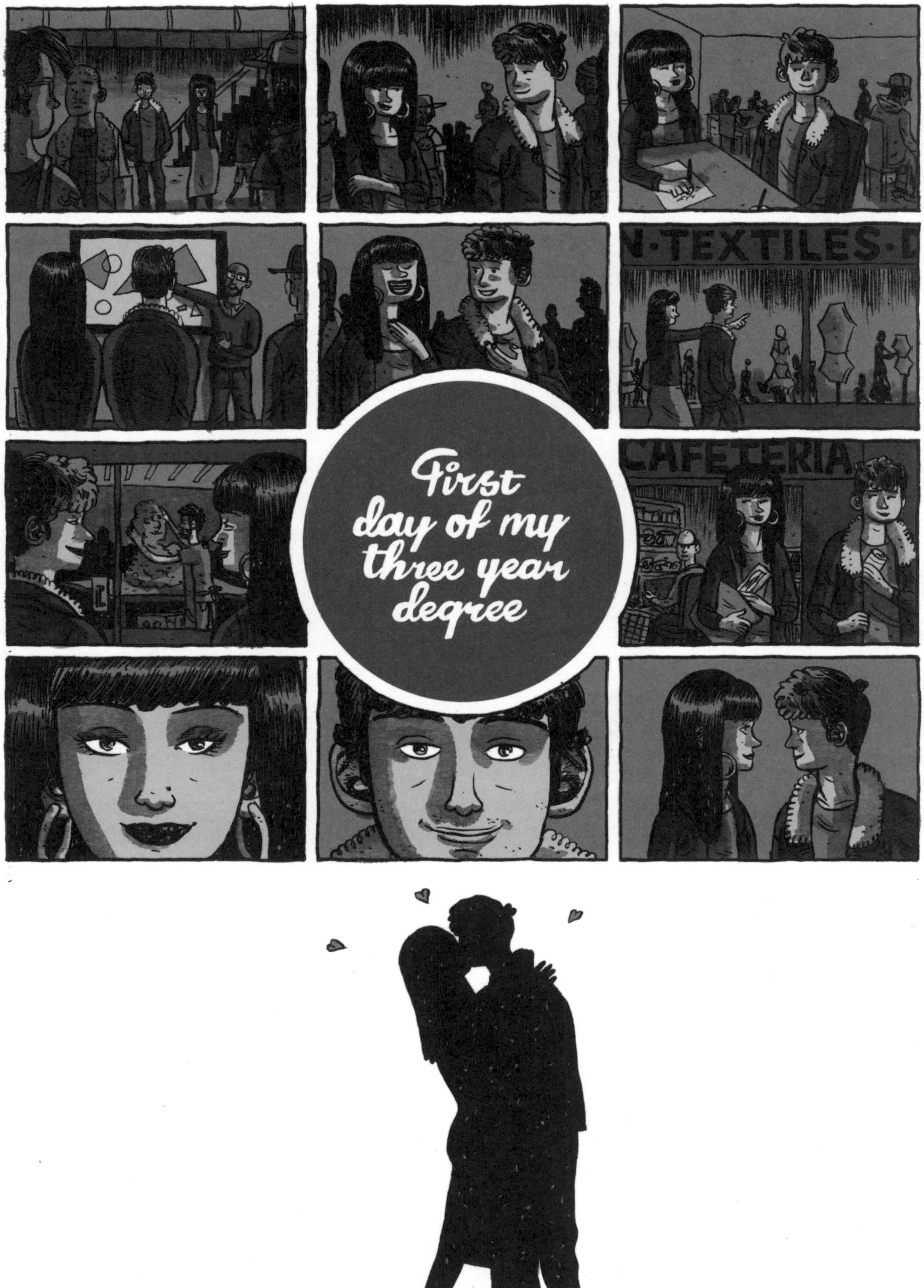

N·TEXTILES·D
First day of my three year degree
CAFETERIA

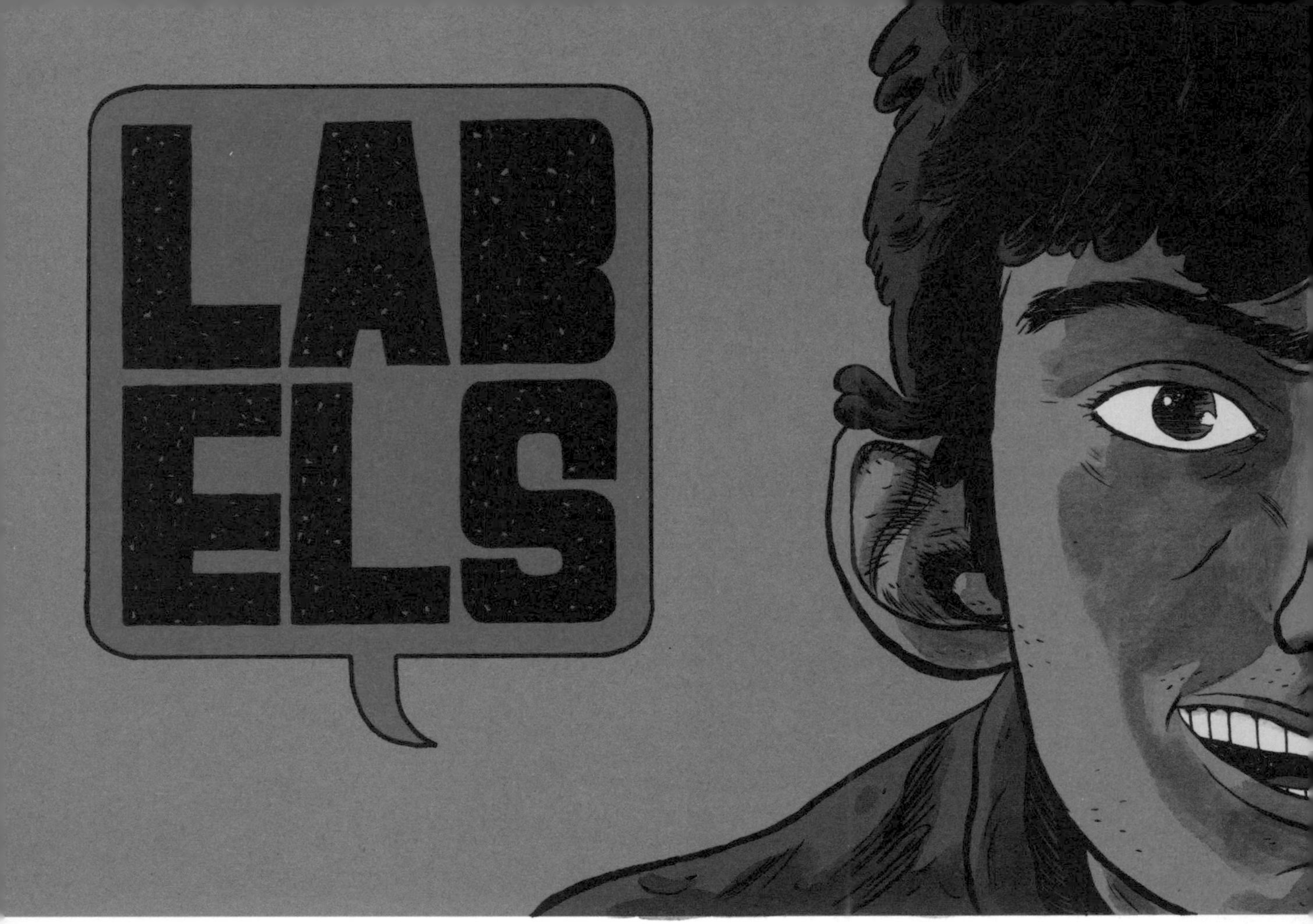
LAB
ELS

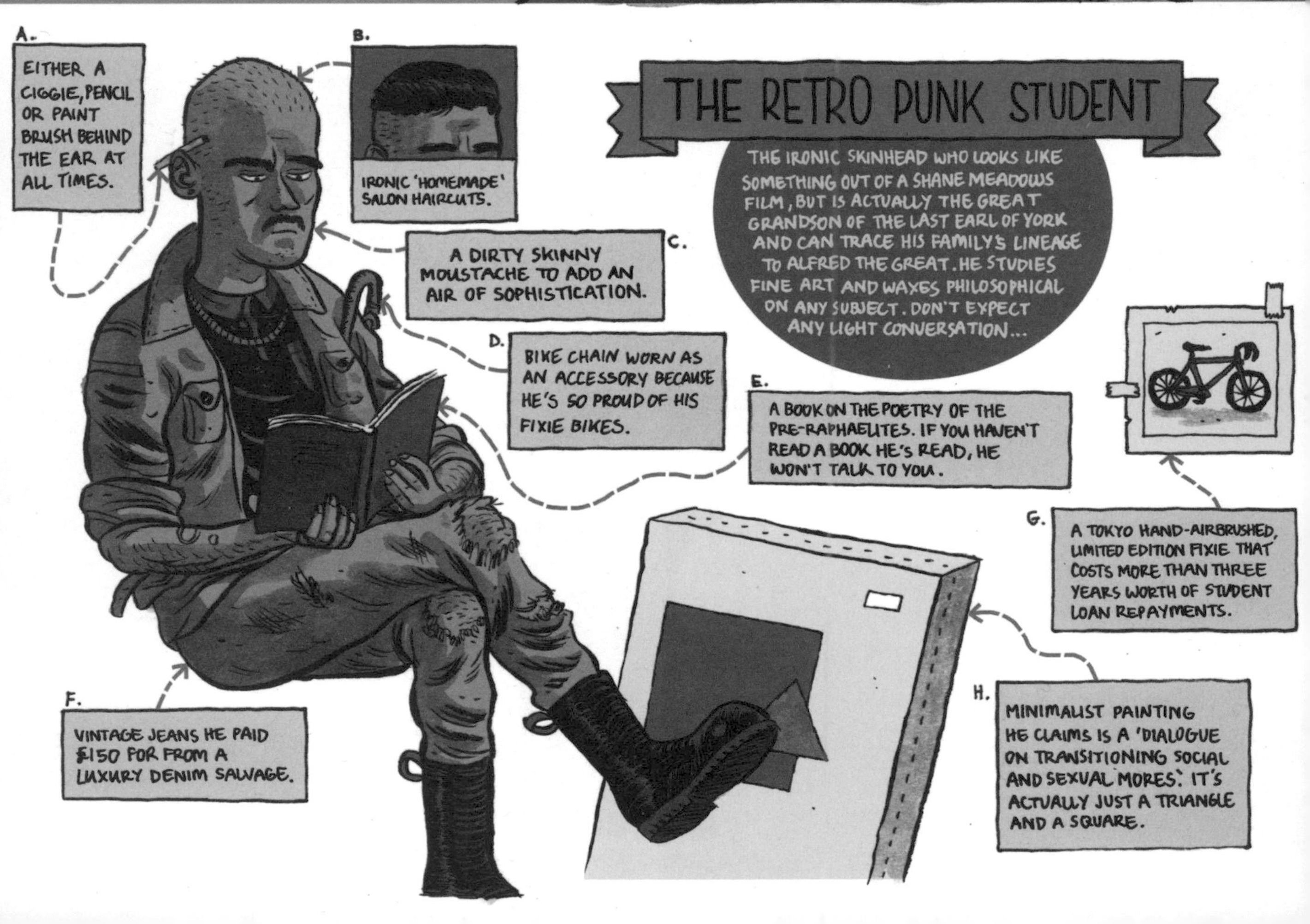
THE RETRO PUNK STUDENT
THE IRONIC SKINHEAD WHO LOOKS LIKE SOMETHING OUT OF A SHANE MEADOWS FILM, BUT IS ACTUALLY THE GREAT GRANDSON OF THE LAST EARL OF YORK AND CAN TRACE HIS FAMILY'S LINEAGE TO ALFRED THE GREAT. HE STUDIES FINE ART AND WAXES PHILOSOPHICAL ON ANY SUBJECT. DON'T EXPECT ANY LIGHT CONVERSATION...
A. EITHER A CIGGIE, PENCIL OR PAINT BRUSH BEHIND THE EAR AT ALL TIMES.
B. IRONIC 'HOMEMADE' SALON HAIRCUTS.
C. A DIRTY SKINNY MOUSTACHE TO ADD AN AIR OF SOPHISTICATION.
D. BIKE CHAIN WORN AS AN ACCESSORY BECAUSE HE'S SO PROUD OF HIS FIXIE BIKES.
E. A BOOK ON THE POETRY OF THE PRE-RAPHAELITES. IF YOU HAVEN'T READ A BOOK HE'S READ, HE WON'T TALK TO YOU.
F. VINTAGE JEANS HE PAID £150 FOR FROM A LUXURY DENIM SALVAGE.
G. A TOKYO HAND-AIRBRUSHED, LIMITED EDITION FIXIE THAT COSTS MORE THAN THREE YEARS WORTH OF STUDENT LOAN REPAYMENTS.
H. MINIMALIST PAINTING HE CLAIMS IS A 'DIALOGUE ON TRANSITIONING SOCIAL AND SEXUAL MORES'. IT'S ACTUALLY JUST A TRIANGLE AND A SQUARE.

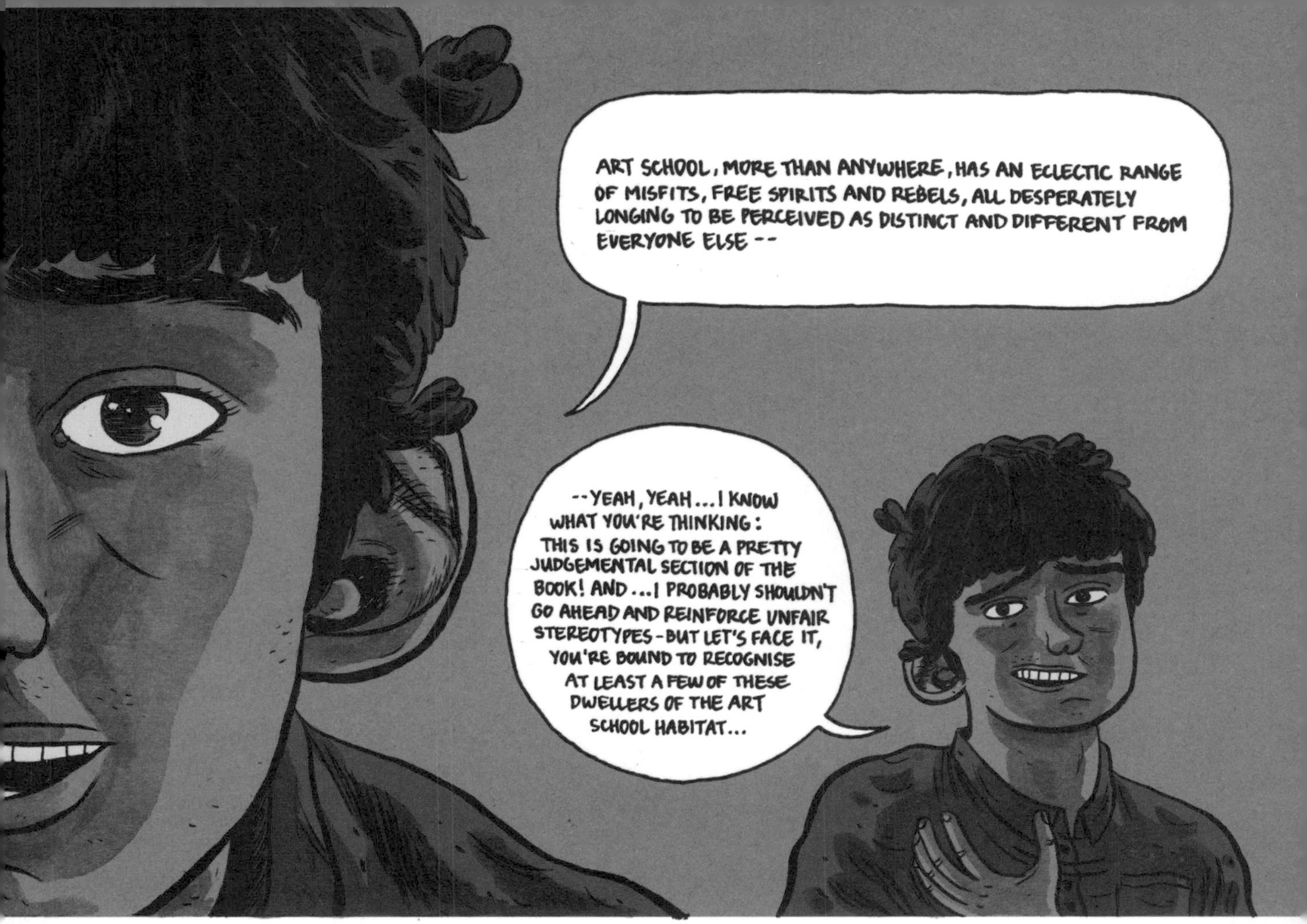
ART SCHOOL, MORE THAN ANYWHERE, HAS AN ECLECTIC RANGE OF MISFITS, FREE SPIRITS AND REBELS, ALL DESPERATELY LONGING TO BE PERCEIVED AS DISTINCT AND DIFFERENT FROM EVERYONE ELSE --
--YEAH, YEAH... I KNOW WHAT YOU'RE THINKING: THIS IS GOING TO BE A PRETTY JUDGEMENTAL SECTION OF THE BOOK! AND... I PROBABLY SHOULDN'T GO AHEAD AND REINFORCE UNFAIR STEREOTYPES - BUT LET'S FACE IT, YOU'RE BOUND TO RECOGNISE AT LEAST A FEW OF THESE DWELLERS OF THE ART SCHOOL HABITAT...

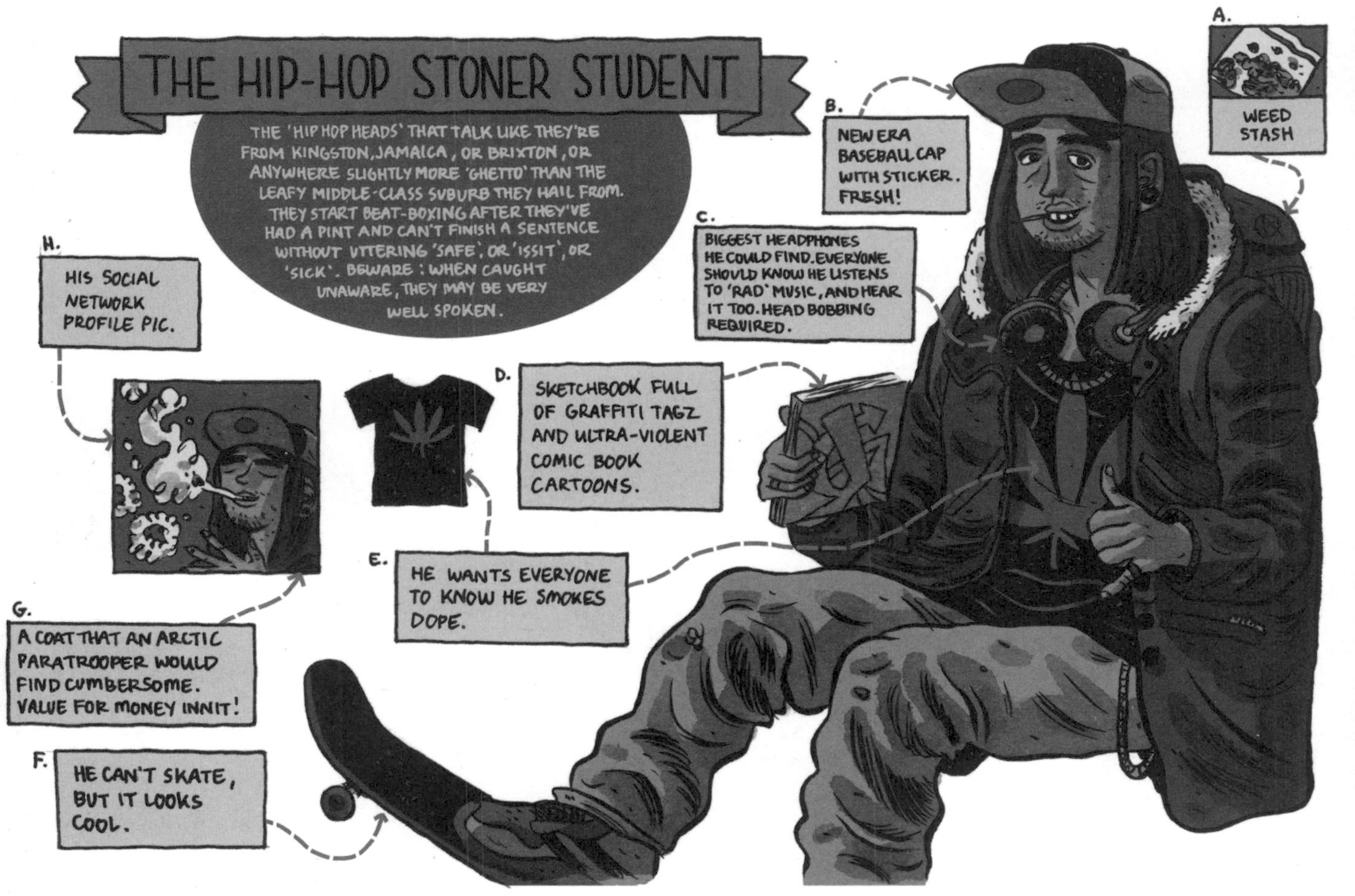
THE HIP-HOP STONER STUDENT
THE 'HIP HOP HEADS' THAT TALK LIKE THEY'RE FROM KINGSTON, JAMAICA, OR BRIXTON, OR ANYWHERE SLIGHTLY MORE 'GHETTO' THAN THE LEAFY MIDDLE-CLASS SUBURB THEY HAIL FROM. THEY START BEAT-BOXING AFTER THEY'VE HAD A PINT AND CAN'T FINISH A SENTENCE WITHOUT UTTERING 'SAFE', OR 'ISSIT', OR 'SICK'. BEWARE: WHEN CAUGHT UNAWARE, THEY MAY BE VERY WELL SPOKEN.
A. WEED STASH
B. NEW ERA BASEBALL CAP WITH STICKER. FRESH!
C. BIGGEST HEADPHONES HE COULD FIND. EVERYONE SHOULD KNOW HE LISTENS TO 'RAD' MUSIC, AND HEAR IT TOO. HEAD BOBBING REQUIRED.
D. SKETCHBOOK FULL OF GRAFFITI TAGZ AND ULTRA-VIOLENT COMIC BOOK CARTOONS.
E. HE WANTS EVERYONE TO KNOW HE SMOKES DOPE.
F. HE CAN'T SKATE, BUT IT LOOKS COOL.
G. A COAT THAT AN ARCTIC PARATROOPER WOULD FIND CUMBERSOME. VALUE FOR MONEY INNIT!
H. HIS SOCIAL NETWORK PROFILE PIC.

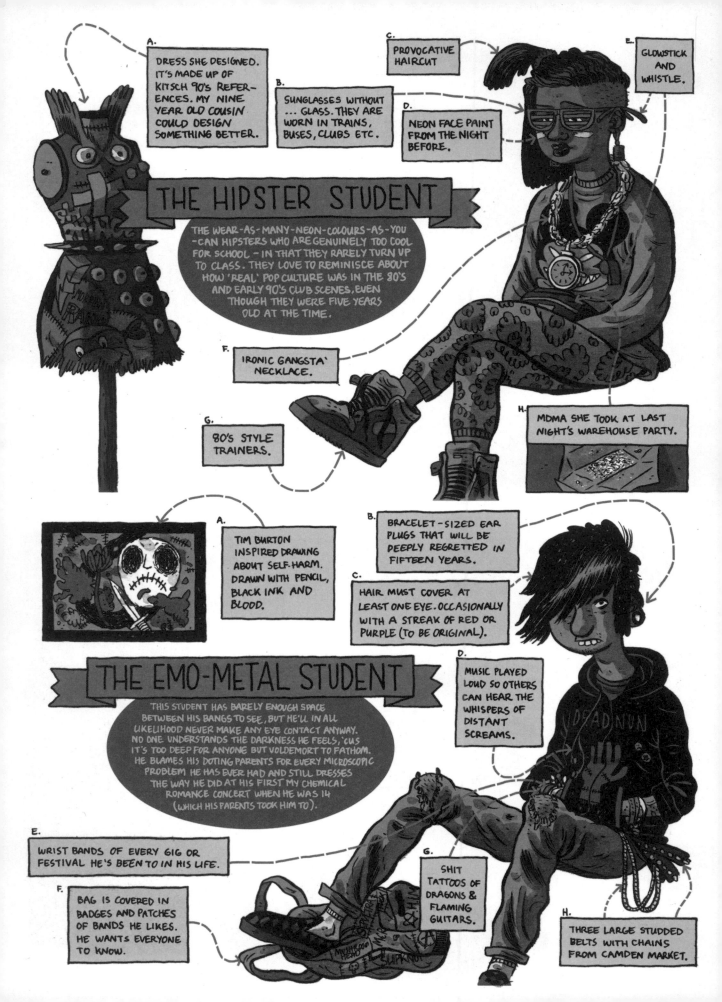

A. DRESS SHE DESIGNED. IT'S MADE UP OF KITSCH 90'S REFERENCES. MY NINE YEAR OLD COUSIN COULD DESIGN SOMETHING BETTER.

B. SUNGLASSES WITHOUT ... GLASS. THEY ARE WORN IN TRAINS, BUSES, CLUBS ETC.

C. PROVOCATIVE HAIRCUT

D. NEON FACE PAINT FROM THE NIGHT BEFORE.

E. GLOWSTICK AND WHISTLE.

THE HIPSTER STUDENT

THE WEAR-AS-MANY-NEON-COLOURS-AS-YOU-CAN HIPSTERS WHO ARE GENUINELY TOO COOL FOR SCHOOL – IN THAT THEY RARELY TURN UP TO CLASS. THEY LOVE TO REMINISCE ABOUT HOW 'REAL' POP CULTURE WAS IN THE 80'S AND EARLY 90'S CLUB SCENES, EVEN THOUGH THEY WERE FIVE YEARS OLD AT THE TIME.

F. IRONIC GANGSTA' NECKLACE.

G. 80'S STYLE TRAINERS.

H. MDMA SHE TOOK AT LAST NIGHT'S WAREHOUSE PARTY.

A. TIM BURTON INSPIRED DRAWING ABOUT SELF-HARM. DRAWN WITH PENCIL, BLACK INK AND BLOOD.

B. BRACELET-SIZED EAR PLUGS THAT WILL BE DEEPLY REGRETTED IN FIFTEEN YEARS.

C. HAIR MUST COVER AT LEAST ONE EYE. OCCASIONALLY WITH A STREAK OF RED OR PURPLE (TO BE ORIGINAL).

D. MUSIC PLAYED LOUD SO OTHERS CAN HEAR THE WHISPERS OF DISTANT SCREAMS.

THE EMO-METAL STUDENT

THIS STUDENT HAS BARELY ENOUGH SPACE BETWEEN HIS BANGS TO SEE, BUT HE'LL IN ALL LIKELIHOOD NEVER MAKE ANY EYE CONTACT ANYWAY. NO ONE UNDERSTANDS THE DARKNESS HE FEELS, 'CUS IT'S TOO DEEP FOR ANYONE BUT VOLDEMORT TO FATHOM. HE BLAMES HIS DOTING PARENTS FOR EVERY MICROSCOPIC PROBLEM HE HAS EVER HAD AND STILL DRESSES THE WAY HE DID AT HIS FIRST MY CHEMICAL ROMANCE CONCERT WHEN HE WAS 14 (WHICH HIS PARENTS TOOK HIM TO).

E. WRIST BANDS OF EVERY GIG OR FESTIVAL HE'S BEEN TO IN HIS LIFE.

F. BAG IS COVERED IN BADGES AND PATCHES OF BANDS HE LIKES. HE WANTS EVERYONE TO KNOW.

G. SHIT TATTOOS OF DRAGONS & FLAMING GUITARS.

H. THREE LARGE STUDDED BELTS WITH CHAINS FROM CAMDEN MARKET.

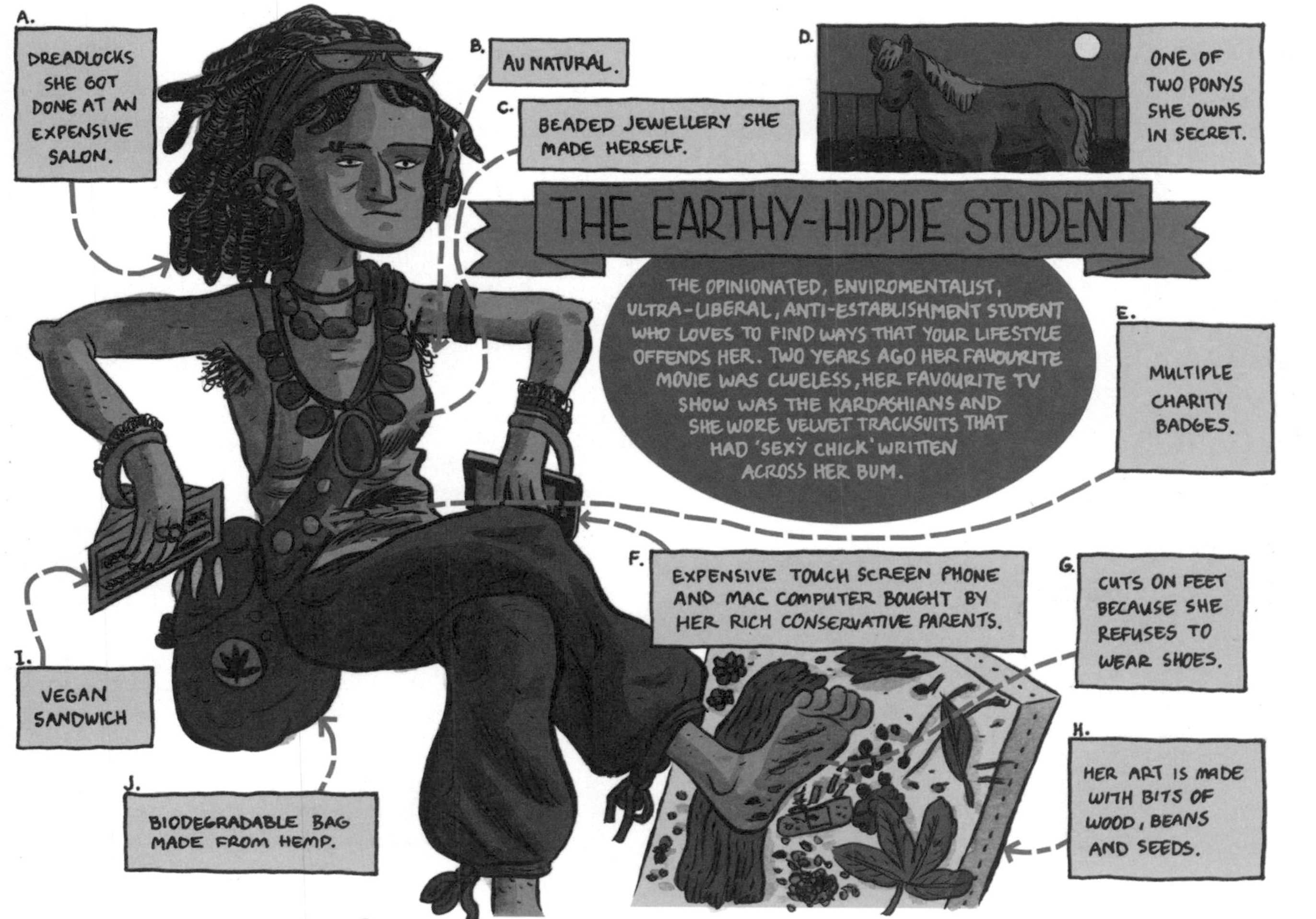
THE EARTHY-HIPPIE STUDENT
THE OPINIONATED, ENVIRONMENTALIST, ULTRA-LIBERAL, ANTI-ESTABLISHMENT STUDENT WHO LOVES TO FIND WAYS THAT YOUR LIFESTYLE OFFENDS HER. TWO YEARS AGO HER FAVOURITE MOVIE WAS CLUELESS, HER FAVOURITE TV SHOW WAS THE KARDASHIANS AND SHE WORE VELVET TRACKSUITS THAT HAD 'SEXY CHICK' WRITTEN ACROSS HER BUM.
A. DREADLOCKS SHE GOT DONE AT AN EXPENSIVE SALON.
B. AU NATURAL.
C. BEADED JEWELLERY SHE MADE HERSELF.
D. ONE OF TWO PONYS SHE OWNS IN SECRET.
E. MULTIPLE CHARITY BADGES.
F. EXPENSIVE TOUCH SCREEN PHONE AND MAC COMPUTER BOUGHT BY HER RICH CONSERVATIVE PARENTS.
G. CUTS ON FEET BECAUSE SHE REFUSES TO WEAR SHOES.
H. HER ART IS MADE WITH BITS OF WOOD, BEANS AND SEEDS.
I. VEGAN SANDWICH
J. BIODEGRADABLE BAG MADE FROM HEMP.

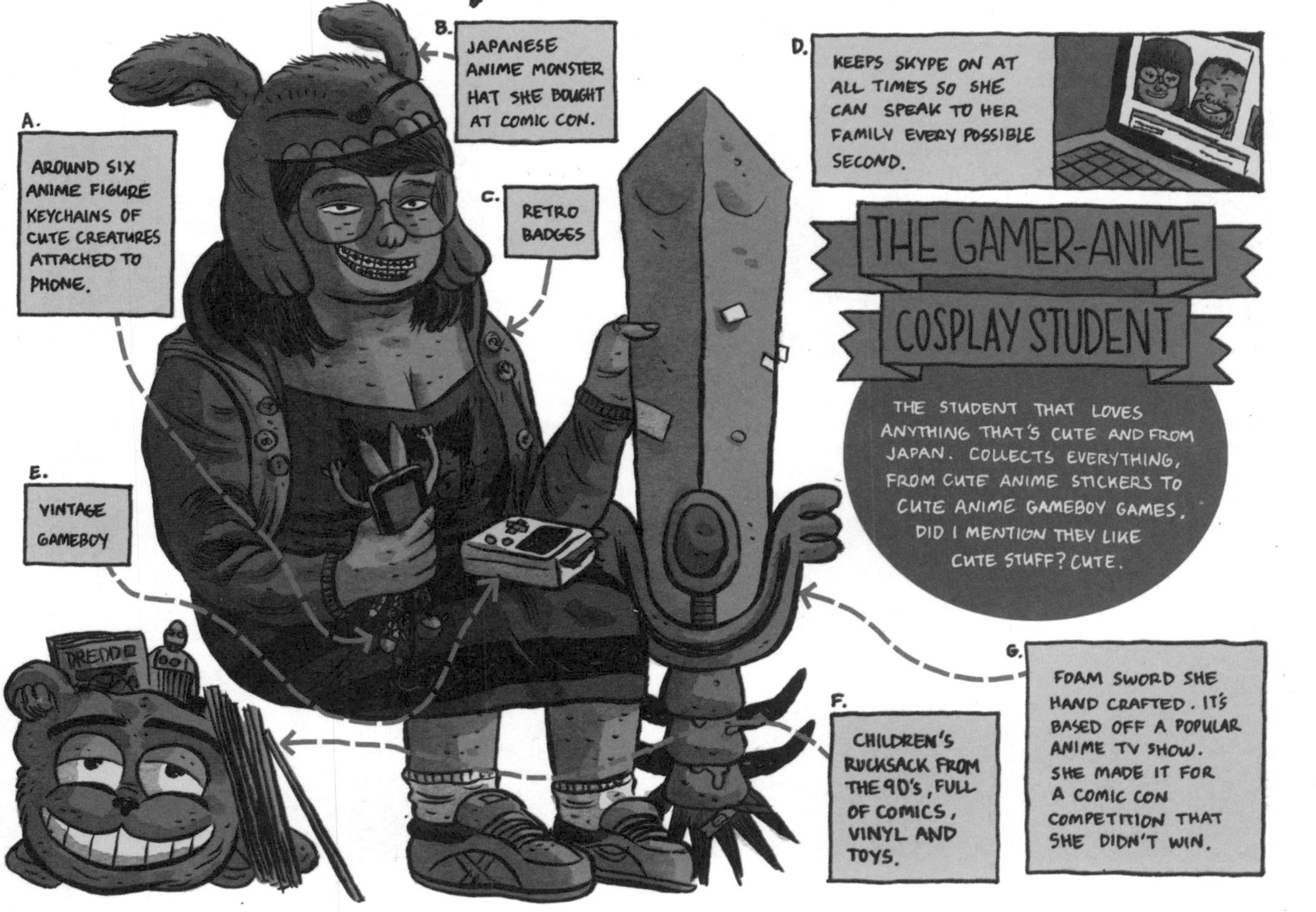
THE GAMER-ANIME COSPLAY STUDENT
THE STUDENT THAT LOVES ANYTHING THAT'S CUTE AND FROM JAPAN. COLLECTS EVERYTHING, FROM CUTE ANIME STICKERS TO CUTE ANIME GAMEBOY GAMES. DID I MENTION THEY LIKE CUTE STUFF? CUTE.
A. AROUND SIX ANIME FIGURE KEYCHAINS OF CUTE CREATURES ATTACHED TO PHONE.
B. JAPANESE ANIME MONSTER HAT SHE BOUGHT AT COMIC CON.
C. RETRO BADGES
D. KEEPS SKYPE ON AT ALL TIMES SO SHE CAN SPEAK TO HER FAMILY EVERY POSSIBLE SECOND.
E. VINTAGE GAMEBOY
F. CHILDREN'S RUCKSACK FROM THE 90'S, FULL OF COMICS, VINYL AND TOYS.
G. FOAM SWORD SHE HAND CRAFTED. IT'S BASED OFF A POPULAR ANIME TV SHOW. SHE MADE IT FOR A COMIC CON COMPETITION THAT SHE DIDN'T WIN.

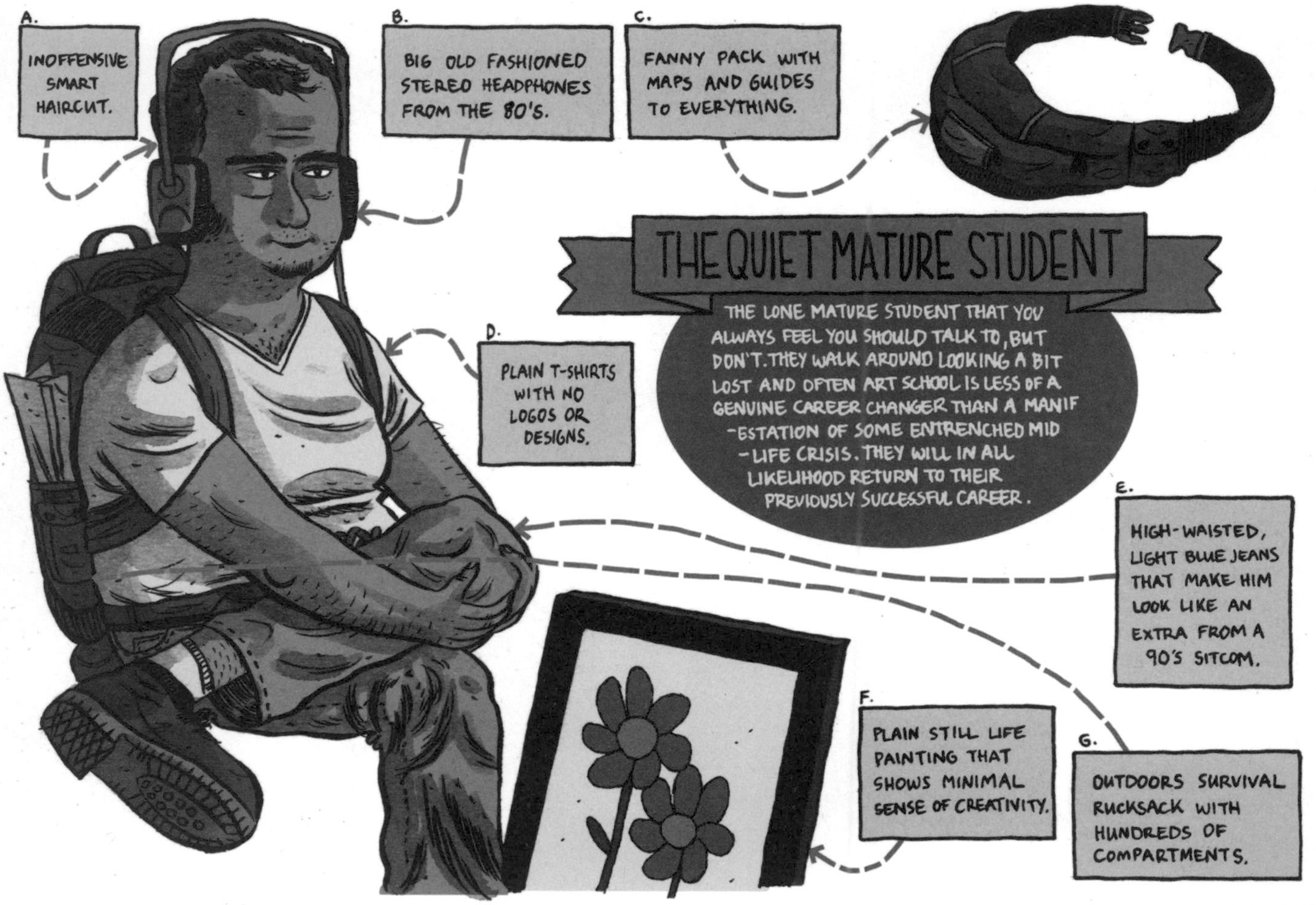
A.
INOFFENSIVE SMART HAIRCUT.
B.
BIG OLD FASHIONED STEREO HEADPHONES FROM THE 80'S.
C.
FANNY PACK WITH MAPS AND GUIDES TO EVERYTHING.
THE QUIET MATURE STUDENT
THE LONE MATURE STUDENT THAT YOU ALWAYS FEEL YOU SHOULD TALK TO, BUT DON'T. THEY WALK AROUND LOOKING A BIT LOST AND OFTEN ART SCHOOL IS LESS OF A GENUINE CAREER CHANGER THAN A MANIF-ESTATION OF SOME ENTRENCHED MID-LIFE CRISIS. THEY WILL IN ALL LIKELIHOOD RETURN TO THEIR PREVIOUSLY SUCCESSFUL CAREER.
D.
PLAIN T-SHIRTS WITH NO LOGOS OR DESIGNS.
E.
HIGH-WAISTED, LIGHT BLUE JEANS THAT MAKE HIM LOOK LIKE AN EXTRA FROM A 90'S SITCOM.
F.
PLAIN STILL LIFE PAINTING THAT SHOWS MINIMAL SENSE OF CREATIVITY.
G.
OUTDOORS SURVIVAL RUCKSACK WITH HUNDREDS OF COMPARTMENTS.

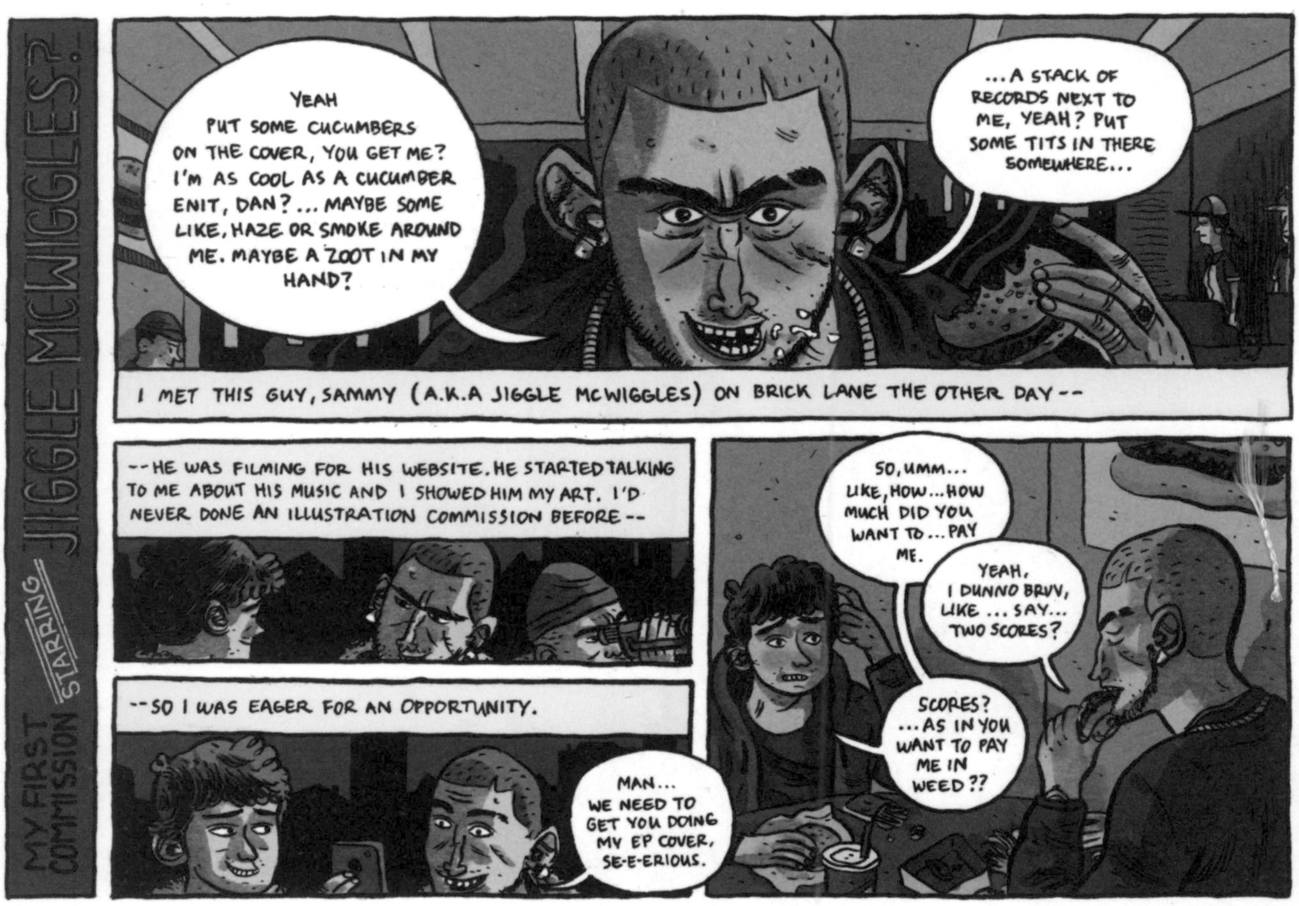
MY FIRST COMMISSION STARRING JIGGLE MCWIGGLES?
YEAH PUT SOME CUCUMBERS ON THE COVER, YOU GET ME? I'M AS COOL AS A CUCUMBER ENIT, DAN?... MAYBE SOME LIKE, HAZE OR SMOKE AROUND ME. MAYBE A ZOOT IN MY HAND?
...A STACK OF RECORDS NEXT TO ME, YEAH? PUT SOME TITS IN THERE SOMEWHERE...
I MET THIS GUY, SAMMY (A.K.A JIGGLE MCWIGGLES) ON BRICK LANE THE OTHER DAY--
--HE WAS FILMING FOR HIS WEBSITE. HE STARTED TALKING TO ME ABOUT HIS MUSIC AND I SHOWED HIM MY ART. I'D NEVER DONE AN ILLUSTRATION COMMISSION BEFORE--
--SO I WAS EAGER FOR AN OPPORTUNITY.
MAN... WE NEED TO GET YOU DOING MY EP COVER, SE-E-ERIOUS.
SO, UMM... LIKE, HOW... HOW MUCH DID YOU WANT TO... PAY ME.
YEAH, I DUNNO BRUV, LIKE ... SAY... TWO SCORES?
SCORES? ...AS IN YOU WANT TO PAY ME IN WEED??

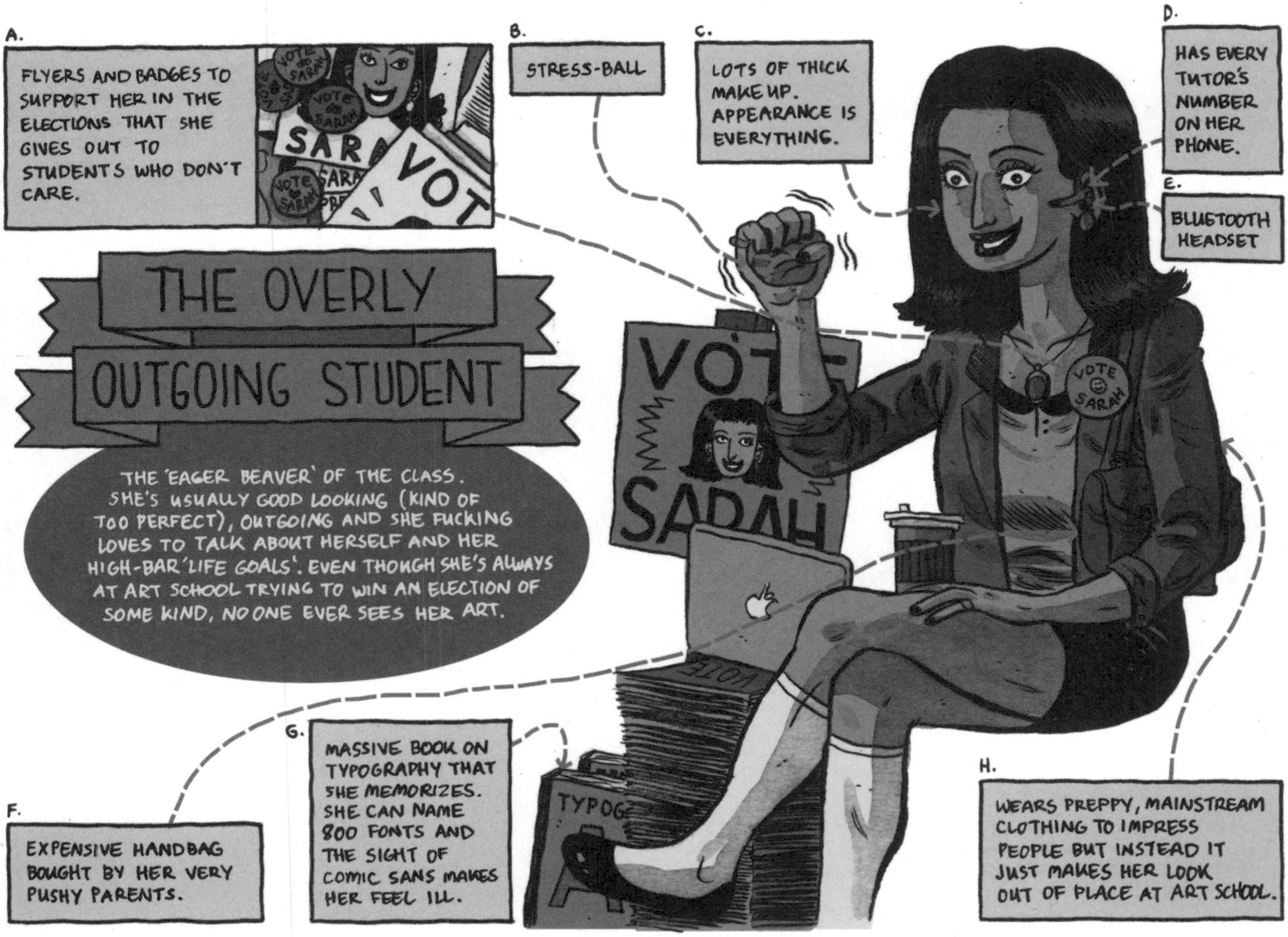
A.
FLYERS AND BADGES TO SUPPORT HER IN THE ELECTIONS THAT SHE GIVES OUT TO STUDENTS WHO DON'T CARE.
VOTE SARAH
B.
STRESS-BALL
C.
LOTS OF THICK MAKE UP. APPEARANCE IS EVERYTHING.
D.
HAS EVERY TUTOR'S NUMBER ON HER PHONE.
E.
BLUETOOTH HEADSET
THE OVERLY
OUTGOING STUDENT
THE 'EAGER BEAVER' OF THE CLASS. SHE'S USUALLY GOOD LOOKING (KIND OF TOO PERFECT), OUTGOING AND SHE FUCKING LOVES TO TALK ABOUT HERSELF AND HER HIGH-BAR 'LIFE GOALS'. EVEN THOUGH SHE'S ALWAYS AT ART SCHOOL TRYING TO WIN AN ELECTION OF SOME KIND, NO ONE EVER SEES HER ART.
VOTE SARAH
F.
EXPENSIVE HANDBAG BOUGHT BY HER VERY PUSHY PARENTS.
G.
MASSIVE BOOK ON TYPOGRAPHY THAT SHE MEMORIZES. SHE CAN NAME 800 FONTS AND THE SIGHT OF COMIC SANS MAKES HER FEEL ILL.
H.
WEARS PREPPY, MAINSTREAM CLOTHING TO IMPRESS PEOPLE BUT INSTEAD IT JUST MAKES HER LOOK OUT OF PLACE AT ART SCHOOL.

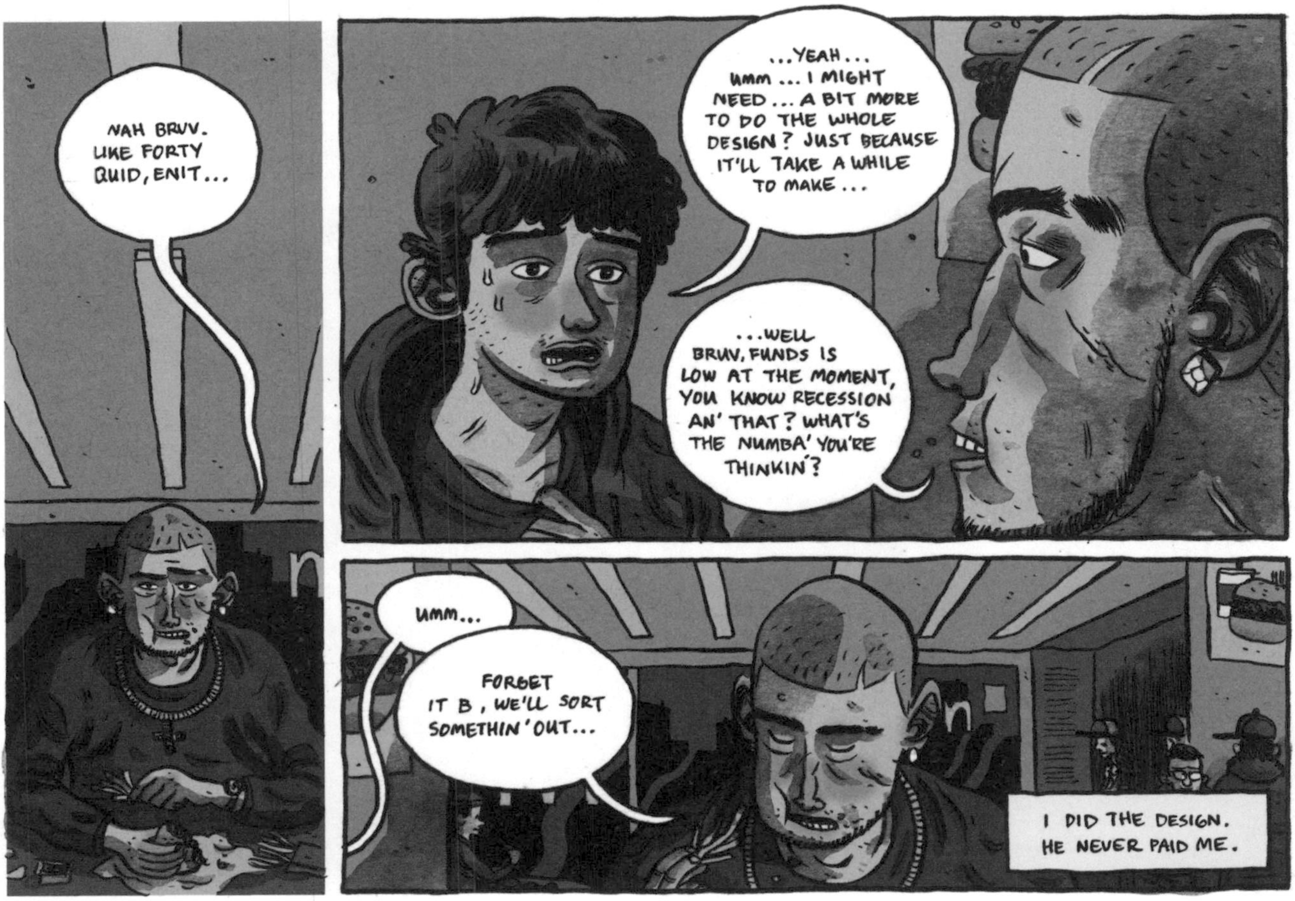
NAH BRUV. LIKE FORTY QUID, ENIT...
...YEAH... UMM... I MIGHT NEED... A BIT MORE TO DO THE WHOLE DESIGN? JUST BECAUSE IT'LL TAKE A WHILE TO MAKE...
...WELL BRUV, FUNDS IS LOW AT THE MOMENT, YOU KNOW RECESSION AN' THAT? WHAT'S THE NUMBA' YOU'RE THINKIN'?
UMM...
FORGET IT B, WE'LL SORT SOMETHIN' OUT...
I DID THE DESIGN. HE NEVER PAID ME.

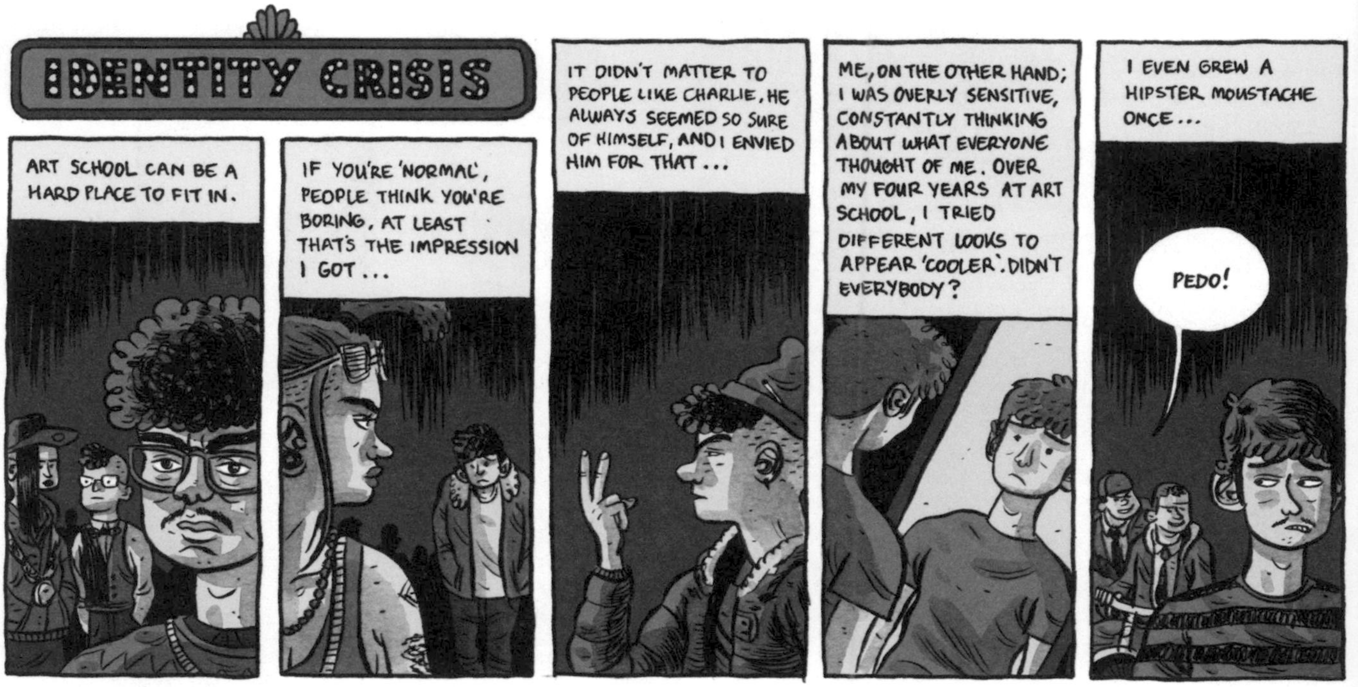
IDENTITY CRISIS
ART SCHOOL CAN BE A HARD PLACE TO FIT IN.
IF YOU'RE 'NORMAL', PEOPLE THINK YOU'RE BORING, AT LEAST THAT'S THE IMPRESSION I GOT...
IT DIDN'T MATTER TO PEOPLE LIKE CHARLIE, HE ALWAYS SEEMED SO SURE OF HIMSELF, AND I ENVIED HIM FOR THAT...
ME, ON THE OTHER HAND; I WAS OVERLY SENSITIVE, CONSTANTLY THINKING ABOUT WHAT EVERYONE THOUGHT OF ME. OVER MY FOUR YEARS AT ART SCHOOL, I TRIED DIFFERENT LOOKS TO APPEAR 'COOLER'. DIDN'T EVERYBODY?
I EVEN GREW A HIPSTER MOUSTACHE ONCE...
PEDO!

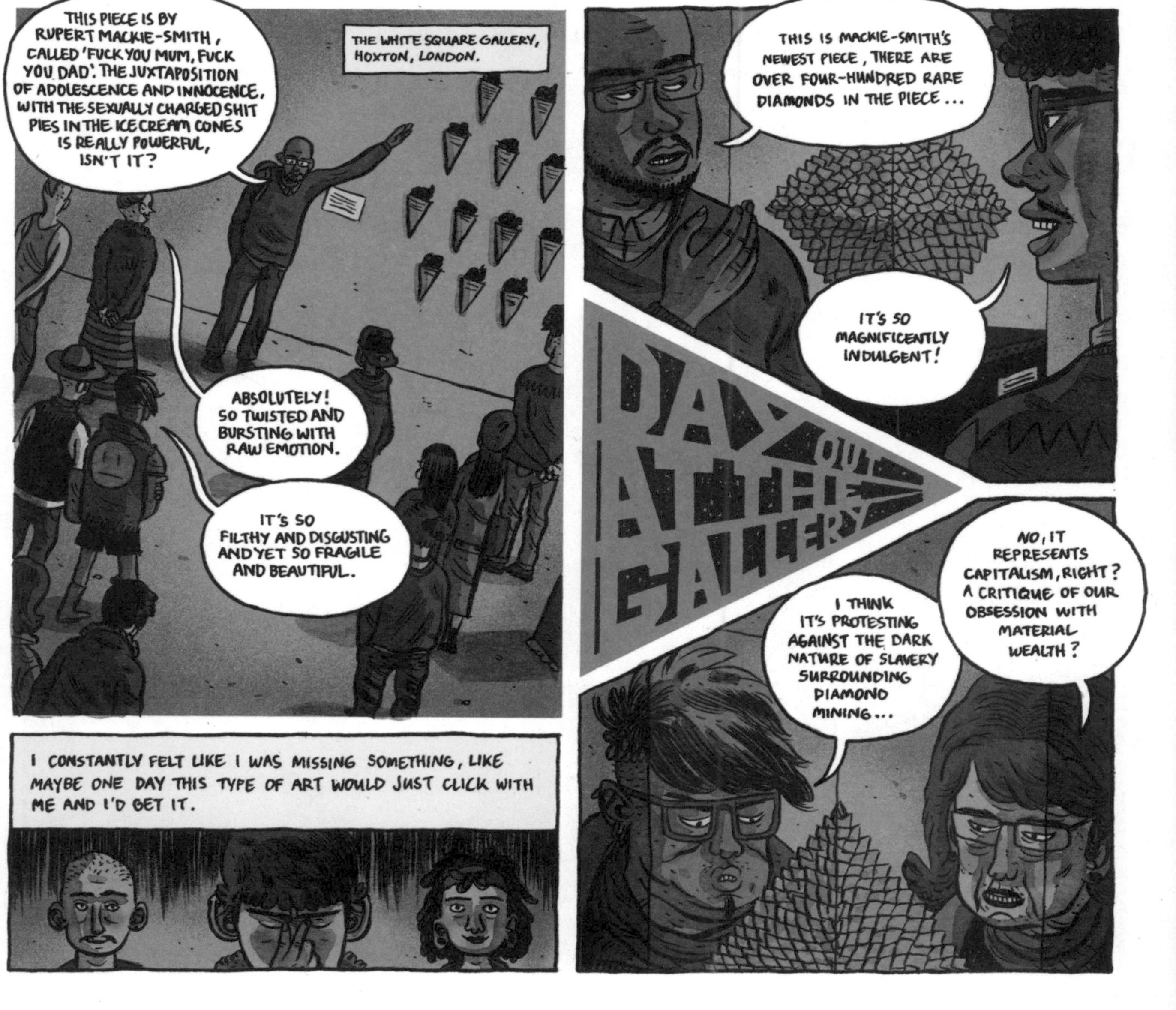
THE WHITE SQUARE GALLERY, HOXTON, LONDON.
THIS PIECE IS BY RUPERT MACKIE-SMITH, CALLED 'FUCK YOU MUM, FUCK YOU DAD'. THE JUXTAPOSITION OF ADOLESCENCE AND INNOCENCE, WITH THE SEXUALLY CHARGED SHIT PIES IN THE ICE CREAM CONES IS REALLY POWERFUL, ISN'T IT?
ABSOLUTELY! SO TWISTED AND BURSTING WITH RAW EMOTION.
IT'S SO FILTHY AND DISGUSTING AND YET SO FRAGILE AND BEAUTIFUL.
DAY OUT AT THE GALLERY
THIS IS MACKIE-SMITH'S NEWEST PIECE, THERE ARE OVER FOUR-HUNDRED RARE DIAMONDS IN THE PIECE...
IT'S SO MAGNIFICENTLY INDULGENT!
I THINK IT'S PROTESTING AGAINST THE DARK NATURE OF SLAVERY SURROUNDING DIAMOND MINING...
NO, IT REPRESENTS CAPITALISM, RIGHT? A CRITIQUE OF OUR OBSESSION WITH MATERIAL WEALTH?
I CONSTANTLY FELT LIKE I WAS MISSING SOMETHING, LIKE MAYBE ONE DAY THIS TYPE OF ART WOULD JUST CLICK WITH ME AND I'D GET IT.

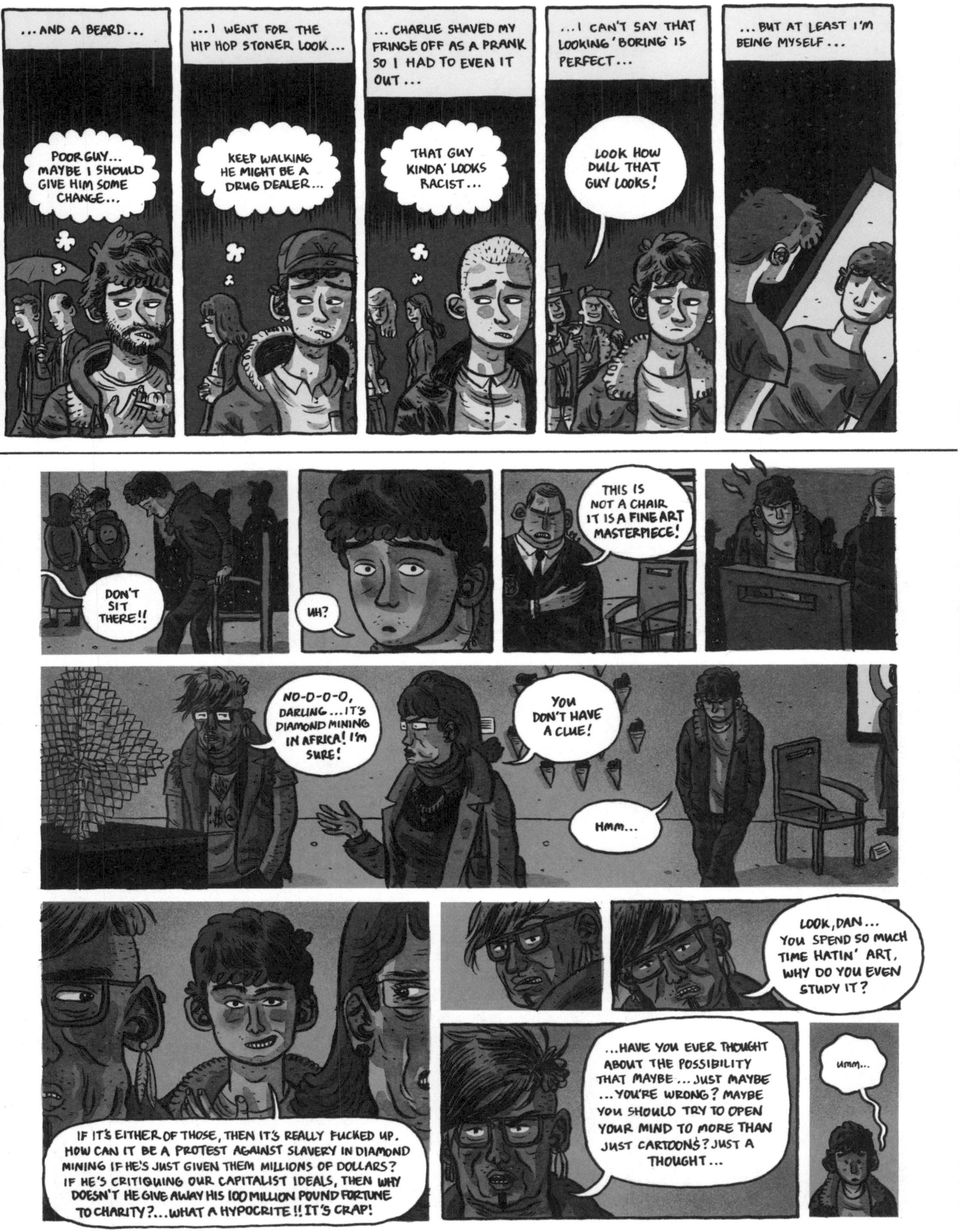
...AND A BEARD...
POOR GUY... MAYBE I SHOULD GIVE HIM SOME CHANGE...
...I WENT FOR THE HIP HOP STONER LOOK...
KEEP WALKING HE MIGHT BE A DRUG DEALER...
...CHARLIE SHAVED MY FRINGE OFF AS A PRANK SO I HAD TO EVEN IT OUT...
THAT GUY KINDA' LOOKS RACIST...
...I CAN'T SAY THAT LOOKING 'BORING' IS PERFECT...
LOOK HOW DULL THAT GUY LOOKS!
...BUT AT LEAST I'M BEING MYSELF...
DON'T SIT THERE!!
UH?
THIS IS NOT A CHAIR IT IS A FINE ART MASTERPIECE!
NO-O-O-O, DARLING...IT'S DIAMOND MINING IN AFRICA! I'M SURE!
YOU DON'T HAVE A CLUE!
HMM...
IF IT'S EITHER OF THOSE, THEN IT'S REALLY FUCKED UP. HOW CAN IT BE A PROTEST AGAINST SLAVERY IN DIAMOND MINING IF HE'S JUST GIVEN THEM MILLIONS OF DOLLARS? IF HE'S CRITIQUING OUR CAPITALIST IDEALS, THEN WHY DOESN'T HE GIVE AWAY HIS 100 MILLION POUND FORTUNE TO CHARITY?...WHAT A HYPOCRITE!! IT'S CRAP!
LOOK, DAN... YOU SPEND SO MUCH TIME HATIN' ART, WHY DO YOU EVEN STUDY IT?
...HAVE YOU EVER THOUGHT ABOUT THE POSSIBILITY THAT MAYBE... JUST MAYBE ...YOU'RE WRONG? MAYBE YOU SHOULD TRY TO OPEN YOUR MIND TO MORE THAN JUST CARTOONS? JUST A THOUGHT...
UMM...

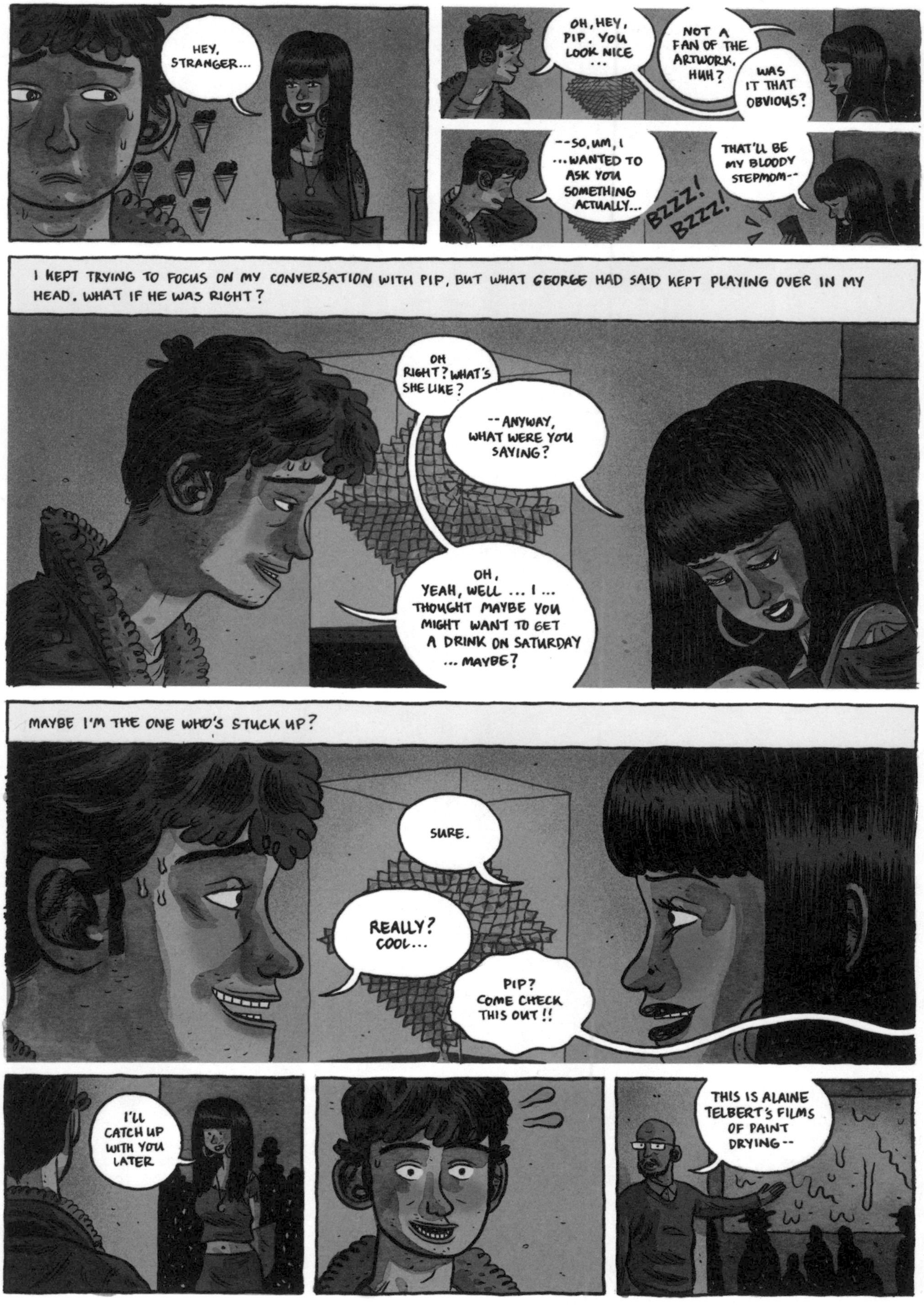
HEY, STRANGER...
OH, HEY, PIP. YOU LOOK NICE ...
NOT A FAN OF THE ARTWORK, HUH?
WAS IT THAT OBVIOUS?
--SO, UM, I ...WANTED TO ASK YOU SOMETHING ACTUALLY...
BZZZ! BZZZ!
THAT'LL BE MY BLOODY STEPMOM--
I KEPT TRYING TO FOCUS ON MY CONVERSATION WITH PIP, BUT WHAT GEORGE HAD SAID KEPT PLAYING OVER IN MY HEAD. WHAT IF HE WAS RIGHT?
OH RIGHT? WHAT'S SHE LIKE?
--ANYWAY, WHAT WERE YOU SAYING?
OH, YEAH, WELL ... I ... THOUGHT MAYBE YOU MIGHT WANT TO GET A DRINK ON SATURDAY ... MAYBE?
MAYBE I'M THE ONE WHO'S STUCK UP?
SURE.
REALLY? COOL...
PIP? COME CHECK THIS OUT!!
I'LL CATCH UP WITH YOU LATER
THIS IS ALAINE TELBERT'S FILMS OF PAINT DRYING--

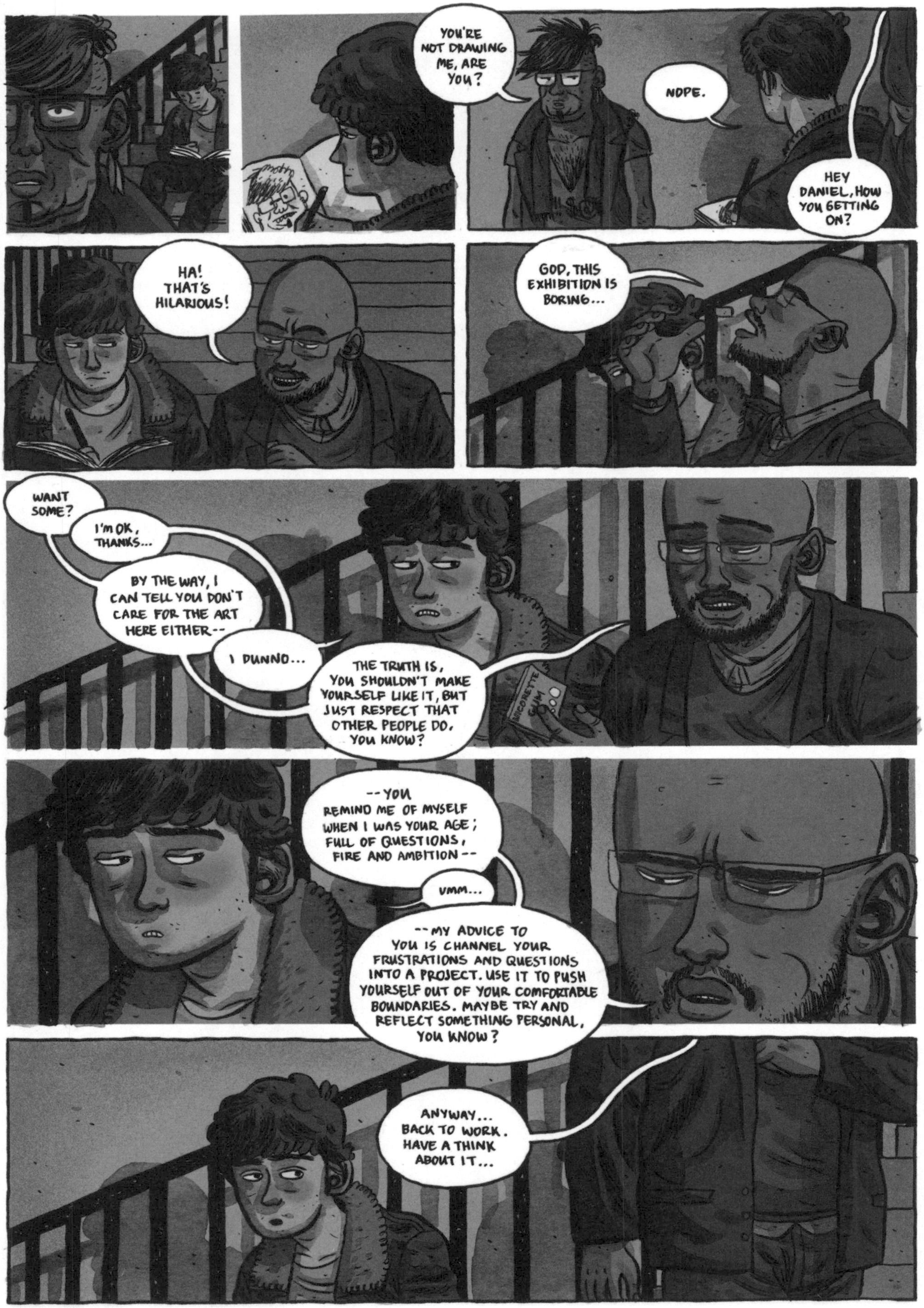
YOU'RE NOT DRAWING ME, ARE YOU?
NOPE.
HEY DANIEL, HOW YOU GETTING ON?
HA! THAT'S HILARIOUS!
GOD, THIS EXHIBITION IS BORING...
WANT SOME?
I'M OK, THANKS...
BY THE WAY, I CAN TELL YOU DON'T CARE FOR THE ART HERE EITHER--
I DUNNO...
THE TRUTH IS, YOU SHOULDN'T MAKE YOURSELF LIKE IT, BUT JUST RESPECT THAT OTHER PEOPLE DO, YOU KNOW?
NICORETTE GUM
--YOU REMIND ME OF MYSELF WHEN I WAS YOUR AGE; FULL OF QUESTIONS, FIRE AND AMBITION--
UMM...
--MY ADVICE TO YOU IS CHANNEL YOUR FRUSTRATIONS AND QUESTIONS INTO A PROJECT. USE IT TO PUSH YOURSELF OUT OF YOUR COMFORTABLE BOUNDARIES. MAYBE TRY AND REFLECT SOMETHING PERSONAL, YOU KNOW?
ANYWAY... BACK TO WORK. HAVE A THINK ABOUT IT...

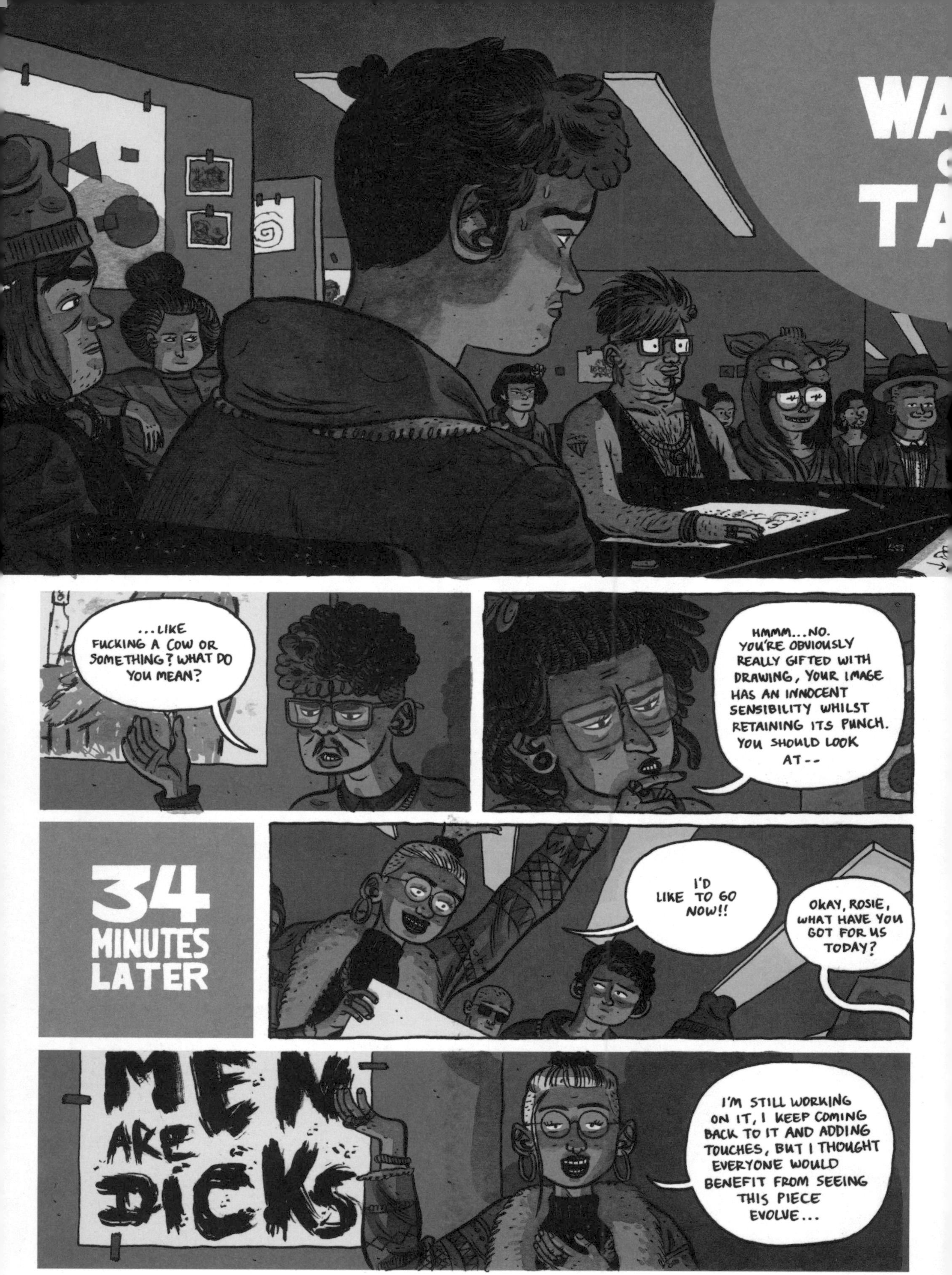
...LIKE FUCKING A COW OR SOMETHING? WHAT DO YOU MEAN?
HMMM...NO. YOU'RE OBVIOUSLY REALLY GIFTED WITH DRAWING, YOUR IMAGE HAS AN INNOCENT SENSIBILITY WHILST RETAINING ITS PUNCH. YOU SHOULD LOOK AT--
34 MINUTES LATER
I'D LIKE TO GO NOW!!
OKAY, ROSIE, WHAT HAVE YOU GOT FOR US TODAY?
MEN ARE DICKS
I'M STILL WORKING ON IT, I KEEP COMING BACK TO IT AND ADDING TOUCHES, BUT I THOUGHT EVERYONE WOULD BENEFIT FROM SEEING THIS PIECE EVOLVE...

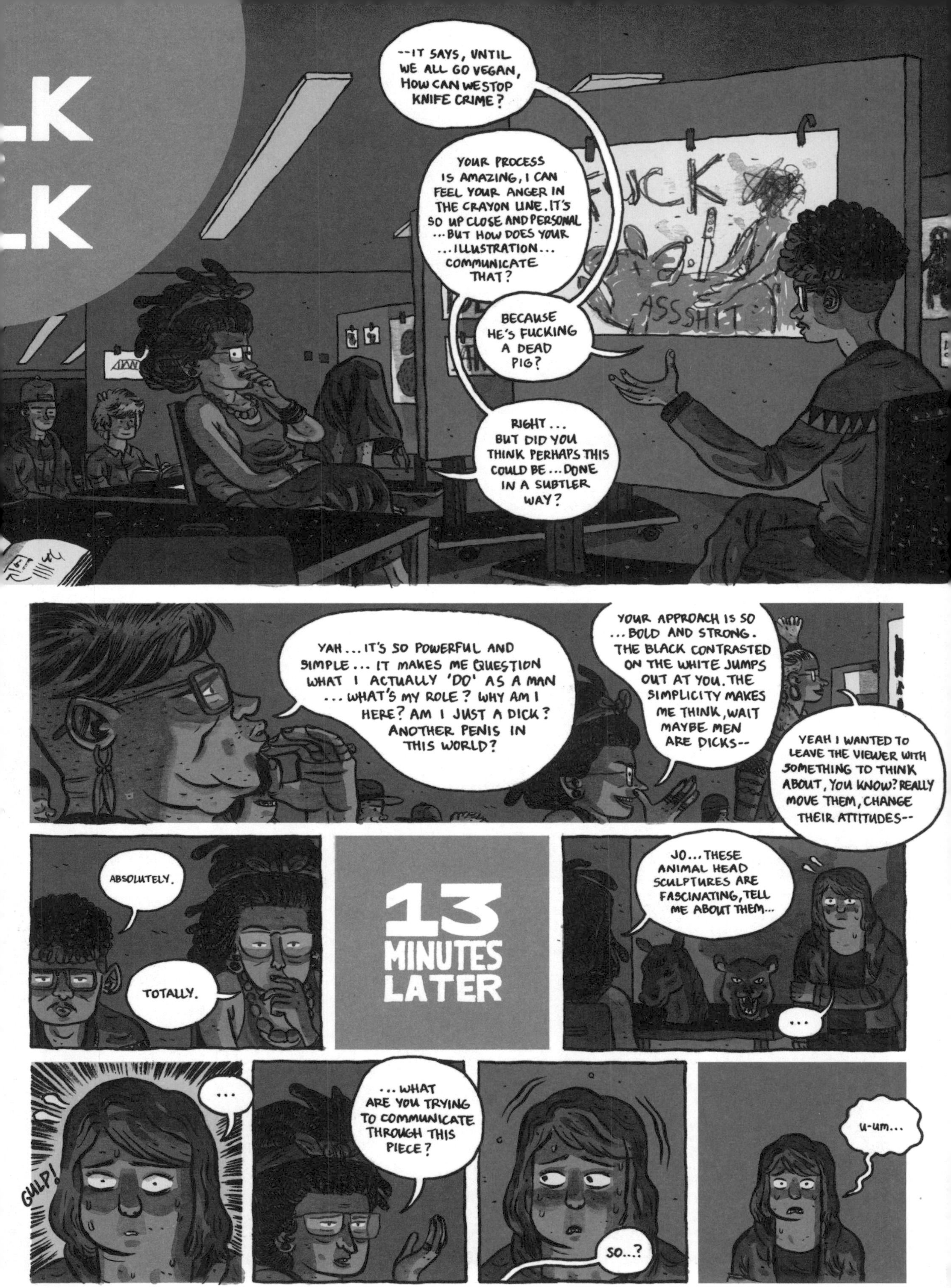
LK
LK
--IT SAYS, UNTIL WE ALL GO VEGAN, HOW CAN WE STOP KNIFE CRIME?
YOUR PROCESS IS AMAZING, I CAN FEEL YOUR ANGER IN THE CRAYON LINE. IT'S SO UP CLOSE AND PERSONAL ...BUT HOW DOES YOUR ...ILLUSTRATION... COMMUNICATE THAT?
BECAUSE HE'S FUCKING A DEAD PIG?
RIGHT... BUT DID YOU THINK PERHAPS THIS COULD BE...DONE IN A SUBTLER WAY?
FUCK
ASSSHIT
YAH...IT'S SO POWERFUL AND SIMPLE... IT MAKES ME QUESTION WHAT I ACTUALLY 'DO' AS A MAN ...WHAT'S MY ROLE? WHY AM I HERE? AM I JUST A DICK? ANOTHER PENIS IN THIS WORLD?
YOUR APPROACH IS SO ...BOLD AND STRONG. THE BLACK CONTRASTED ON THE WHITE JUMPS OUT AT YOU. THE SIMPLICITY MAKES ME THINK, WAIT MAYBE MEN ARE DICKS--
YEAH I WANTED TO LEAVE THE VIEWER WITH SOMETHING TO THINK ABOUT, YOU KNOW? REALLY MOVE THEM, CHANGE THEIR ATTITUDES--
ABSOLUTELY.
TOTALLY.
13 MINUTES LATER
JO... THESE ANIMAL HEAD SCULPTURES ARE FASCINATING, TELL ME ABOUT THEM...
...
...
GULP!
...WHAT ARE YOU TRYING TO COMMUNICATE THROUGH THIS PIECE?
SO...?
U-UM...

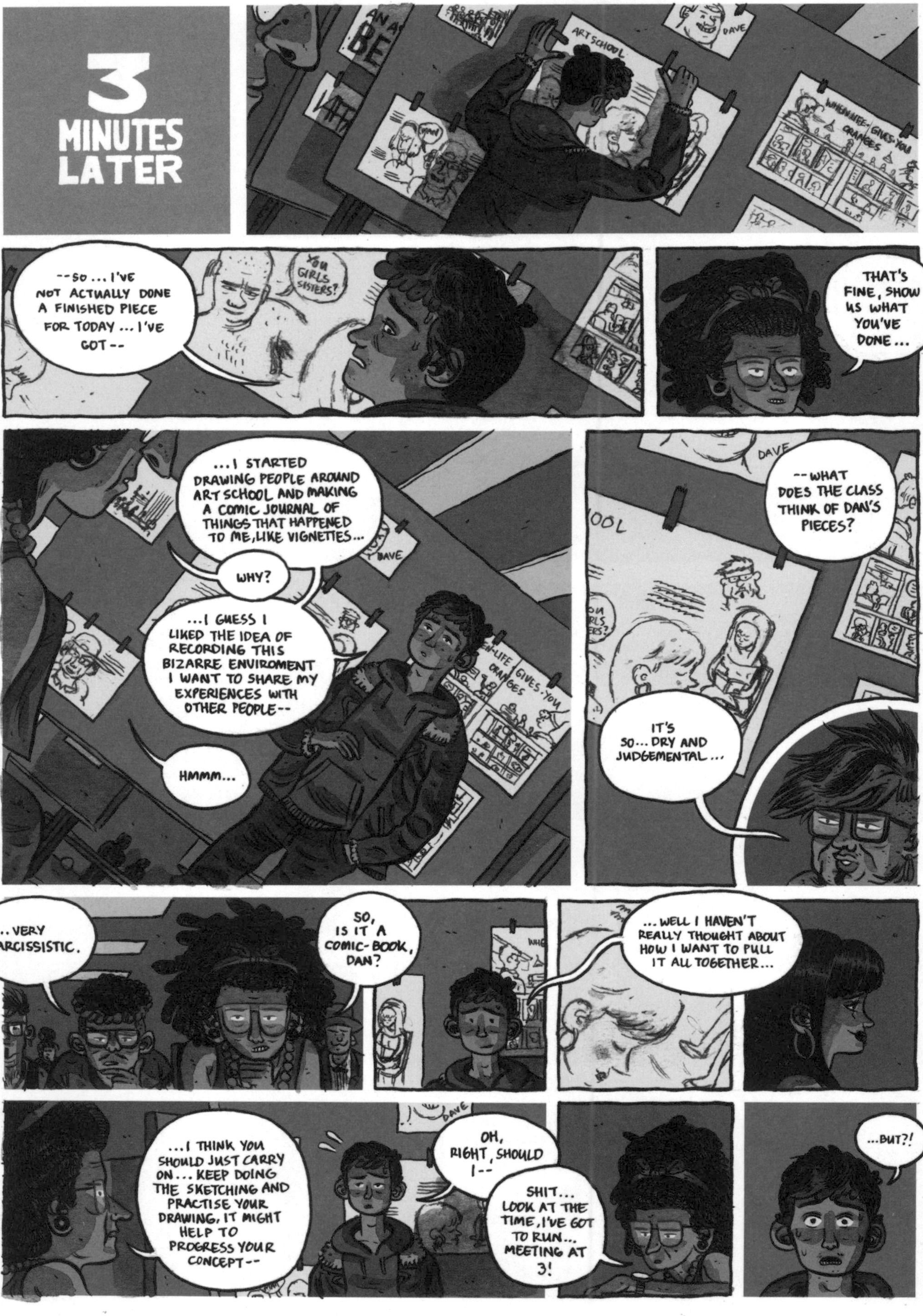
3 MINUTES LATER
--SO ... I'VE NOT ACTUALLY DONE A FINISHED PIECE FOR TODAY ... I'VE GOT--
THAT'S FINE, SHOW US WHAT YOU'VE DONE...
...I STARTED DRAWING PEOPLE AROUND ART SCHOOL AND MAKING A COMIC JOURNAL OF THINGS THAT HAPPENED TO ME, LIKE VIGNETTES...
WHY?
...I GUESS I LIKED THE IDEA OF RECORDING THIS BIZARRE ENVIROMENT I WANT TO SHARE MY EXPERIENCES WITH OTHER PEOPLE--
HMMM...
--WHAT DOES THE CLASS THINK OF DAN'S PIECES?
IT'S SO... DRY AND JUDGEMENTAL...
...VERY NARCISSISTIC.
SO, IS IT A COMIC-BOOK, DAN?
...WELL I HAVEN'T REALLY THOUGHT ABOUT HOW I WANT TO PULL IT ALL TOGETHER...
...I THINK YOU SHOULD JUST CARRY ON... KEEP DOING THE SKETCHING AND PRACTISE YOUR DRAWING, IT MIGHT HELP TO PROGRESS YOUR CONCEPT--
OH, RIGHT, SHOULD I--
SHIT... LOOK AT THE TIME, I'VE GOT TO RUN... MEETING AT 3!
...BUT?!

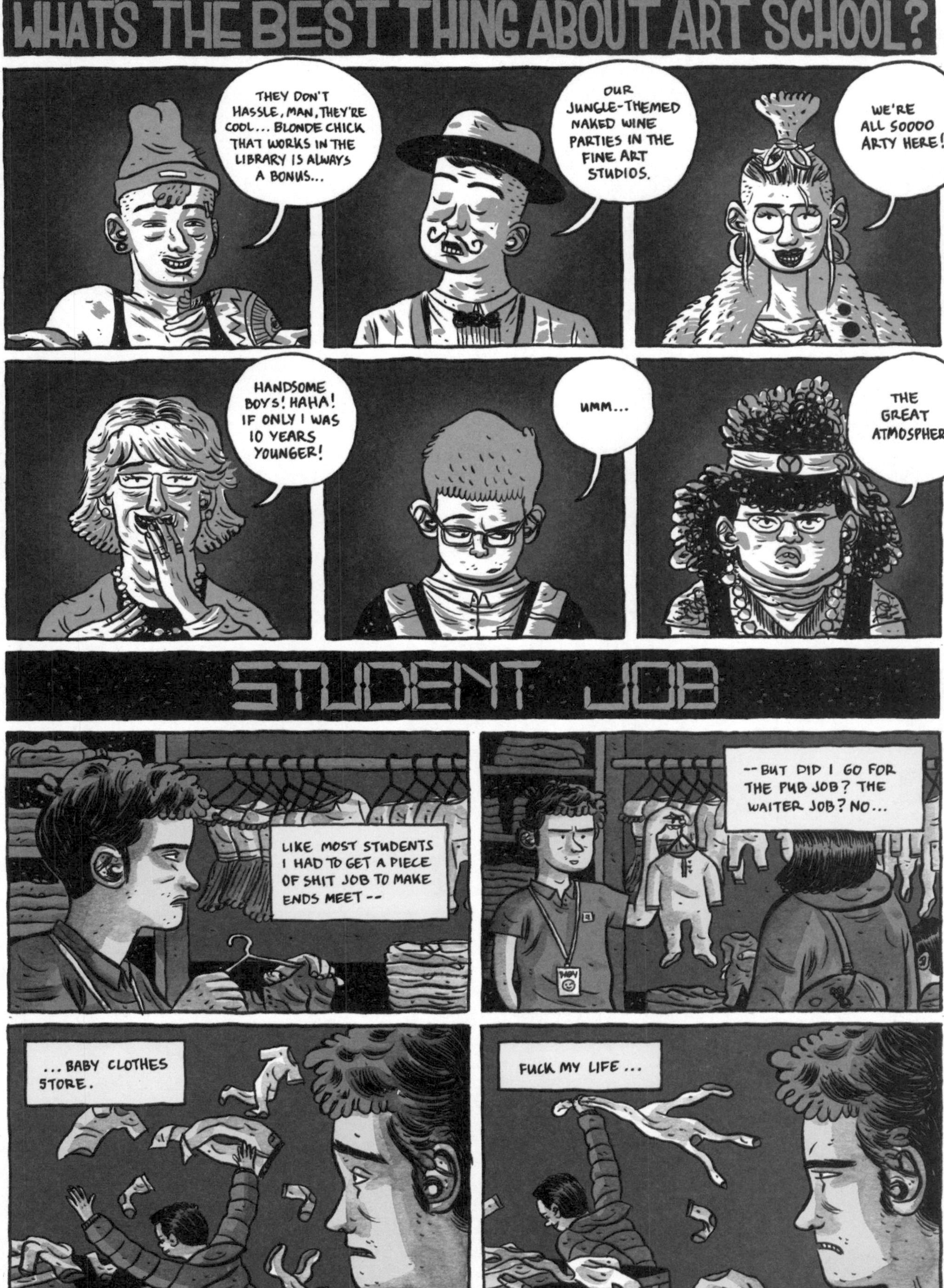
WHAT'S THE BEST THING ABOUT ART SCHOOL?
THEY DON'T HASSLE, MAN, THEY'RE COOL... BLONDE CHICK THAT WORKS IN THE LIBRARY IS ALWAYS A BONUS...
OUR JUNGLE-THEMED NAKED WINE PARTIES IN THE FINE ART STUDIOS.
WE'RE ALL SOOOO ARTY HERE!
HANDSOME BOYS! HAHA! IF ONLY I WAS 10 YEARS YOUNGER!
UMM...
THE GREAT ATMOSPHERE.
STUDENT JOB
LIKE MOST STUDENTS I HAD TO GET A PIECE OF SHIT JOB TO MAKE ENDS MEET --
-- BUT DID I GO FOR THE PUB JOB? THE WAITER JOB? NO...
... BABY CLOTHES STORE.
FUCK MY LIFE ...

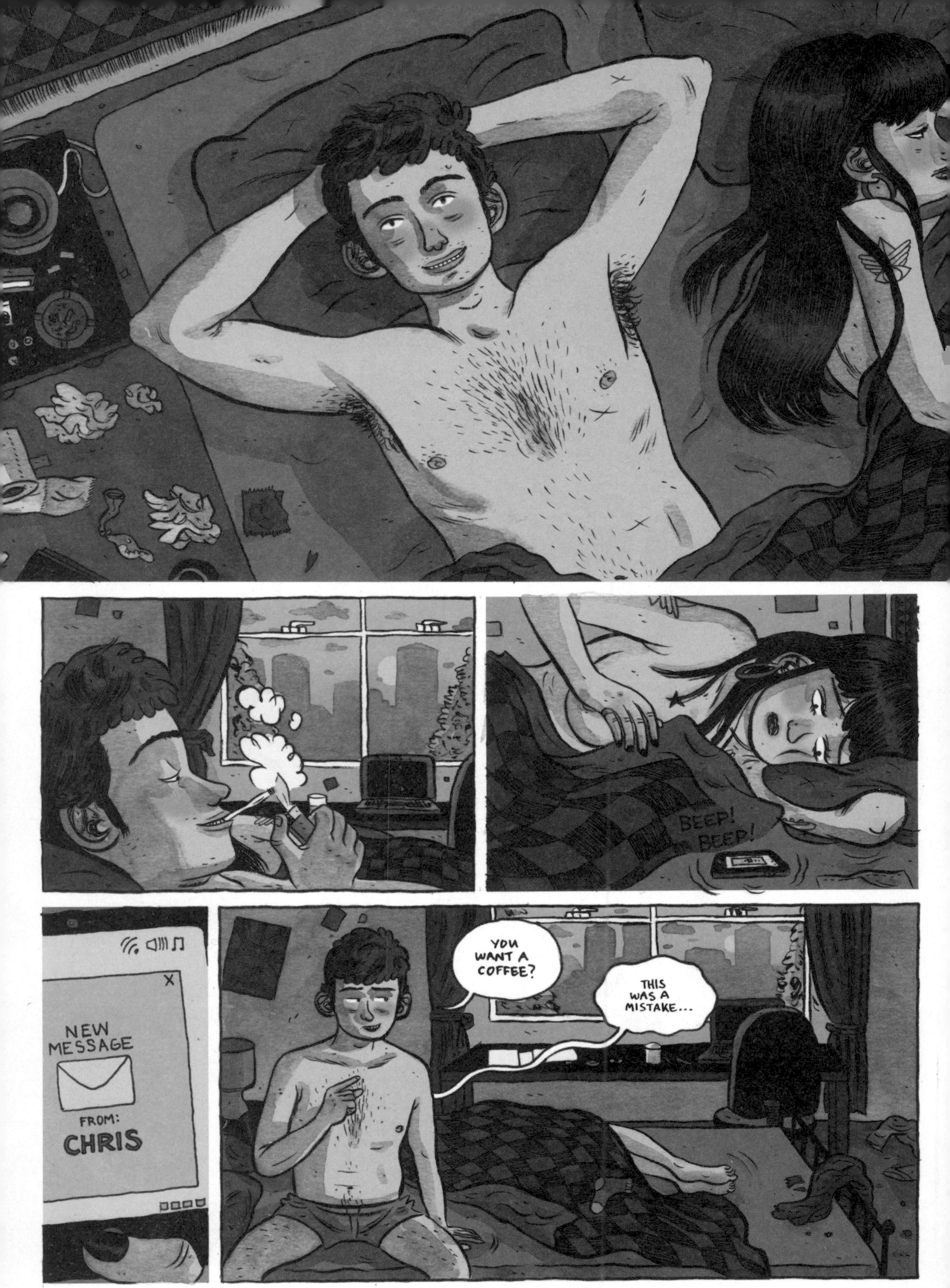
BEEP! BEEP!
NEW MESSAGE
FROM:
CHRIS
YOU WANT A COFFEE?
THIS WAS A MISTAKE...

HUH?

...I THOUGHT YOU WANTED THIS?

I DON'T KNOW WHAT I WANT, DANIEL...

...ALL I KNOW IS THAT YESTERDAY YOU WERE MY FRIEND AND NOW...

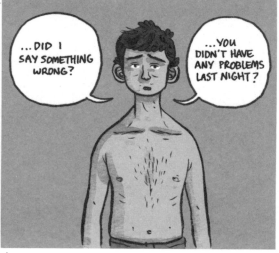

...DID I SAY SOMETHING WRONG?

...YOU DIDN'T HAVE ANY PROBLEMS LAST NIGHT?

...AND NOW...EVERYTHING IS TOTALLY FUCKED UP--

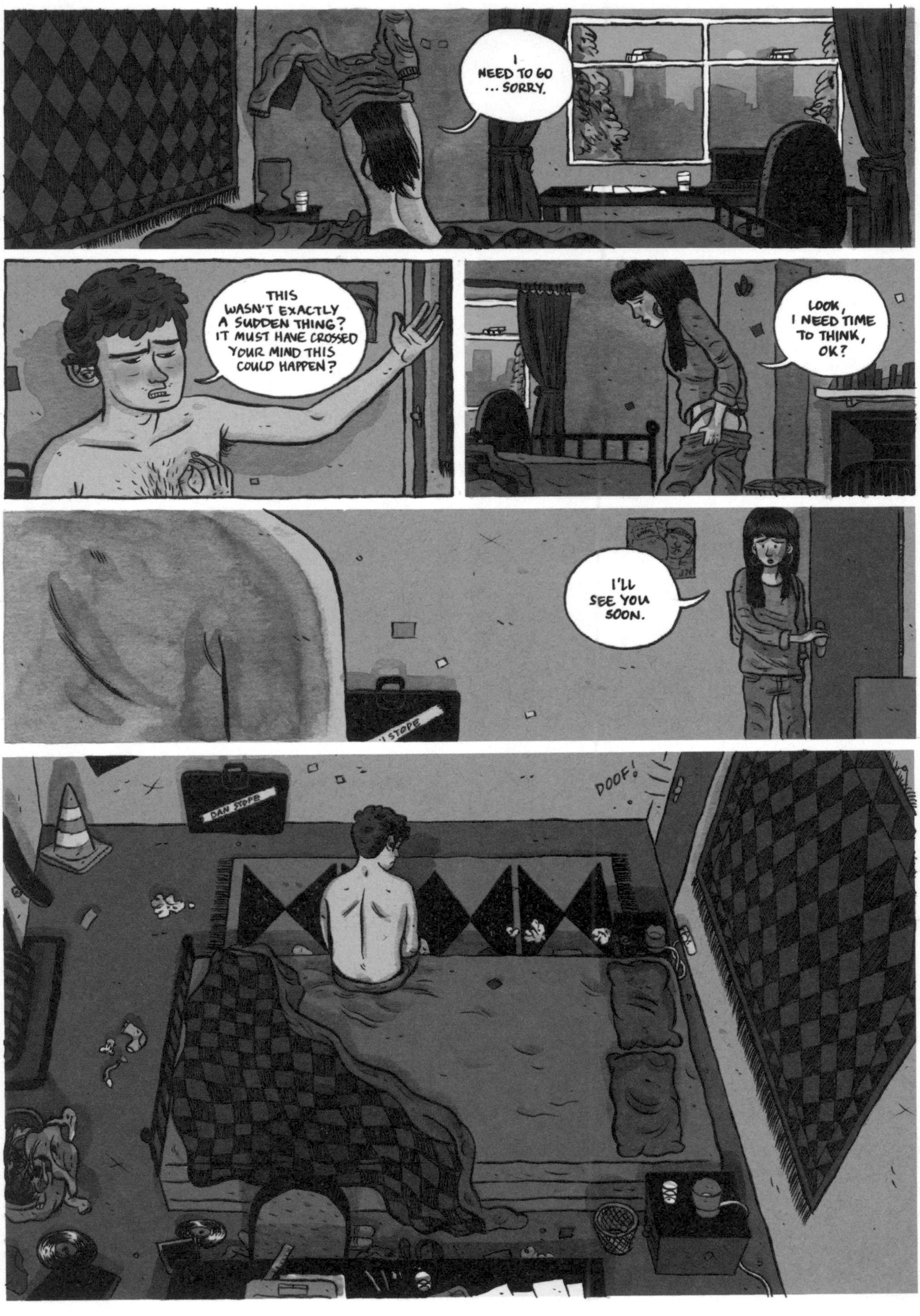
I NEED TO GO ... SORRY.
THIS WASN'T EXACTLY A SUDDEN THING? IT MUST HAVE CROSSED YOUR MIND THIS COULD HAPPEN?
LOOK, I NEED TIME TO THINK, OK?
I'LL SEE YOU SOON.
DOOF!
DAN STOPE

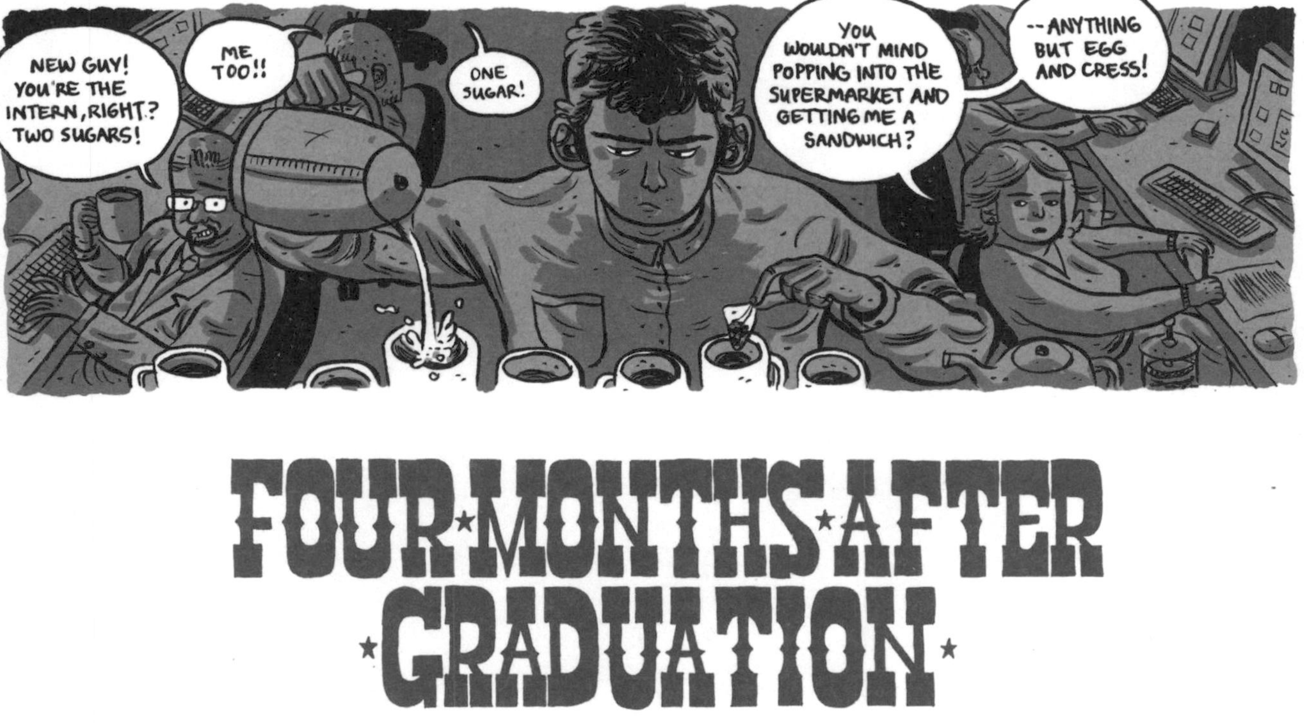
NEW GUY! YOU'RE THE INTERN, RIGHT? TWO SUGARS!
ME TOO!!
ONE SUGAR!
YOU WOULDN'T MIND POPPING INTO THE SUPERMARKET AND GETTING ME A SANDWICH?
--ANYTHING BUT EGG AND CRESS!

FOUR MONTHS AFTER GRADUATION

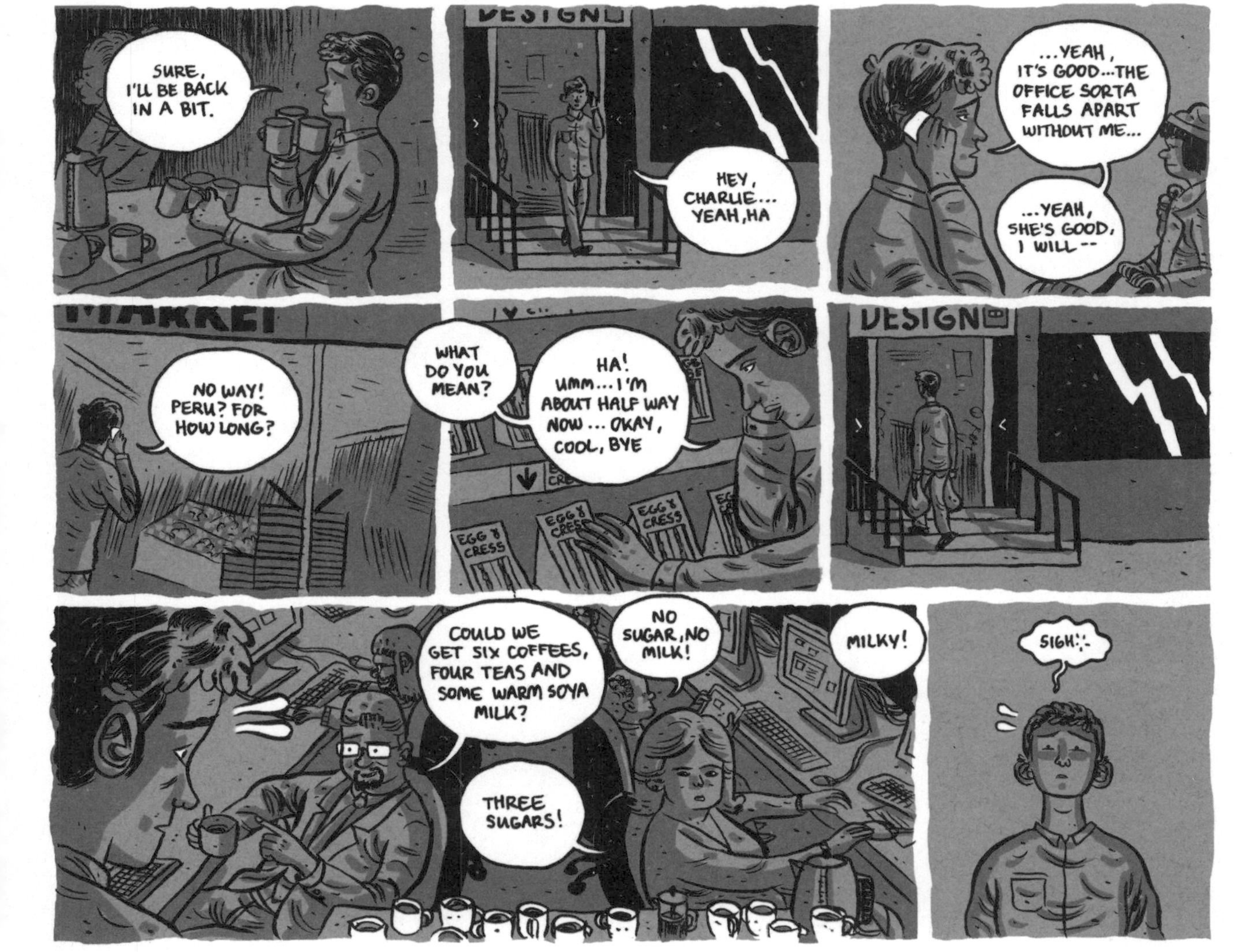
SURE, I'LL BE BACK IN A BIT.
DESIGN
HEY, CHARLIE... YEAH, HA
...YEAH, IT'S GOOD...THE OFFICE SORTA FALLS APART WITHOUT ME...
...YEAH, SHE'S GOOD, I WILL--
NO WAY! PERU? FOR HOW LONG?
WHAT DO YOU MEAN?
HA! UMM...I'M ABOUT HALF WAY NOW... OKAY, COOL, BYE
EGG & CRESS
DESIGN
COULD WE GET SIX COFFEES, FOUR TEAS AND SOME WARM SOYA MILK?
NO SUGAR, NO MILK!
MILKY!
THREE SUGARS!
SIGH

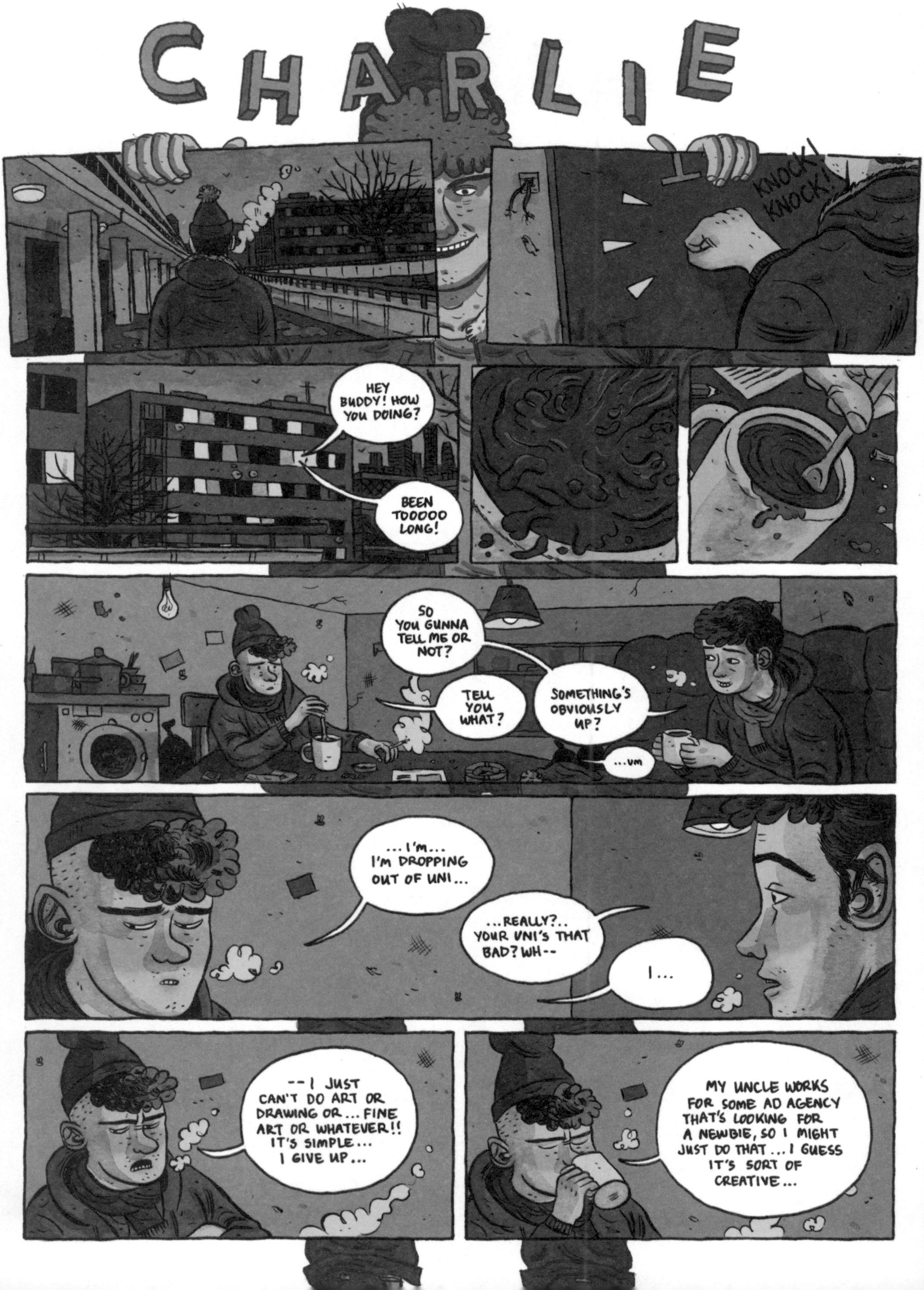
CHARLIE
KNOCK KNOCK!
HEY BUDDY! HOW YOU DOING?
BEEN TOOOOO LONG!
SO YOU GUNNA TELL ME OR NOT?
TELL YOU WHAT?
SOMETHING'S OBVIOUSLY UP?
...UM
...I'M... I'M DROPPING OUT OF UNI...
...REALLY?.. YOUR UNI'S THAT BAD? WH--
I...
--I JUST CAN'T DO ART OR DRAWING OR... FINE ART OR WHATEVER!! IT'S SIMPLE... I GIVE UP...
MY UNCLE WORKS FOR SOME AD AGENCY THAT'S LOOKING FOR A NEWBIE, SO I MIGHT JUST DO THAT... I GUESS IT'S SORT OF CREATIVE...

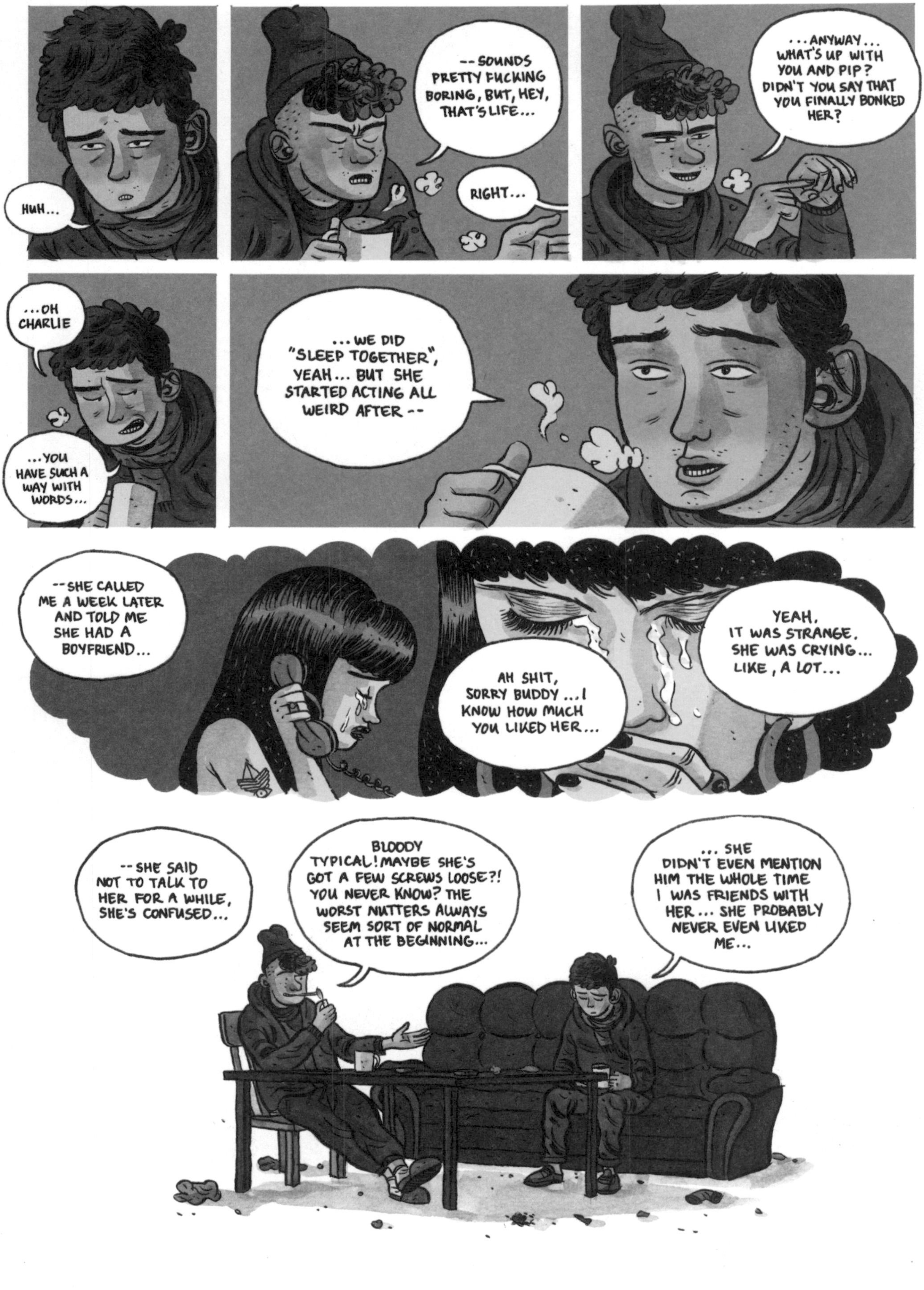
HUH...
-- SOUNDS PRETTY FUCKING BORING, BUT, HEY, THAT'S LIFE...
RIGHT...
...ANYWAY... WHAT'S UP WITH YOU AND PIP? DIDN'T YOU SAY THAT YOU FINALLY BONKED HER?
...OH CHARLIE
...YOU HAVE SUCH A WAY WITH WORDS...
...WE DID "SLEEP TOGETHER", YEAH... BUT SHE STARTED ACTING ALL WEIRD AFTER --
--SHE CALLED ME A WEEK LATER AND TOLD ME SHE HAD A BOYFRIEND...
AH SHIT, SORRY BUDDY... I KNOW HOW MUCH YOU LIKED HER...
YEAH, IT WAS STRANGE. SHE WAS CRYING... LIKE, A LOT...
--SHE SAID NOT TO TALK TO HER FOR A WHILE, SHE'S CONFUSED...
BLOODY TYPICAL! MAYBE SHE'S GOT A FEW SCREWS LOOSE?! YOU NEVER KNOW? THE WORST NUTTERS ALWAYS SEEM SORT OF NORMAL AT THE BEGINNING...
... SHE DIDN'T EVEN MENTION HIM THE WHOLE TIME I WAS FRIENDS WITH HER... SHE PROBABLY NEVER EVEN LIKED ME...

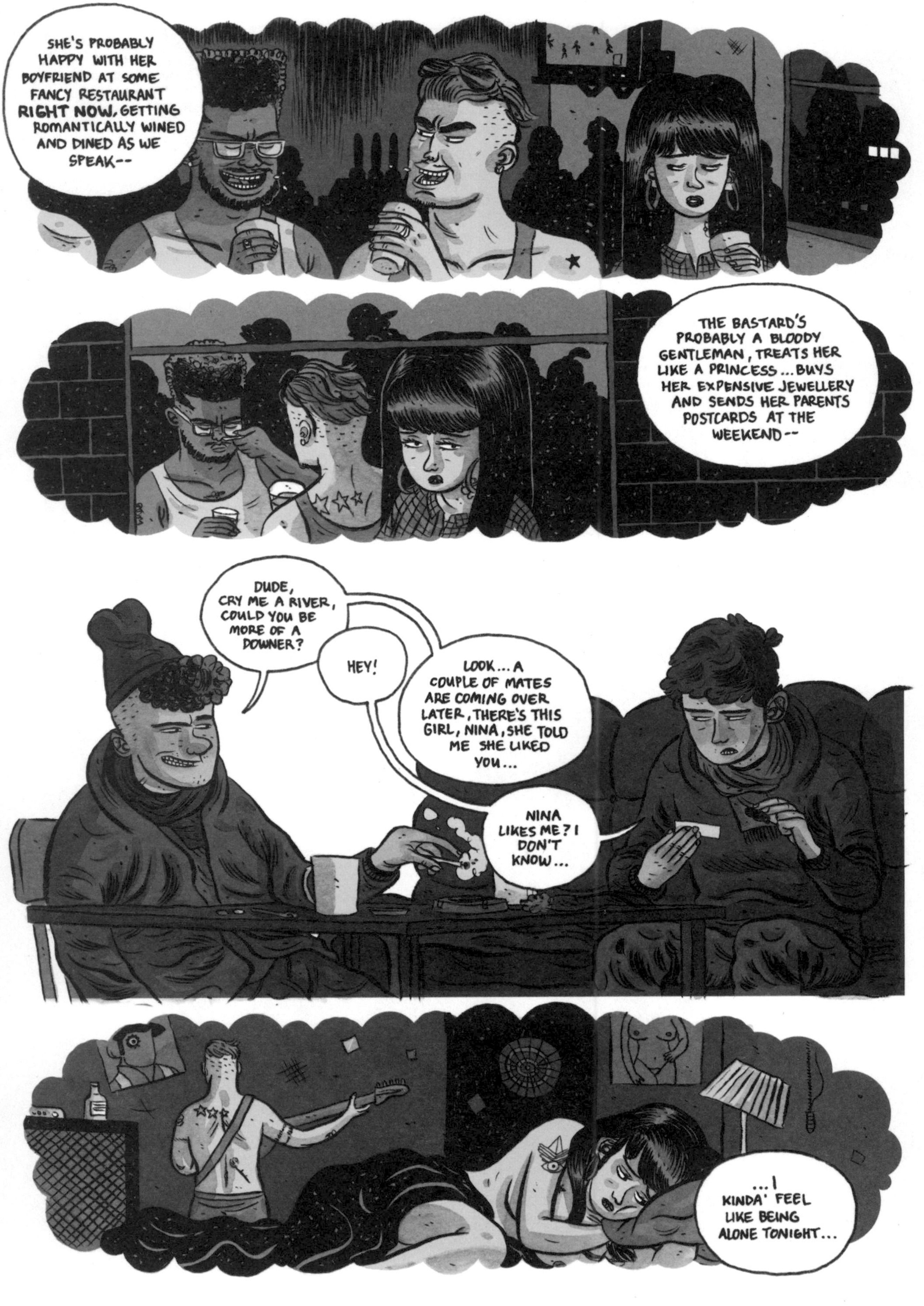
SHE'S PROBABLY HAPPY WITH HER BOYFRIEND AT SOME FANCY RESTAURANT RIGHT NOW, GETTING ROMANTICALLY WINED AND DINED AS WE SPEAK--
THE BASTARD'S PROBABLY A BLOODY GENTLEMAN, TREATS HER LIKE A PRINCESS...BUYS HER EXPENSIVE JEWELLERY AND SENDS HER PARENTS POSTCARDS AT THE WEEKEND--
DUDE, CRY ME A RIVER, COULD YOU BE MORE OF A DOWNER?
HEY!
LOOK... A COUPLE OF MATES ARE COMING OVER LATER, THERE'S THIS GIRL, NINA, SHE TOLD ME SHE LIKED YOU...
NINA LIKES ME? I DON'T KNOW...
...I KINDA' FEEL LIKE BEING ALONE TONIGHT...

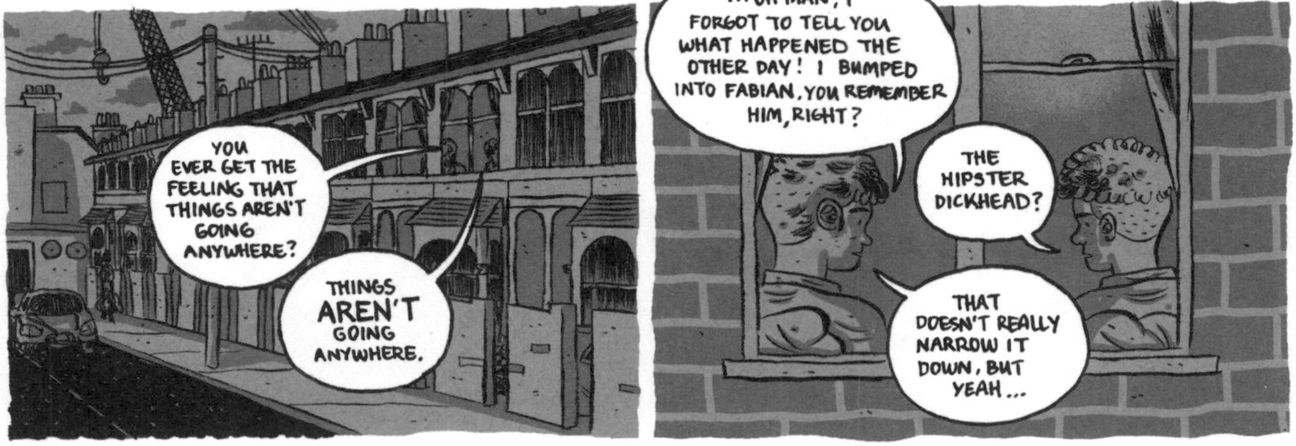
YOU EVER GET THE FEELING THAT THINGS AREN'T GOING ANYWHERE?
THINGS AREN'T GOING ANYWHERE.
...OH MAN, I FORGOT TO TELL YOU WHAT HAPPENED THE OTHER DAY! I BUMPED INTO FABIAN, YOU REMEMBER HIM, RIGHT?
THE HIPSTER DICKHEAD?
THAT DOESN'T REALLY NARROW IT DOWN, BUT YEAH...

TWO MONTHS AFTER GRADUATION

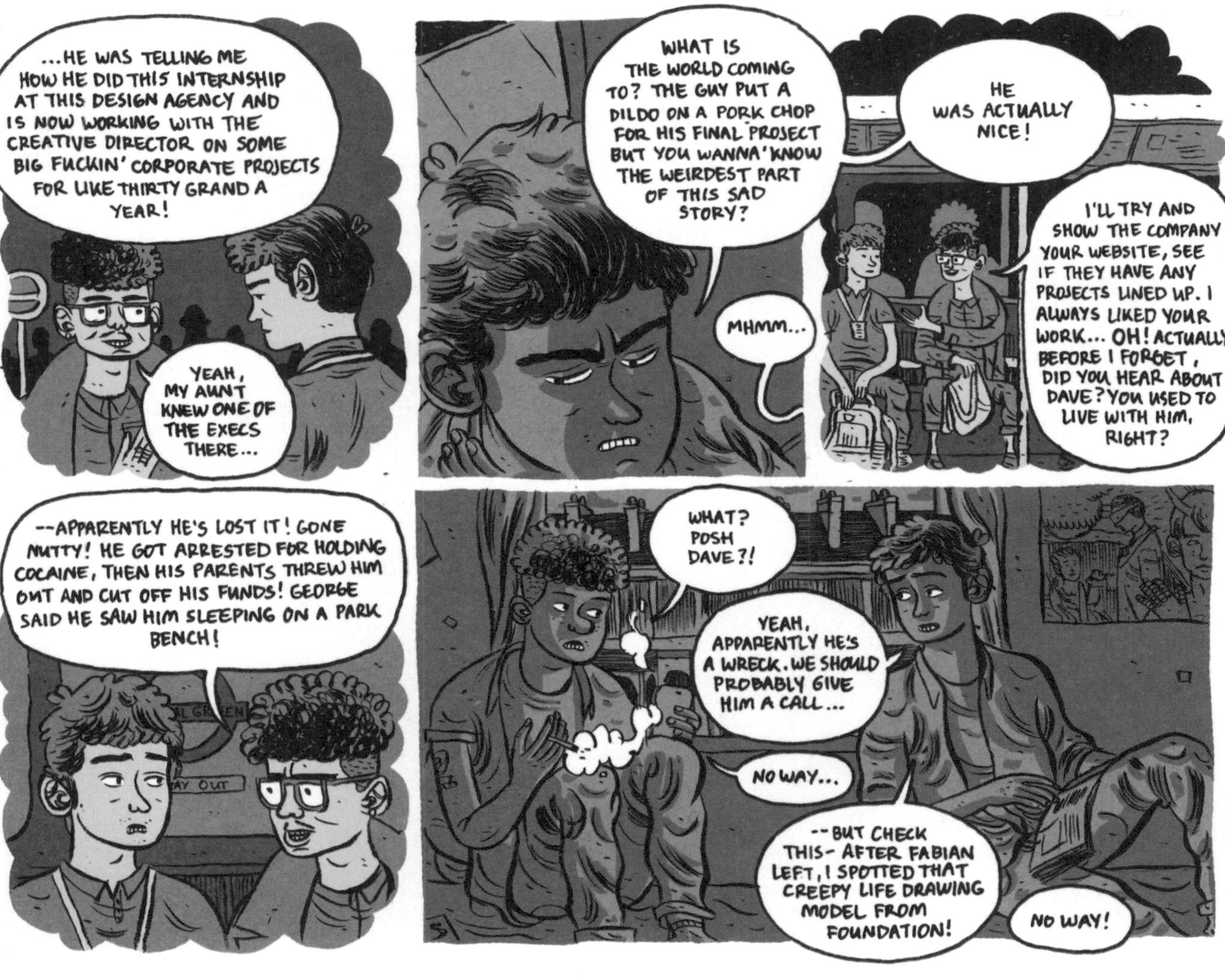
...HE WAS TELLING ME HOW HE DID THIS INTERNSHIP AT THIS DESIGN AGENCY AND IS NOW WORKING WITH THE CREATIVE DIRECTOR ON SOME BIG FUCKIN' CORPORATE PROJECTS FOR LIKE THIRTY GRAND A YEAR!
YEAH, MY AUNT KNEW ONE OF THE EXECS THERE...
WHAT IS THE WORLD COMING TO? THE GUY PUT A DILDO ON A PORK CHOP FOR HIS FINAL PROJECT BUT YOU WANNA' KNOW THE WEIRDEST PART OF THIS SAD STORY?
MHMM...
HE WAS ACTUALLY NICE!
I'LL TRY AND SHOW THE COMPANY YOUR WEBSITE, SEE IF THEY HAVE ANY PROJECTS LINED UP. I ALWAYS LIKED YOUR WORK... OH! ACTUALLY BEFORE I FORGET, DID YOU HEAR ABOUT DAVE? YOU USED TO LIVE WITH HIM, RIGHT?
--APPARENTLY HE'S LOST IT! GONE NUTTY! HE GOT ARRESTED FOR HOLDING COCAINE, THEN HIS PARENTS THREW HIM OUT AND CUT OFF HIS FUNDS! GEORGE SAID HE SAW HIM SLEEPING ON A PARK BENCH!
WHAT? POSH DAVE?!
YEAH, APPARENTLY HE'S A WRECK. WE SHOULD PROBABLY GIVE HIM A CALL...
NO WAY...
--BUT CHECK THIS- AFTER FABIAN LEFT, I SPOTTED THAT CREEPY LIFE DRAWING MODEL FROM FOUNDATION!
NO WAY!

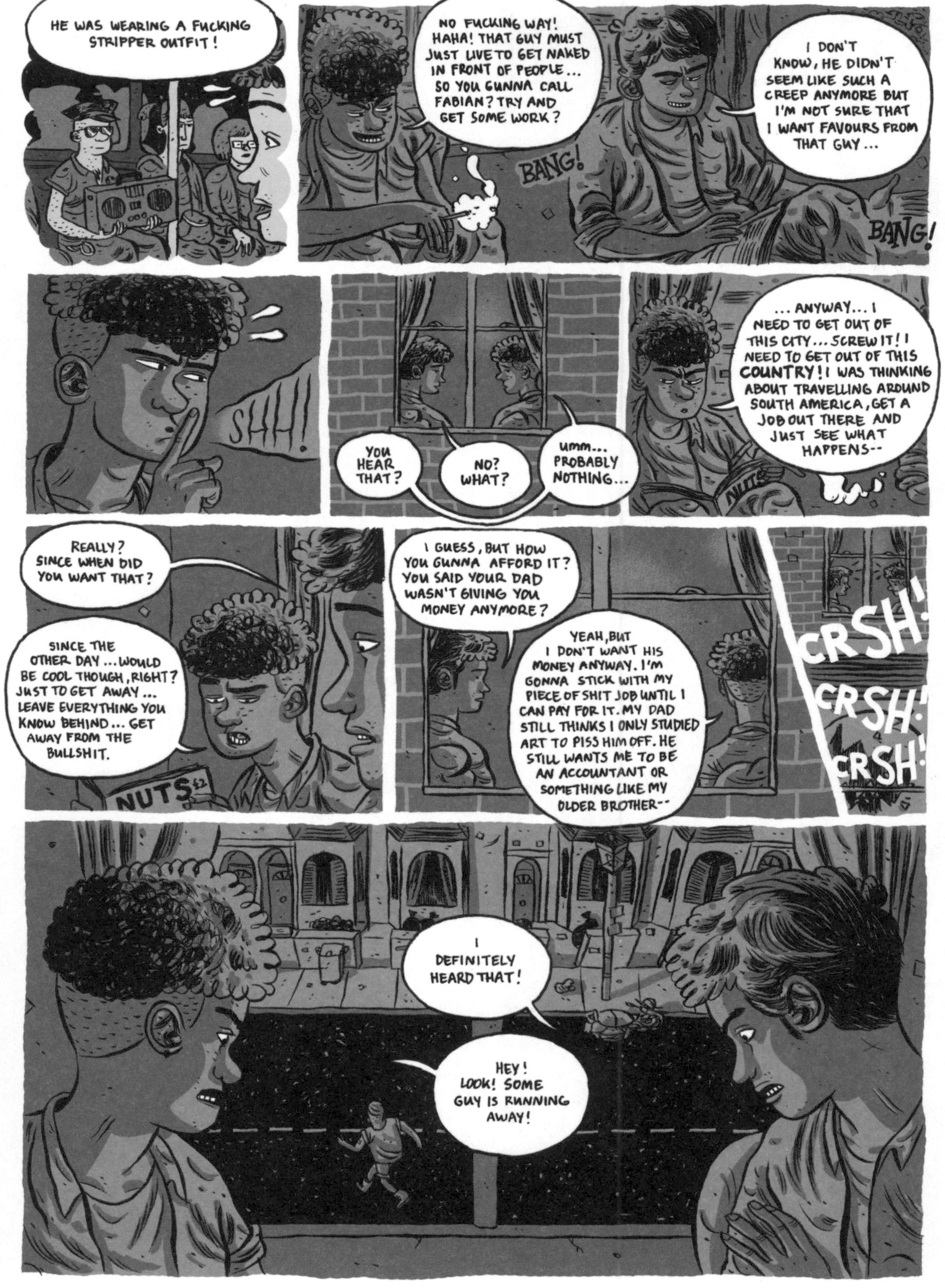
HE WAS WEARING A FUCKING STRIPPER OUTFIT!
NO FUCKING WAY! HAHA! THAT GUY MUST JUST LIVE TO GET NAKED IN FRONT OF PEOPLE... SO YOU GUNNA CALL FABIAN? TRY AND GET SOME WORK?
BANG!
I DON'T KNOW, HE DIDN'T SEEM LIKE SUCH A CREEP ANYMORE BUT I'M NOT SURE THAT I WANT FAVOURS FROM THAT GUY...
BANG!
SHH!
YOU HEAR THAT?
NO? WHAT?
UMM... PROBABLY NOTHING...
... ANYWAY... I NEED TO GET OUT OF THIS CITY... SCREW IT! I NEED TO GET OUT OF THIS COUNTRY! I WAS THINKING ABOUT TRAVELLING AROUND SOUTH AMERICA, GET A JOB OUT THERE AND JUST SEE WHAT HAPPENS--
REALLY? SINCE WHEN DID YOU WANT THAT?
SINCE THE OTHER DAY... WOULD BE COOL THOUGH, RIGHT? JUST TO GET AWAY... LEAVE EVERYTHING YOU KNOW BEHIND... GET AWAY FROM THE BULLSHIT.
NUTS £2
I GUESS, BUT HOW YOU GUNNA AFFORD IT? YOU SAID YOUR DAD WASN'T GIVING YOU MONEY ANYMORE?
YEAH, BUT I DON'T WANT HIS MONEY ANYWAY. I'M GONNA STICK WITH MY PIECE OF SHIT JOB UNTIL I CAN PAY FOR IT. MY DAD STILL THINKS I ONLY STUDIED ART TO PISS HIM OFF. HE STILL WANTS ME TO BE AN ACCOUNTANT OR SOMETHING LIKE MY OLDER BROTHER--
CRSH!
CRSH!
CRSH!
I DEFINITELY HEARD THAT!
HEY! LOOK! SOME GUY IS RUNNING AWAY!

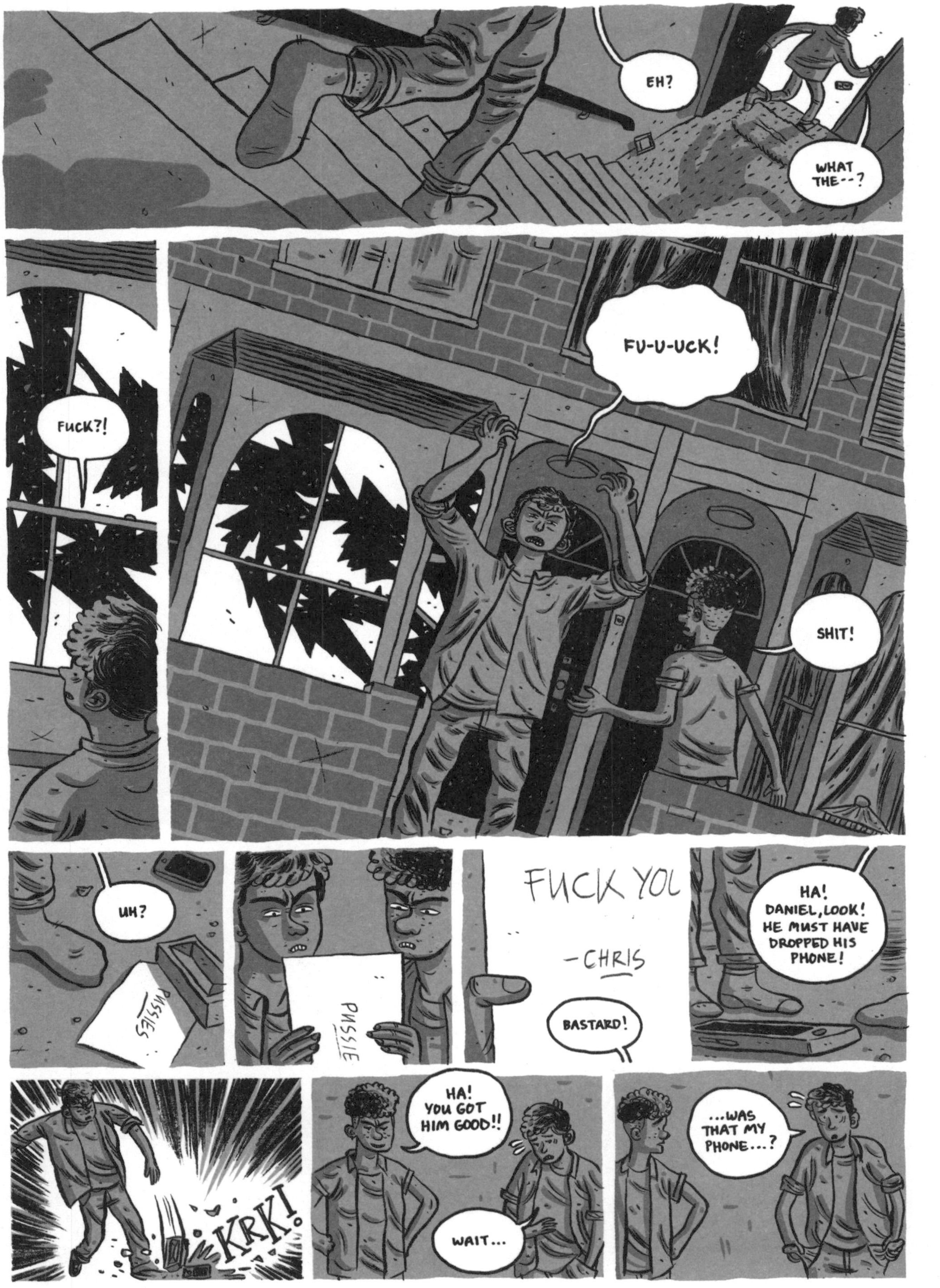
EH?
WHAT THE--?
FUCK?!
FU-U-UCK!
SHIT!
UH?
PUSSIES
PUSSIE
FUCK YOU
-CHRIS
BASTARD!
HA! DANIEL, LOOK! HE MUST HAVE DROPPED HIS PHONE!
KRK!
HA! YOU GOT HIM GOOD!!
WAIT...
...WAS THAT MY PHONE...?

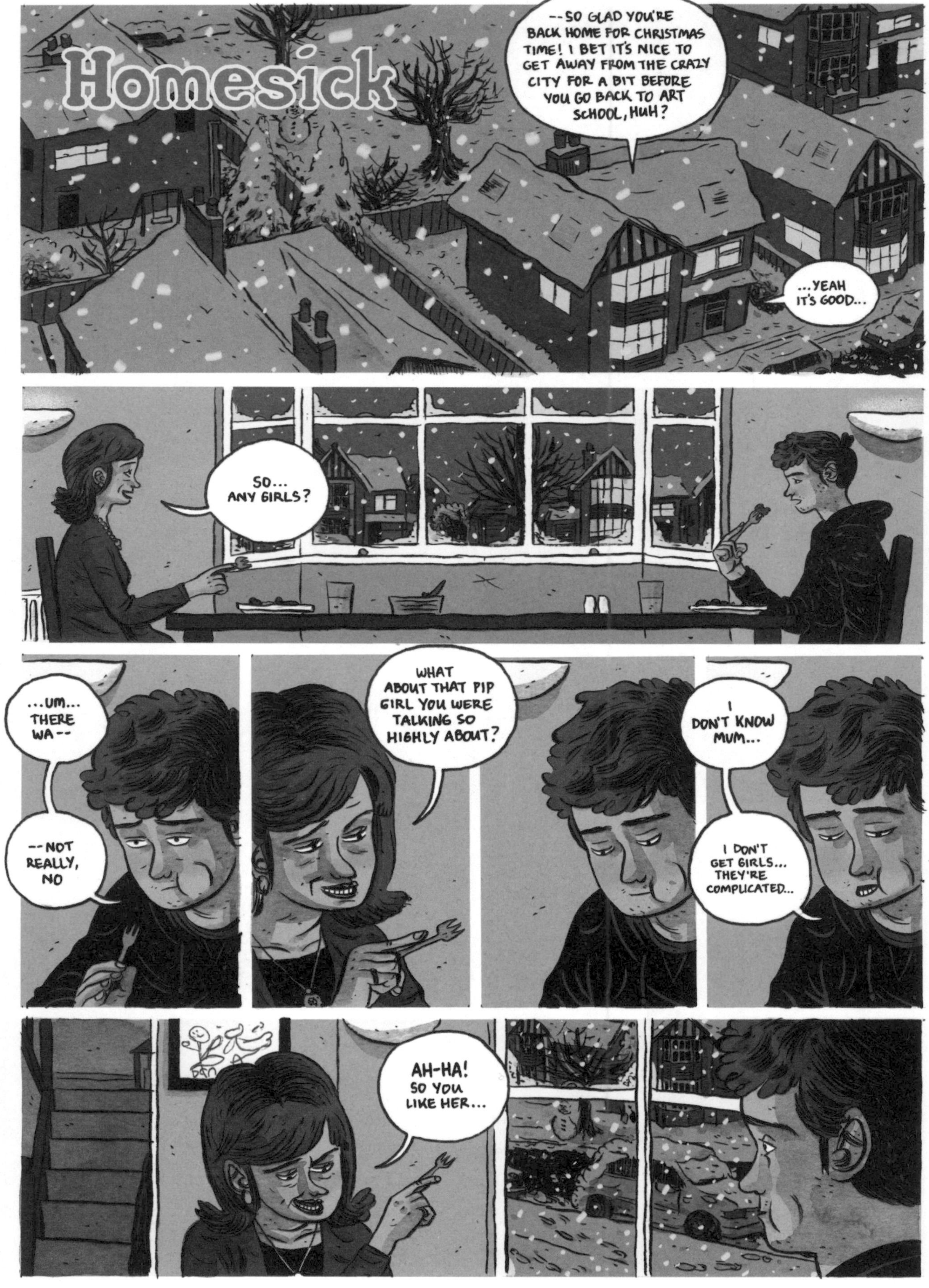
Homesick
--SO GLAD YOU'RE BACK HOME FOR CHRISTMAS TIME! I BET IT'S NICE TO GET AWAY FROM THE CRAZY CITY FOR A BIT BEFORE YOU GO BACK TO ART SCHOOL, HUH?
...YEAH IT'S GOOD...
SO... ANY GIRLS?
...UM... THERE WA--
--NOT REALLY, NO
WHAT ABOUT THAT PIP GIRL YOU WERE TALKING SO HIGHLY ABOUT?
I DON'T KNOW MUM...
I DON'T GET GIRLS... THEY'RE COMPLICATED...
AH-HA! SO YOU LIKE HER...

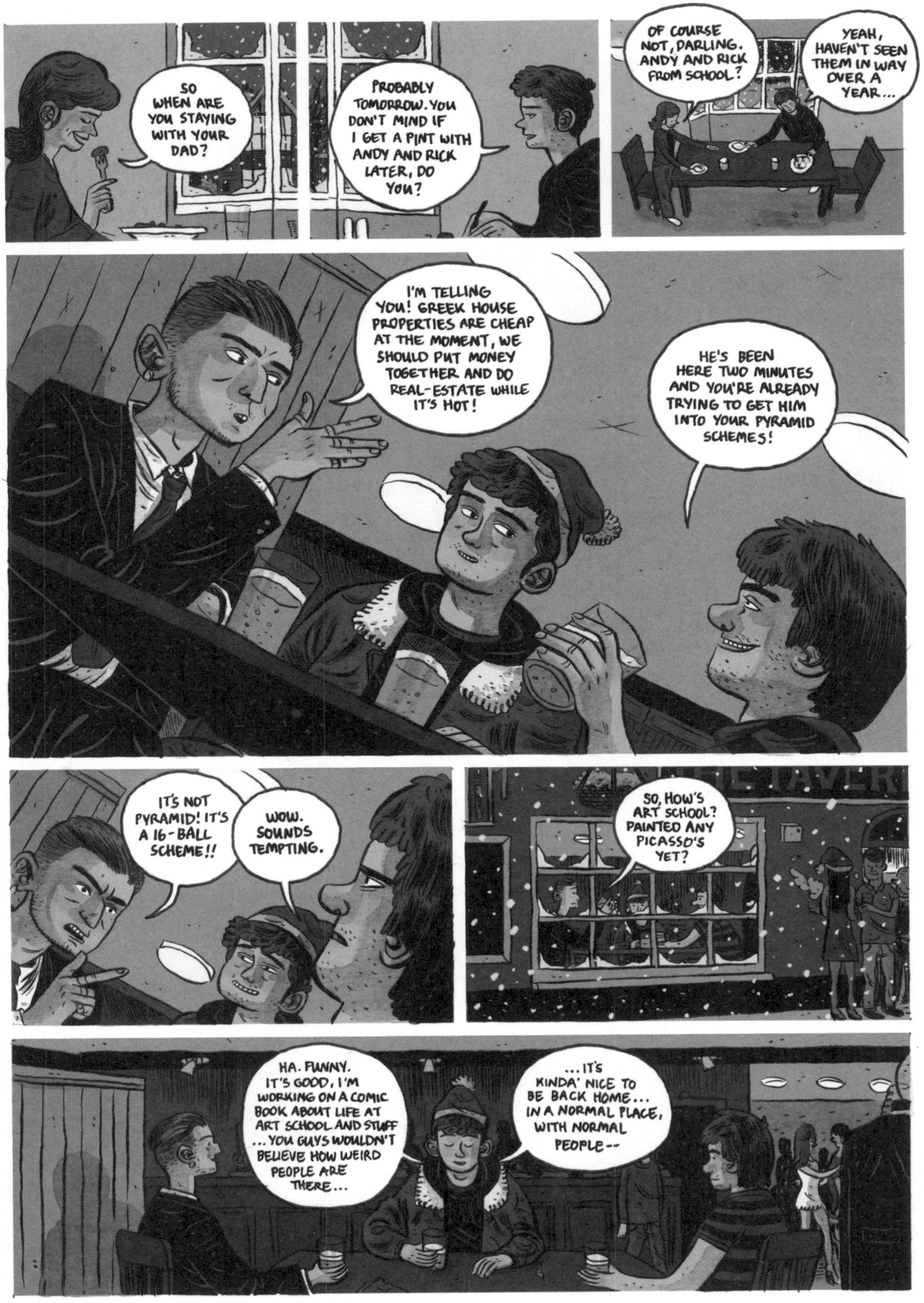
SO WHEN ARE YOU STAYING WITH YOUR DAD?
PROBABLY TOMORROW. YOU DON'T MIND IF I GET A PINT WITH ANDY AND RICK LATER, DO YOU?
OF COURSE NOT, DARLING. ANDY AND RICK FROM SCHOOL?
YEAH, HAVEN'T SEEN THEM IN WAY OVER A YEAR...
I'M TELLING YOU! GREEK HOUSE PROPERTIES ARE CHEAP AT THE MOMENT, WE SHOULD PUT MONEY TOGETHER AND DO REAL-ESTATE WHILE IT'S HOT!
HE'S BEEN HERE TWO MINUTES AND YOU'RE ALREADY TRYING TO GET HIM INTO YOUR PYRAMID SCHEMES!
IT'S NOT PYRAMID! IT'S A 16-BALL SCHEME!!
WOW. SOUNDS TEMPTING.
SO, HOW'S ART SCHOOL? PAINTED ANY PICASSO'S YET?
HA. FUNNY. IT'S GOOD, I'M WORKING ON A COMIC BOOK ABOUT LIFE AT ART SCHOOL AND STUFF ...YOU GUYS WOULDN'T BELIEVE HOW WEIRD PEOPLE ARE THERE...
...IT'S KINDA' NICE TO BE BACK HOME... IN A NORMAL PLACE, WITH NORMAL PEOPLE--

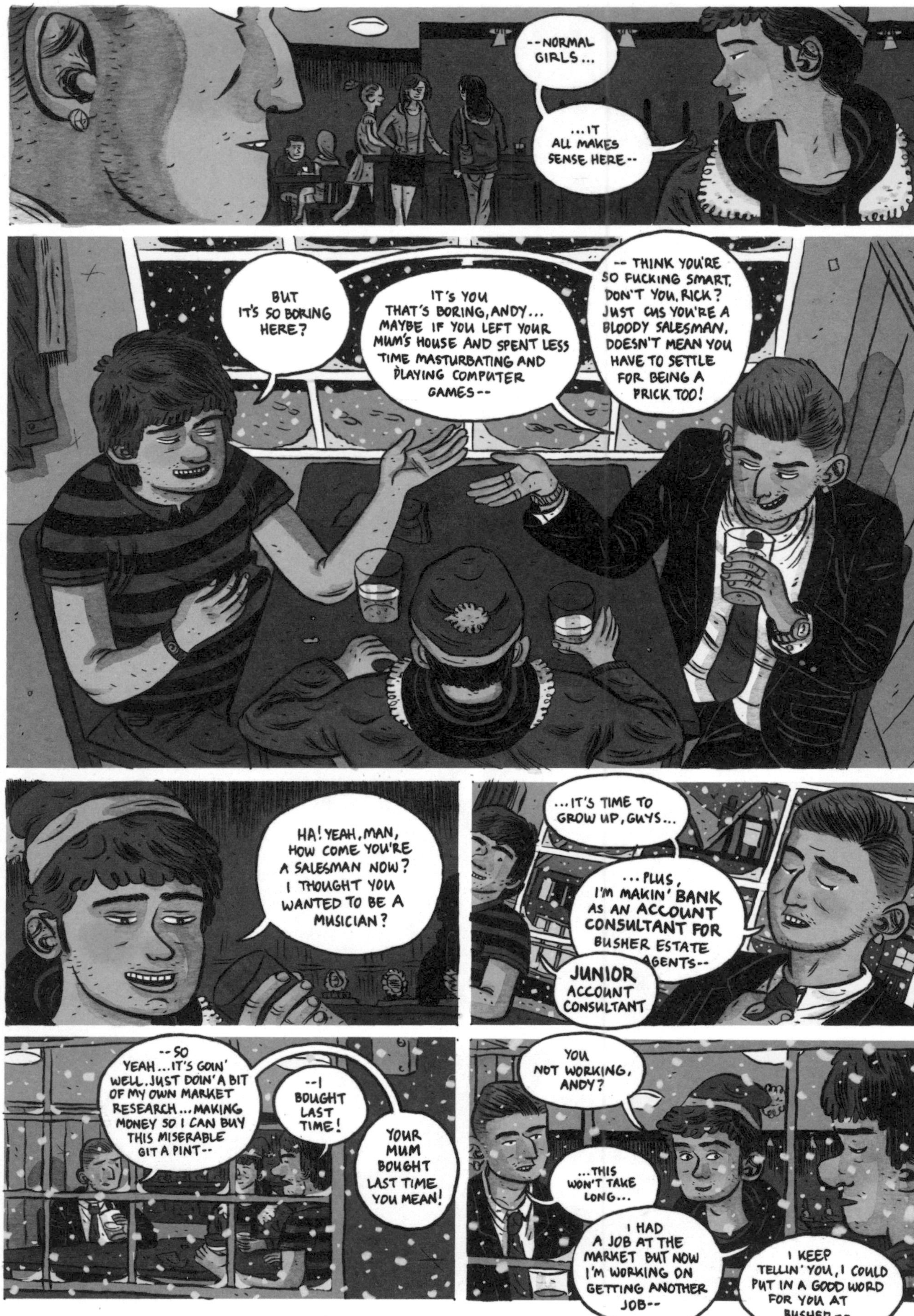
--NORMAL GIRLS...
...IT ALL MAKES SENSE HERE--
BUT IT'S SO BORING HERE?
IT'S YOU THAT'S BORING, ANDY... MAYBE IF YOU LEFT YOUR MUM'S HOUSE AND SPENT LESS TIME MASTURBATING AND PLAYING COMPUTER GAMES--
-- THINK YOU'RE SO FUCKING SMART, DON'T YOU, RICK? JUST CUS YOU'RE A BLOODY SALESMAN, DOESN'T MEAN YOU HAVE TO SETTLE FOR BEING A PRICK TOO!
HA! YEAH, MAN, HOW COME YOU'RE A SALESMAN NOW? I THOUGHT YOU WANTED TO BE A MUSICIAN?
...IT'S TIME TO GROW UP, GUYS...
...PLUS, I'M MAKIN' BANK AS AN ACCOUNT CONSULTANT FOR BUSHER ESTATE AGENTS--
JUNIOR ACCOUNT CONSULTANT
--SO YEAH...IT'S GOIN' WELL. JUST DOIN' A BIT OF MY OWN MARKET RESEARCH...MAKING MONEY SO I CAN BUY THIS MISERABLE GIT A PINT--
--I BOUGHT LAST TIME!
YOUR MUM BOUGHT LAST TIME YOU MEAN!
YOU NOT WORKING, ANDY?
...THIS WON'T TAKE LONG...
I HAD A JOB AT THE MARKET BUT NOW I'M WORKING ON GETTING ANOTHER JOB--
I KEEP TELLIN' YOU, I COULD PUT IN A GOOD WORD FOR YOU AT BUSHER--

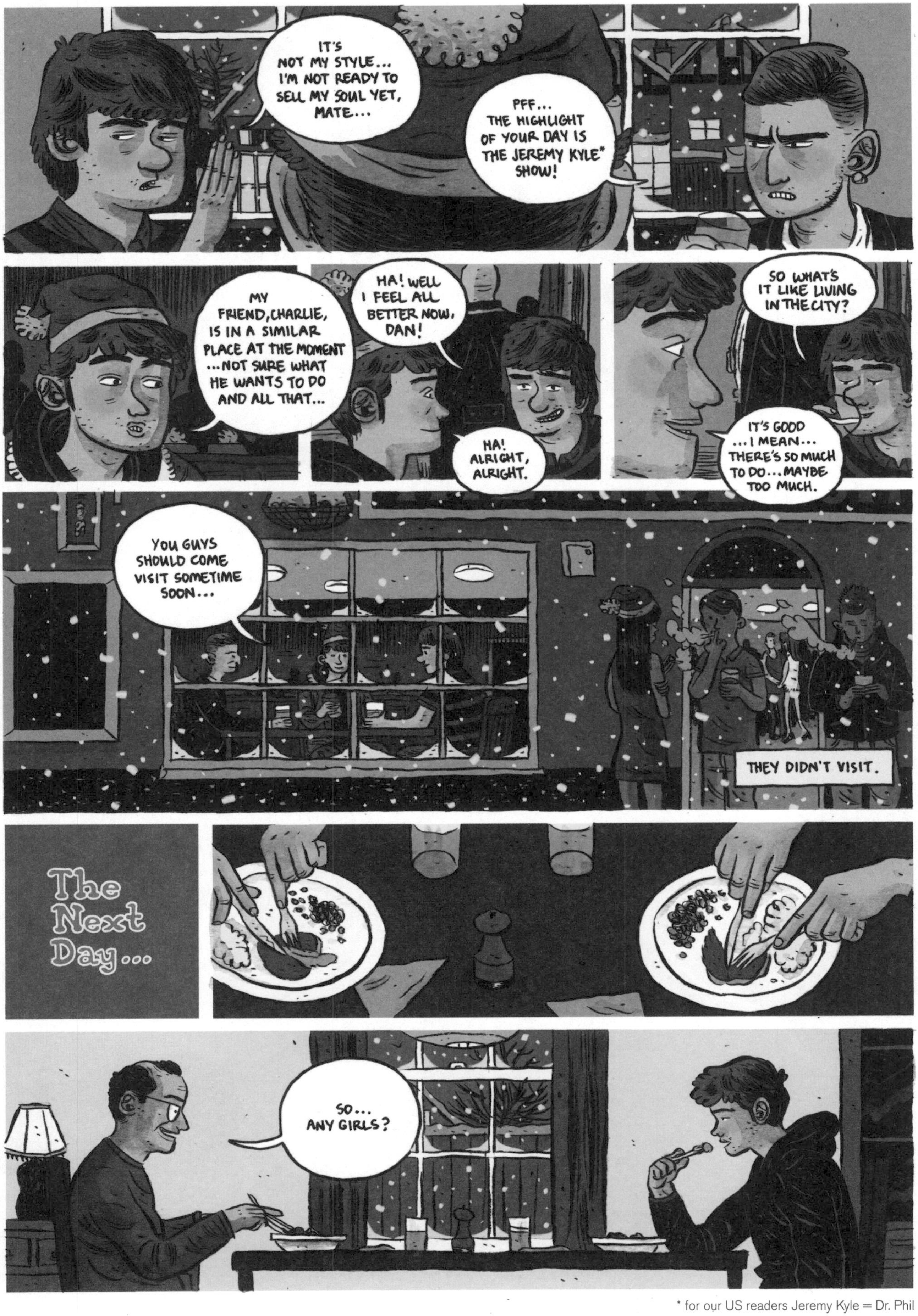

IT'S NOT MY STYLE... I'M NOT READY TO SELL MY SOUL YET, MATE...
PFF... THE HIGHLIGHT OF YOUR DAY IS THE JEREMY KYLE* SHOW!
MY FRIEND, CHARLIE, IS IN A SIMILAR PLACE AT THE MOMENT ...NOT SURE WHAT HE WANTS TO DO AND ALL THAT...
HA! WELL I FEEL ALL BETTER NOW, DAN!
HA! ALRIGHT, ALRIGHT.
SO WHAT'S IT LIKE LIVING IN THE CITY?
IT'S GOOD ...I MEAN... THERE'S SO MUCH TO DO... MAYBE TOO MUCH.
YOU GUYS SHOULD COME VISIT SOMETIME SOON...
THEY DIDN'T VISIT.
The Next Day...
SO... ANY GIRLS?

* for our US readers Jeremy Kyle = Dr. Phil

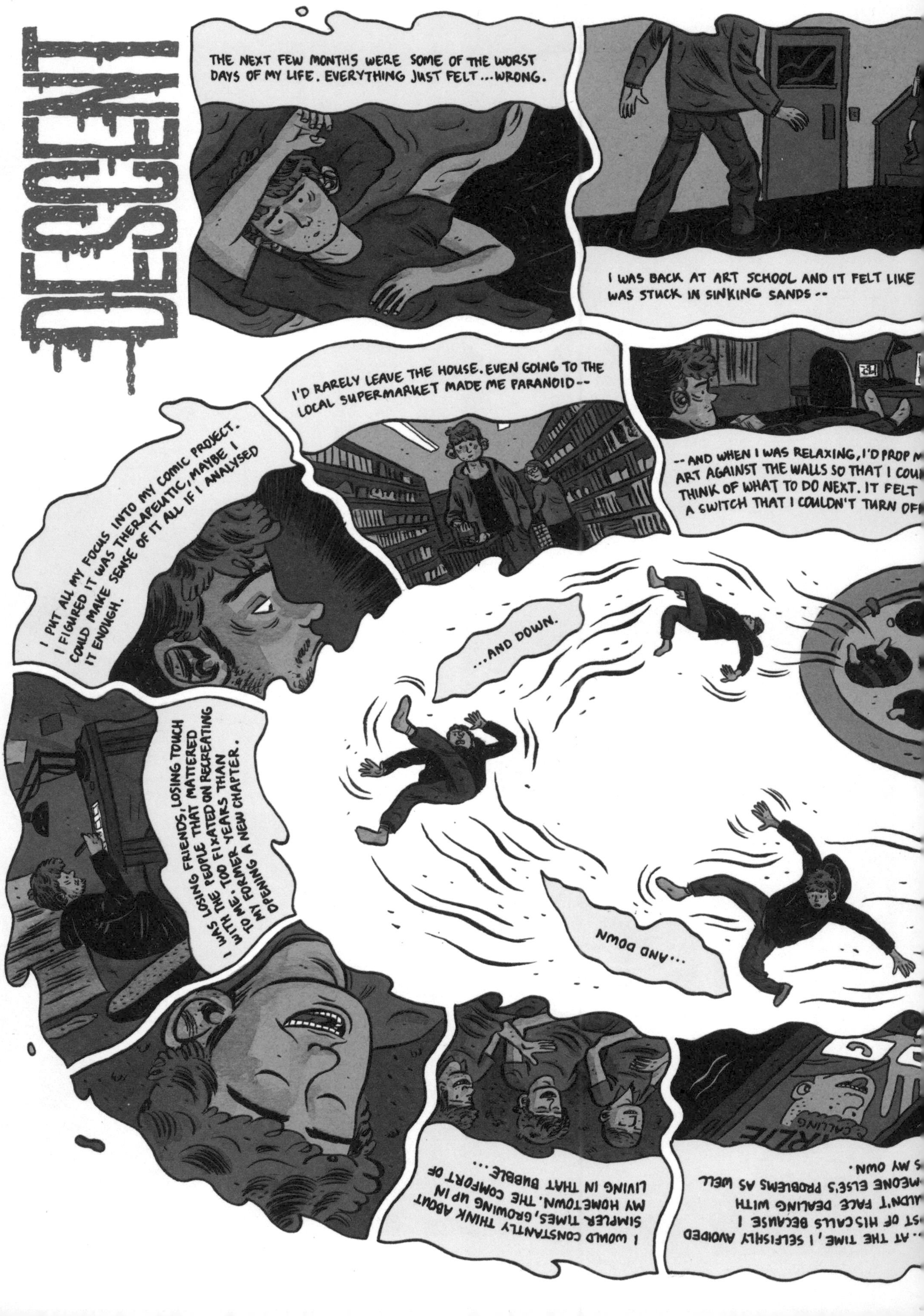
DESCENT
THE NEXT FEW MONTHS WERE SOME OF THE WORST DAYS OF MY LIFE. EVERYTHING JUST FELT...WRONG.
I WAS BACK AT ART SCHOOL AND IT FELT LIKE I WAS STUCK IN SINKING SANDS --
I'D RARELY LEAVE THE HOUSE. EVEN GOING TO THE LOCAL SUPERMARKET MADE ME PARANOID--
-- AND WHEN I WAS RELAXING, I'D PROP MY ART AGAINST THE WALLS SO THAT I COULD THINK OF WHAT TO DO NEXT. IT FELT LIKE A SWITCH THAT I COULDN'T TURN OFF.
I PUT ALL MY FOCUS INTO MY COMIC PROJECT. I FIGURED IT WAS THERAPEUTIC, MAYBE I COULD MAKE SENSE OF IT ALL IF I ANALYSED IT ENOUGH.
...AND DOWN.
I WAS LOSING FRIENDS, LOSING TOUCH WITH THE PEOPLE THAT MATTERED TO ME. TOO FIXATED ON RECREATING MY FORMER YEARS THAN OPENING A NEW CHAPTER.
...AND DOWN
I WOULD CONSTANTLY THINK ABOUT SIMPLER TIMES, GROWING UP IN MY HOMETOWN. THE COMFORT OF LIVING IN THAT BUBBLE...
...AT THE TIME, I SELFISHLY AVOIDED MOST OF HIS CALLS BECAUSE I COULDN'T FACE DEALING WITH SOMEONE ELSE'S PROBLEMS AS WELL AS MY OWN.
CALLING

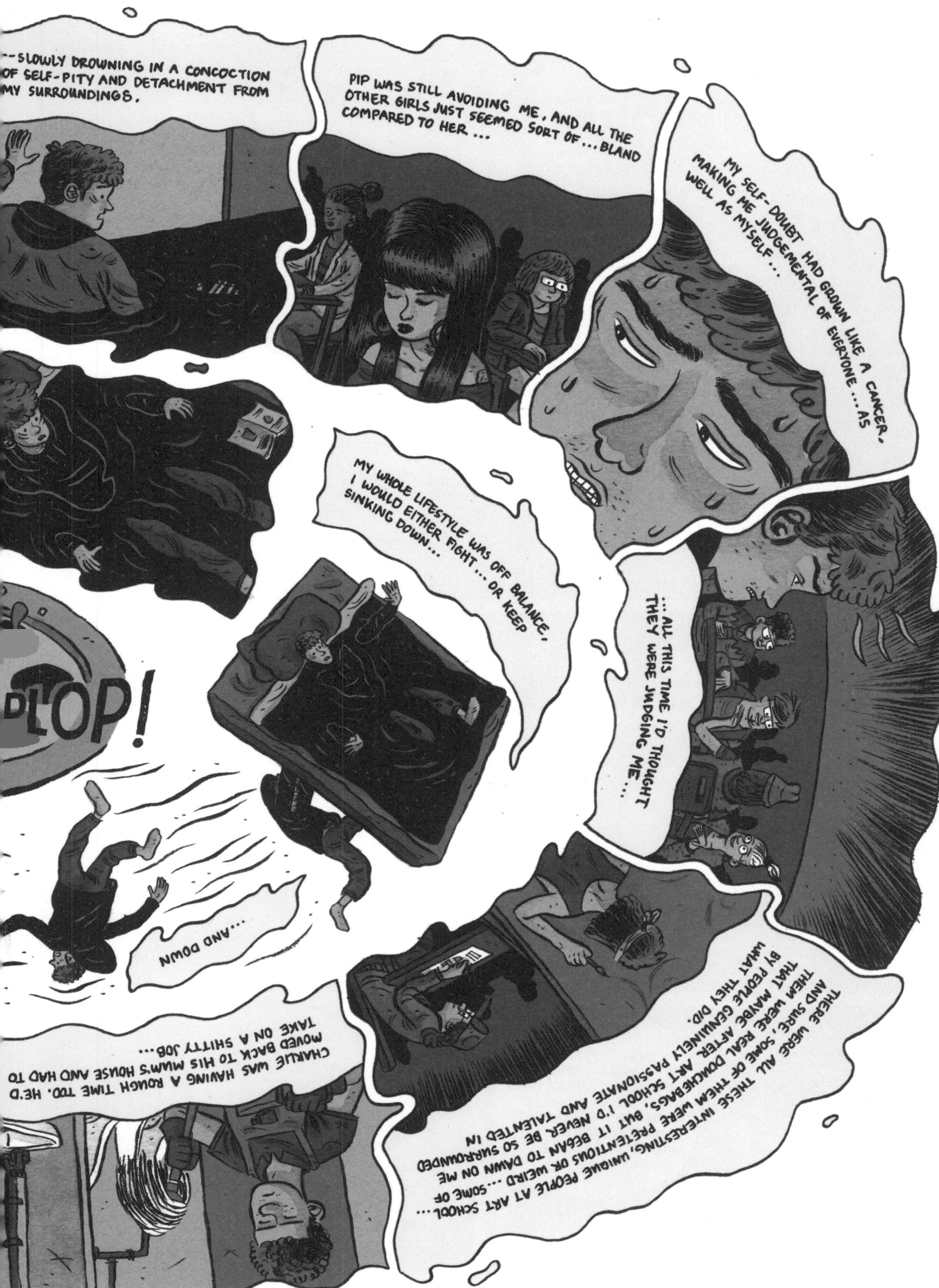

...SLOWLY DROWNING IN A CONCOCTION OF SELF-PITY AND DETACHMENT FROM MY SURROUNDINGS.
PIP WAS STILL AVOIDING ME, AND ALL THE OTHER GIRLS JUST SEEMED SORT OF... BLAND COMPARED TO HER...
MY SELF-DOUBT HAD GROWN LIKE A CANCER, MAKING ME JUDGEMENTAL OF EVERYONE... AS WELL AS MYSELF...
...ALL THIS TIME I'D THOUGHT THEY WERE JUDGING ME...
THERE WERE ALL THESE INTERESTING, UNIQUE PEOPLE AT ART SCHOOL... SOME OF THEM WERE PRETENTIOUS OR WEIRD... AND SURE, SOME REAL DOUCHEBAGS, BUT IT BEGAN TO DAWN ON ME THAT MAYBE AFTER ART SCHOOL I'D NEVER BE SO SURROUNDED BY PEOPLE GENUINELY PASSIONATE AND TALENTED IN WHAT THEY DID.
CHARLIE WAS HAVING A ROUGH TIME TOO. HE'D MOVED BACK TO HIS MUM'S HOUSE AND HAD TO TAKE ON A SHITTY JOB...
...AND DOWN
PLOP!
MY WHOLE LIFESTYLE WAS OFF BALANCE. I WOULD EITHER FIGHT... OR KEEP SINKING DOWN...

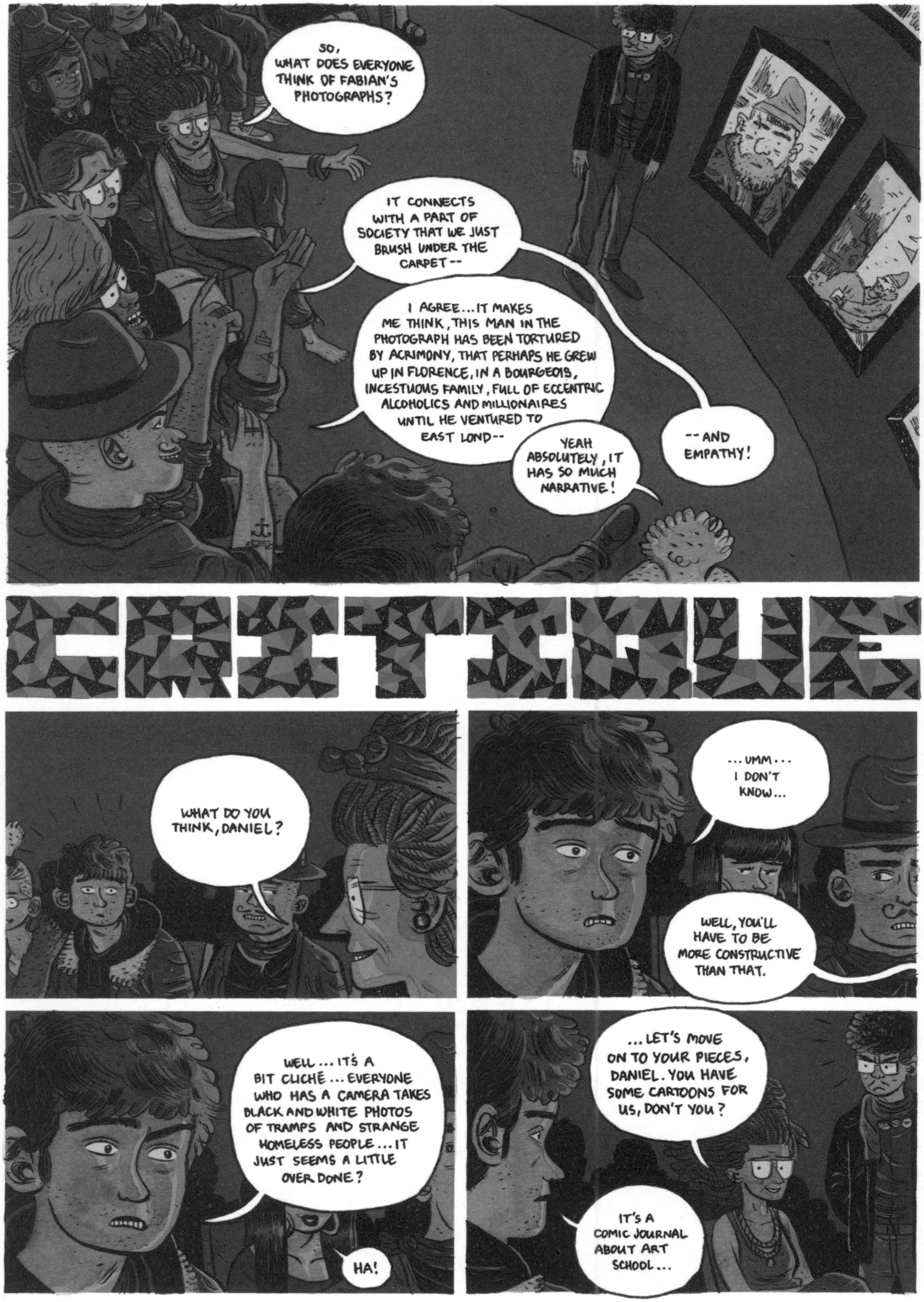
SO, WHAT DOES EVERYONE THINK OF FABIAN'S PHOTOGRAPHS?
IT CONNECTS WITH A PART OF SOCIETY THAT WE JUST BRUSH UNDER THE CARPET--
I AGREE... IT MAKES ME THINK, THIS MAN IN THE PHOTOGRAPH HAS BEEN TORTURED BY ACRIMONY, THAT PERHAPS HE GREW UP IN FLORENCE, IN A BOURGEOIS, INCESTUOUS FAMILY, FULL OF ECCENTRIC ALCOHOLICS AND MILLIONAIRES UNTIL HE VENTURED TO EAST LOND--
YEAH ABSOLUTELY, IT HAS SO MUCH NARRATIVE!
--AND EMPATHY!
CRITIQUE
WHAT DO YOU THINK, DANIEL?
...UMM... I DON'T KNOW...
WELL, YOU'LL HAVE TO BE MORE CONSTRUCTIVE THAN THAT.
WELL... IT'S A BIT CLICHÉ... EVERYONE WHO HAS A CAMERA TAKES BLACK AND WHITE PHOTOS OF TRAMPS AND STRANGE HOMELESS PEOPLE... IT JUST SEEMS A LITTLE OVER DONE?
HA!
...LET'S MOVE ON TO YOUR PIECES, DANIEL. YOU HAVE SOME CARTOONS FOR US, DON'T YOU?
IT'S A COMIC JOURNAL ABOUT ART SCHOOL...

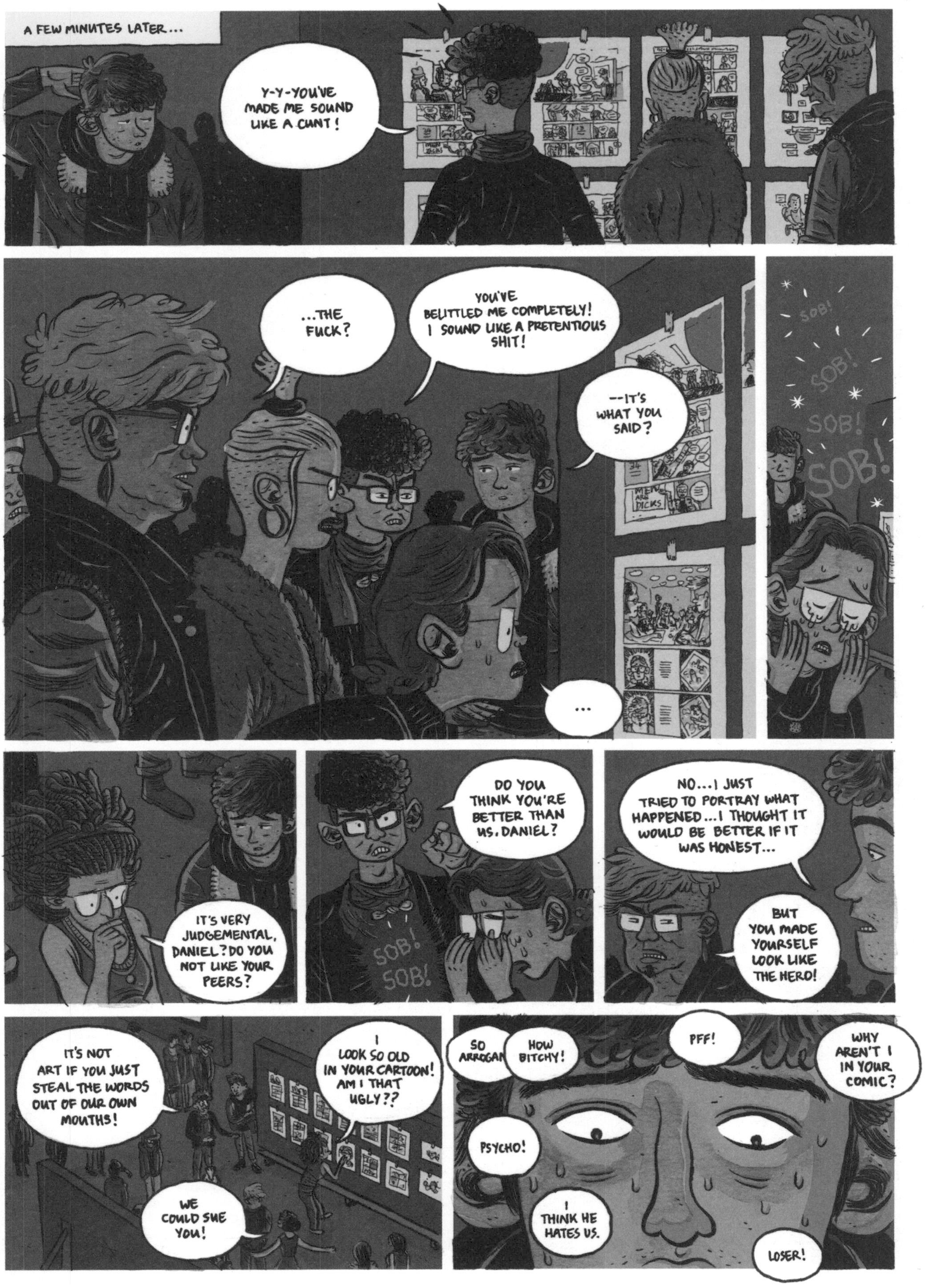
A FEW MINUTES LATER...
Y-Y-YOU'VE MADE ME SOUND LIKE A CUNT!
...THE FUCK?
YOU'VE BELITTLED ME COMPLETELY! I SOUND LIKE A PRETENTIOUS SHIT!
--IT'S WHAT YOU SAID?
...
SOB!
SOB!
SOB!
SOB!
IT'S VERY JUDGEMENTAL, DANIEL? DO YOU NOT LIKE YOUR PEERS?
DO YOU THINK YOU'RE BETTER THAN US, DANIEL?
SOB!
SOB!
NO... I JUST TRIED TO PORTRAY WHAT HAPPENED... I THOUGHT IT WOULD BE BETTER IF IT WAS HONEST...
BUT YOU MADE YOURSELF LOOK LIKE THE HERO!
IT'S NOT ART IF YOU JUST STEAL THE WORDS OUT OF OUR OWN MOUTHS!
I LOOK SO OLD IN YOUR CARTOON! AM I THAT UGLY??
WE COULD SUE YOU!
SO ARROGAN
HOW BITCHY!
PFF!
WHY AREN'T I IN YOUR COMIC?
PSYCHO!
I THINK HE HATES US.
LOSER!

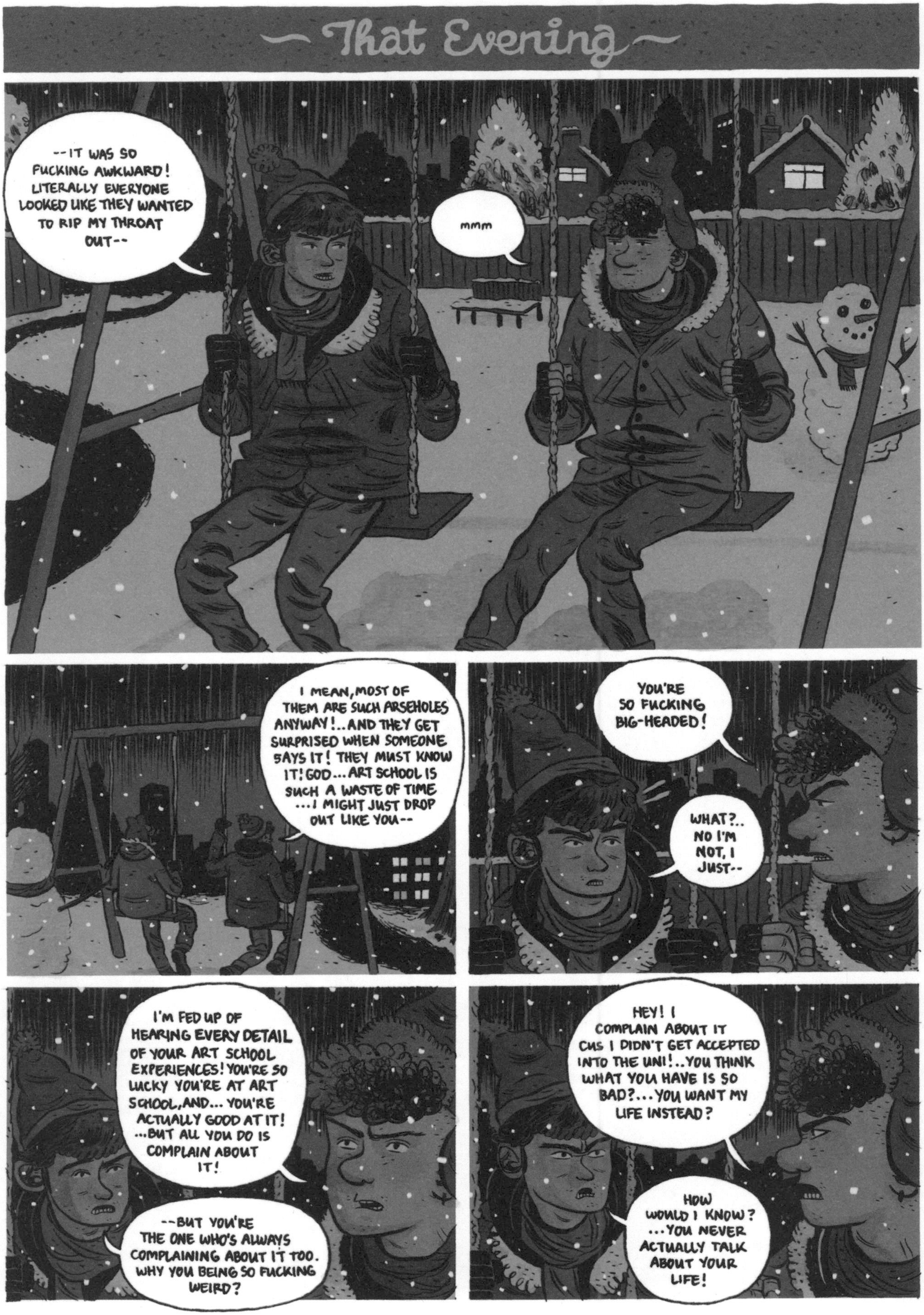
That Evening
--IT WAS SO FUCKING AWKWARD! LITERALLY EVERYONE LOOKED LIKE THEY WANTED TO RIP MY THROAT OUT--
mmm
I MEAN, MOST OF THEM ARE SUCH ARSEHOLES ANYWAY!...AND THEY GET SURPRISED WHEN SOMEONE SAYS IT! THEY MUST KNOW IT! GOD...ART SCHOOL IS SUCH A WASTE OF TIME ...I MIGHT JUST DROP OUT LIKE YOU--
YOU'RE SO FUCKING BIG-HEADED!
WHAT?.. NO I'M NOT, I JUST--
I'M FED UP OF HEARING EVERY DETAIL OF YOUR ART SCHOOL EXPERIENCES! YOU'RE SO LUCKY YOU'RE AT ART SCHOOL, AND... YOU'RE ACTUALLY GOOD AT IT! ...BUT ALL YOU DO IS COMPLAIN ABOUT IT!
--BUT YOU'RE THE ONE WHO'S ALWAYS COMPLAINING ABOUT IT TOO. WHY YOU BEING SO FUCKING WEIRD?
HEY! I COMPLAIN ABOUT IT CUS I DIDN'T GET ACCEPTED INTO THE UNI!...YOU THINK WHAT YOU HAVE IS SO BAD?... YOU WANT MY LIFE INSTEAD?
HOW WOULD I KNOW? ...YOU NEVER ACTUALLY TALK ABOUT YOUR LIFE!

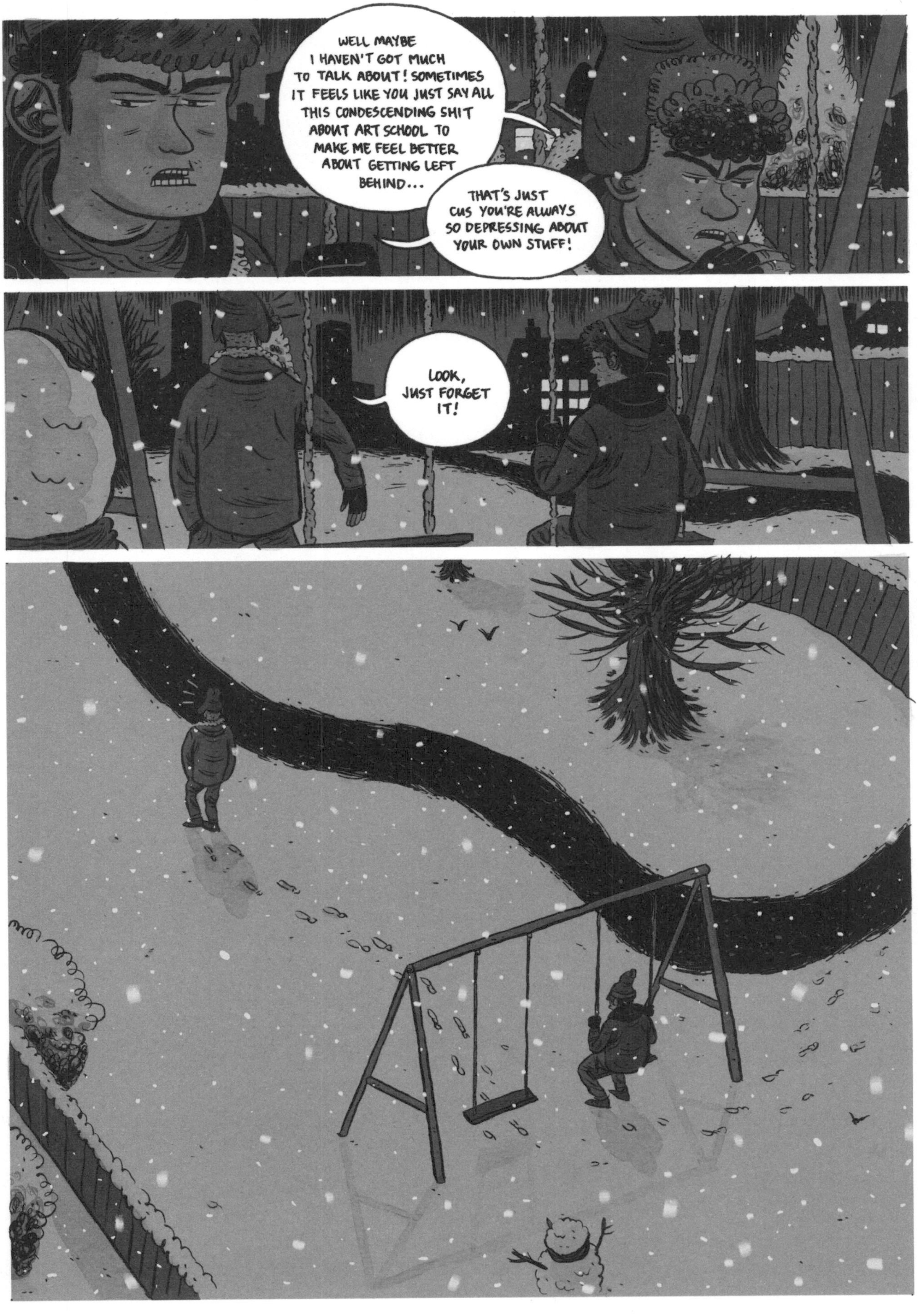
WELL MAYBE I HAVEN'T GOT MUCH TO TALK ABOUT! SOMETIMES IT FEELS LIKE YOU JUST SAY ALL THIS CONDESCENDING SHIT ABOUT ART SCHOOL TO MAKE ME FEEL BETTER ABOUT GETTING LEFT BEHIND...
THAT'S JUST CUS YOU'RE ALWAYS SO DEPRESSING ABOUT YOUR OWN STUFF!
LOOK, JUST FORGET IT!

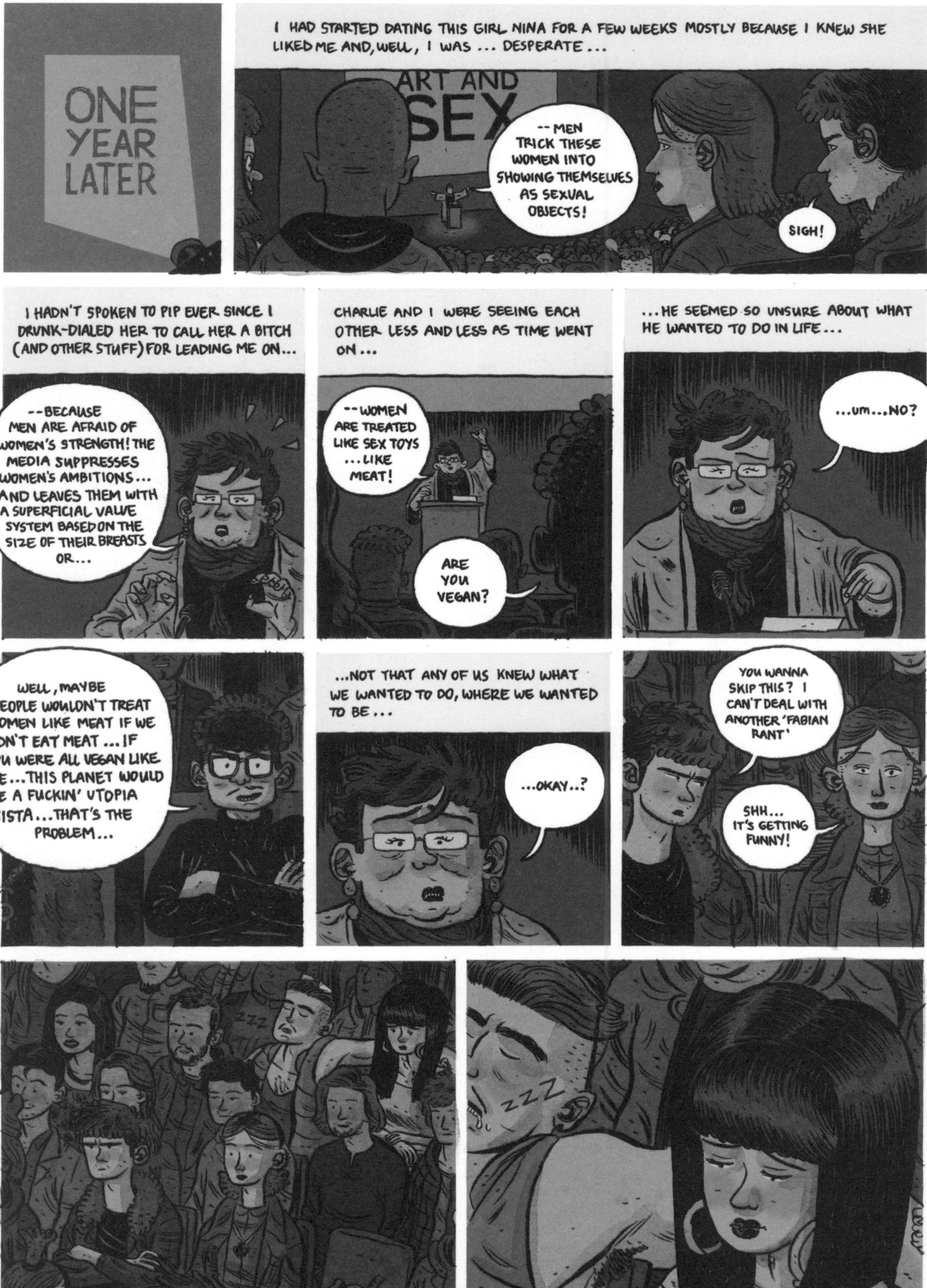
ONE YEAR LATER
I HAD STARTED DATING THIS GIRL NINA FOR A FEW WEEKS MOSTLY BECAUSE I KNEW SHE LIKED ME AND, WELL, I WAS ... DESPERATE ...
ART AND SEX
--MEN TRICK THESE WOMEN INTO SHOWING THEMSELVES AS SEXUAL OBJECTS!
SIGH!
I HADN'T SPOKEN TO PIP EVER SINCE I DRUNK-DIALED HER TO CALL HER A BITCH (AND OTHER STUFF) FOR LEADING ME ON...
--BECAUSE MEN ARE AFRAID OF WOMEN'S STRENGTH! THE MEDIA SUPPRESSES WOMEN'S AMBITIONS... AND LEAVES THEM WITH A SUPERFICIAL VALUE SYSTEM BASED ON THE SIZE OF THEIR BREASTS OR...
CHARLIE AND I WERE SEEING EACH OTHER LESS AND LESS AS TIME WENT ON...
--WOMEN ARE TREATED LIKE SEX TOYS ...LIKE MEAT!
ARE YOU VEGAN?
...HE SEEMED SO UNSURE ABOUT WHAT HE WANTED TO DO IN LIFE...
...um...NO?
WELL, MAYBE PEOPLE WOULDN'T TREAT WOMEN LIKE MEAT IF WE DIDN'T EAT MEAT ... IF YOU WERE ALL VEGAN LIKE ME...THIS PLANET WOULD BE A FUCKIN' UTOPIA SISTA...THAT'S THE PROBLEM...
...NOT THAT ANY OF US KNEW WHAT WE WANTED TO DO, WHERE WE WANTED TO BE...
...OKAY..?
YOU WANNA SKIP THIS? I CAN'T DEAL WITH ANOTHER 'FABIAN RANT'
SHH... IT'S GETTING FUNNY!
ZZZ
ZZZ

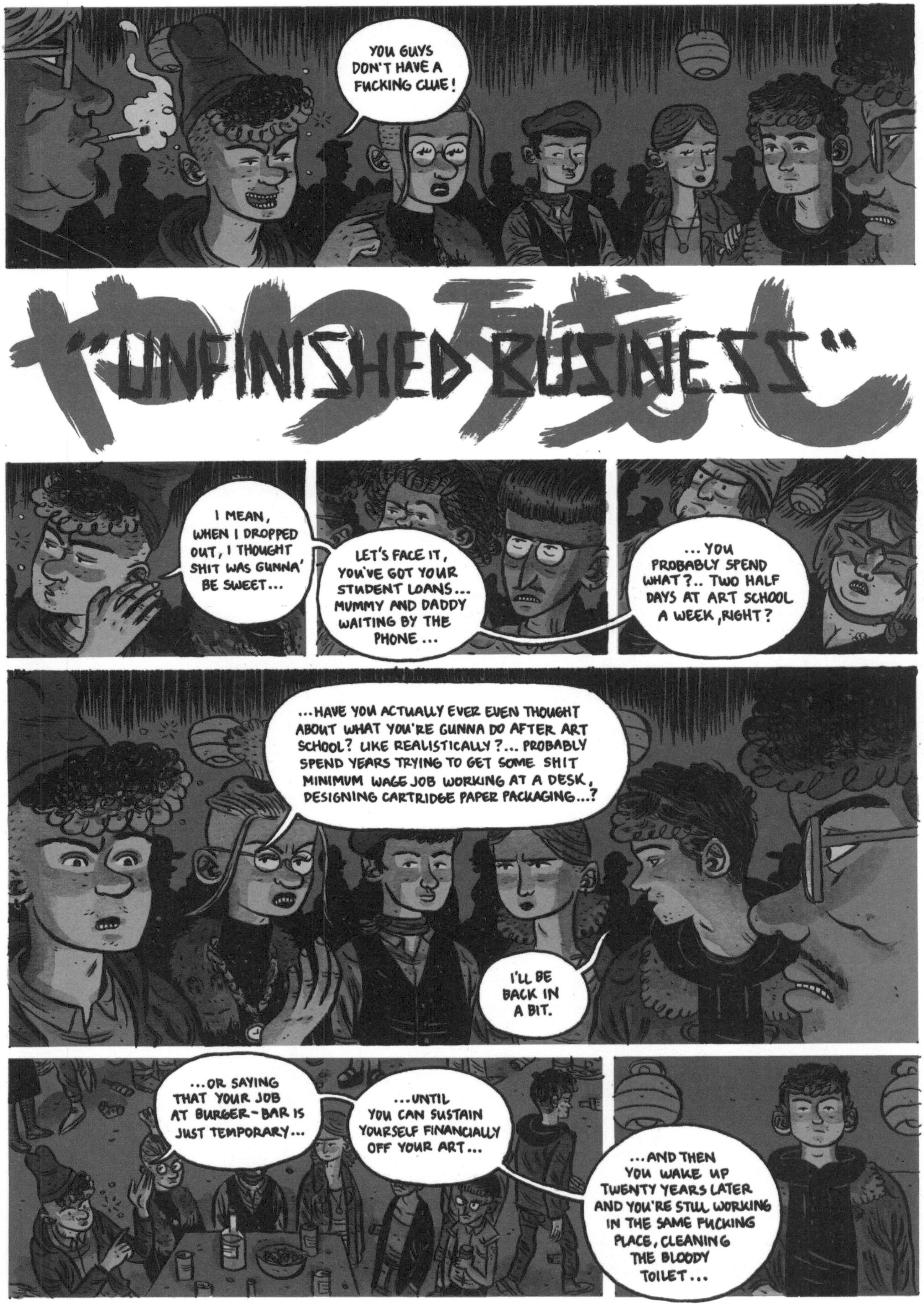
YOU GUYS DON'T HAVE A FUCKING CLUE!
"UNFINISHED BUSINESS"
I MEAN, WHEN I DROPPED OUT, I THOUGHT SHIT WAS GUNNA' BE SWEET...
LET'S FACE IT, YOU'VE GOT YOUR STUDENT LOANS... MUMMY AND DADDY WAITING BY THE PHONE...
...YOU PROBABLY SPEND WHAT?.. TWO HALF DAYS AT ART SCHOOL A WEEK, RIGHT?
...HAVE YOU ACTUALLY EVER EVEN THOUGHT ABOUT WHAT YOU'RE GUNNA DO AFTER ART SCHOOL? LIKE REALISTICALLY?... PROBABLY SPEND YEARS TRYING TO GET SOME SHIT MINIMUM WAGE JOB WORKING AT A DESK, DESIGNING CARTRIDGE PAPER PACKAGING...?
I'LL BE BACK IN A BIT.
...OR SAYING THAT YOUR JOB AT BURGER-BAR IS JUST TEMPORARY...
...UNTIL YOU CAN SUSTAIN YOURSELF FINANCIALLY OFF YOUR ART...
...AND THEN YOU WAKE UP TWENTY YEARS LATER AND YOU'RE STILL WORKING IN THE SAME FUCKING PLACE, CLEANING THE BLOODY TOILET...

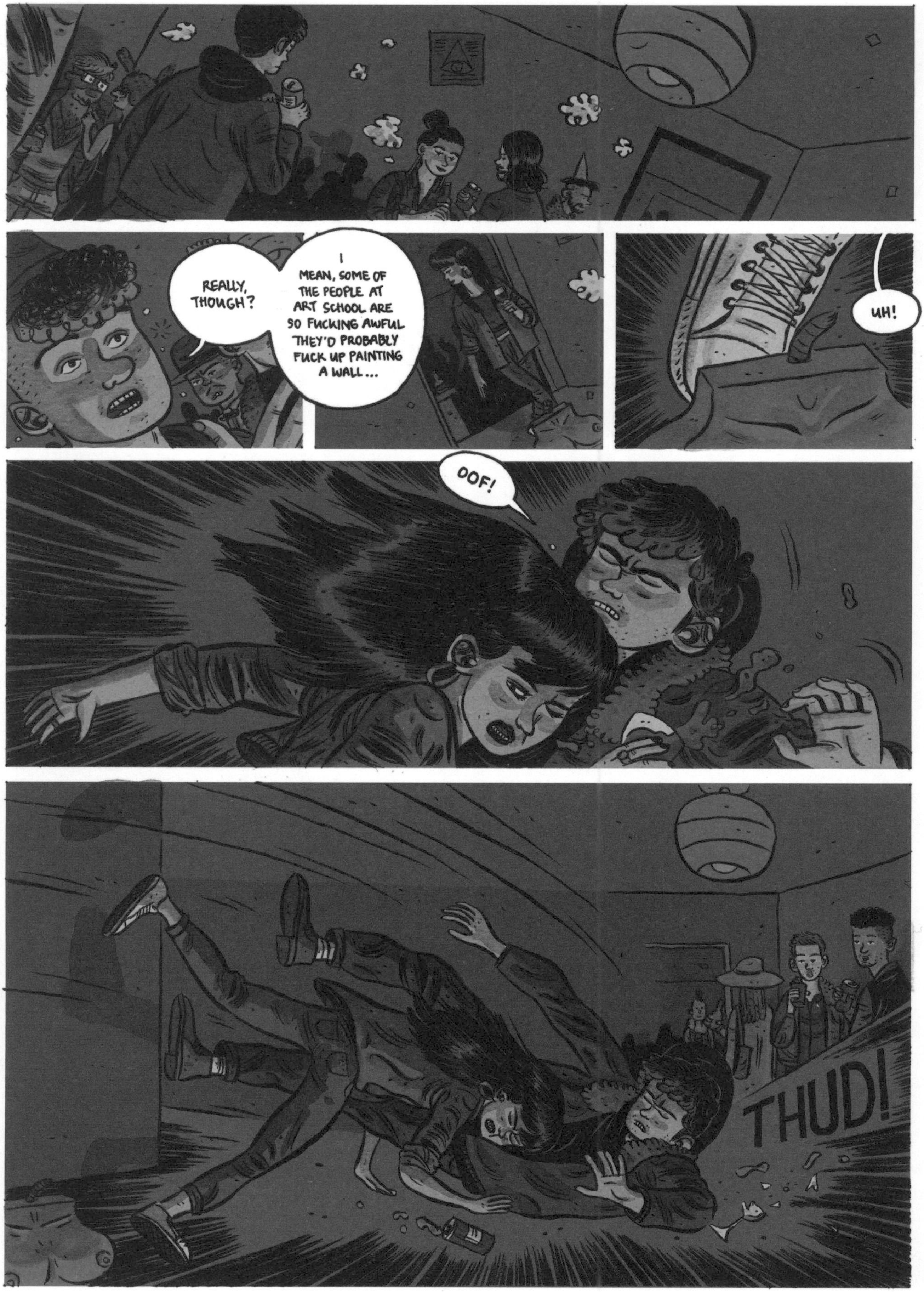

REALLY, THOUGH?
I MEAN, SOME OF THE PEOPLE AT ART SCHOOL ARE SO FUCKING AWFUL THEY'D PROBABLY FUCK UP PAINTING A WALL...
UH!
OOF!
THUD!

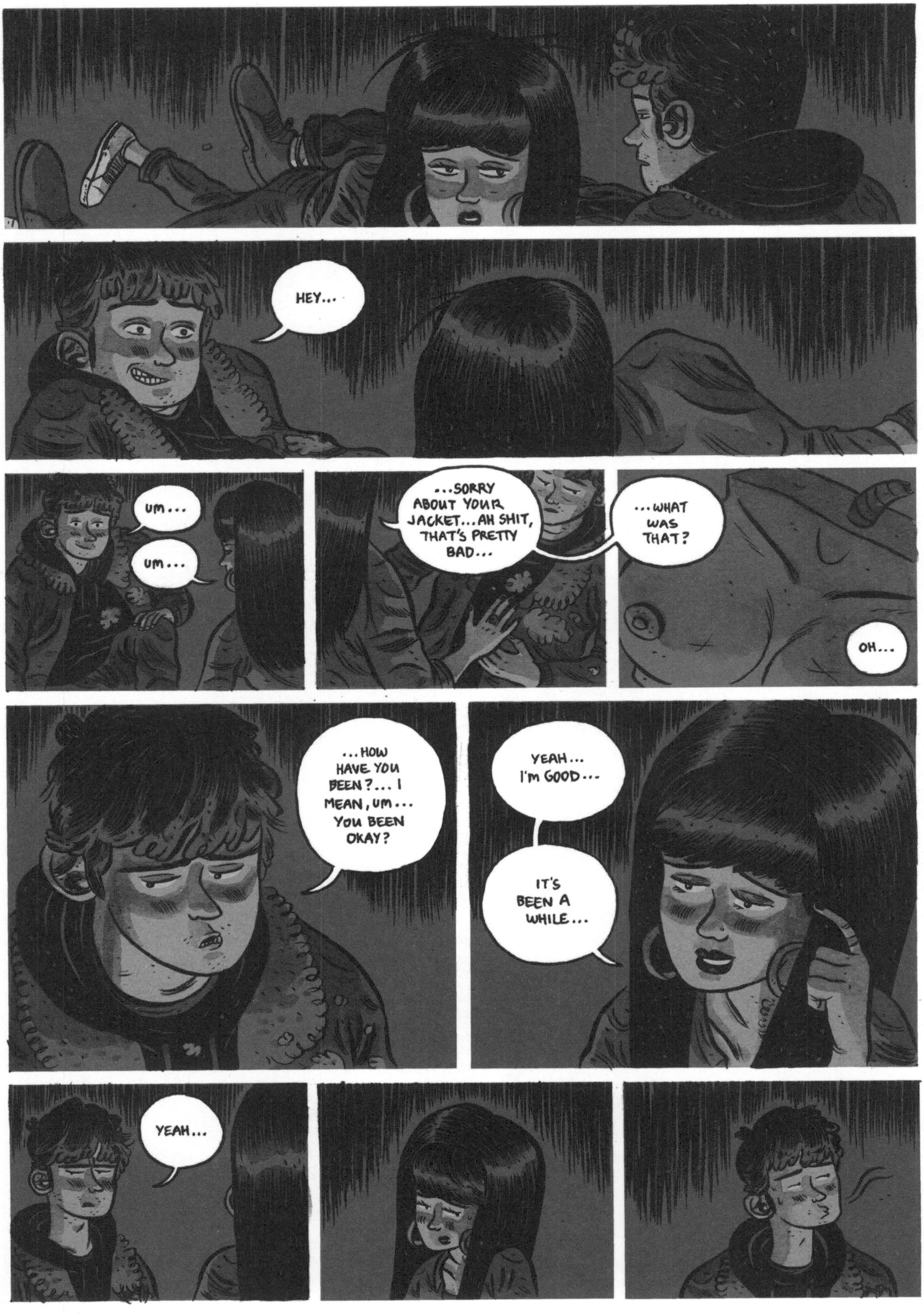
HEY...
UM...
UM...
...SORRY ABOUT YOUR JACKET...AH SHIT, THAT'S PRETTY BAD...
...WHAT WAS THAT?
OH...
...HOW HAVE YOU BEEN?... I MEAN, UM... YOU BEEN OKAY?
YEAH... I'M GOOD...
IT'S BEEN A WHILE...
YEAH...

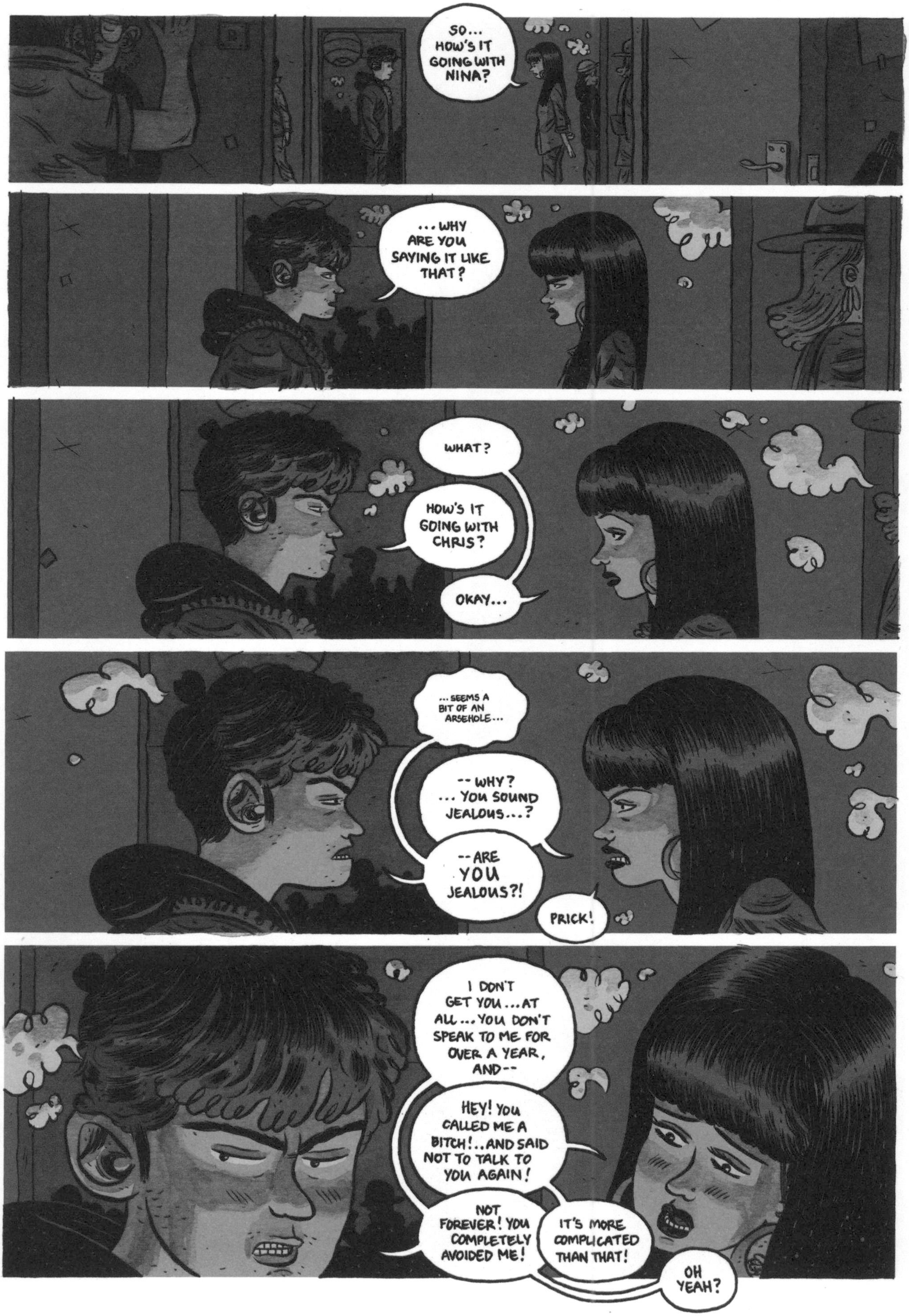
SO... HOW'S IT GOING WITH NINA?
...WHY ARE YOU SAYING IT LIKE THAT?
WHAT?
HOW'S IT GOING WITH CHRIS?
OKAY...
...SEEMS A BIT OF AN ARSEHOLE...
--WHY? ...YOU SOUND JEALOUS...?
--ARE YOU JEALOUS?!
PRICK!
I DON'T GET YOU...AT ALL...YOU DON'T SPEAK TO ME FOR OVER A YEAR, AND--
HEY! YOU CALLED ME A BITCH!..AND SAID NOT TO TALK TO YOU AGAIN!
NOT FOREVER! YOU COMPLETELY AVOIDED ME!
IT'S MORE COMPLICATED THAN THAT!
OH YEAH?

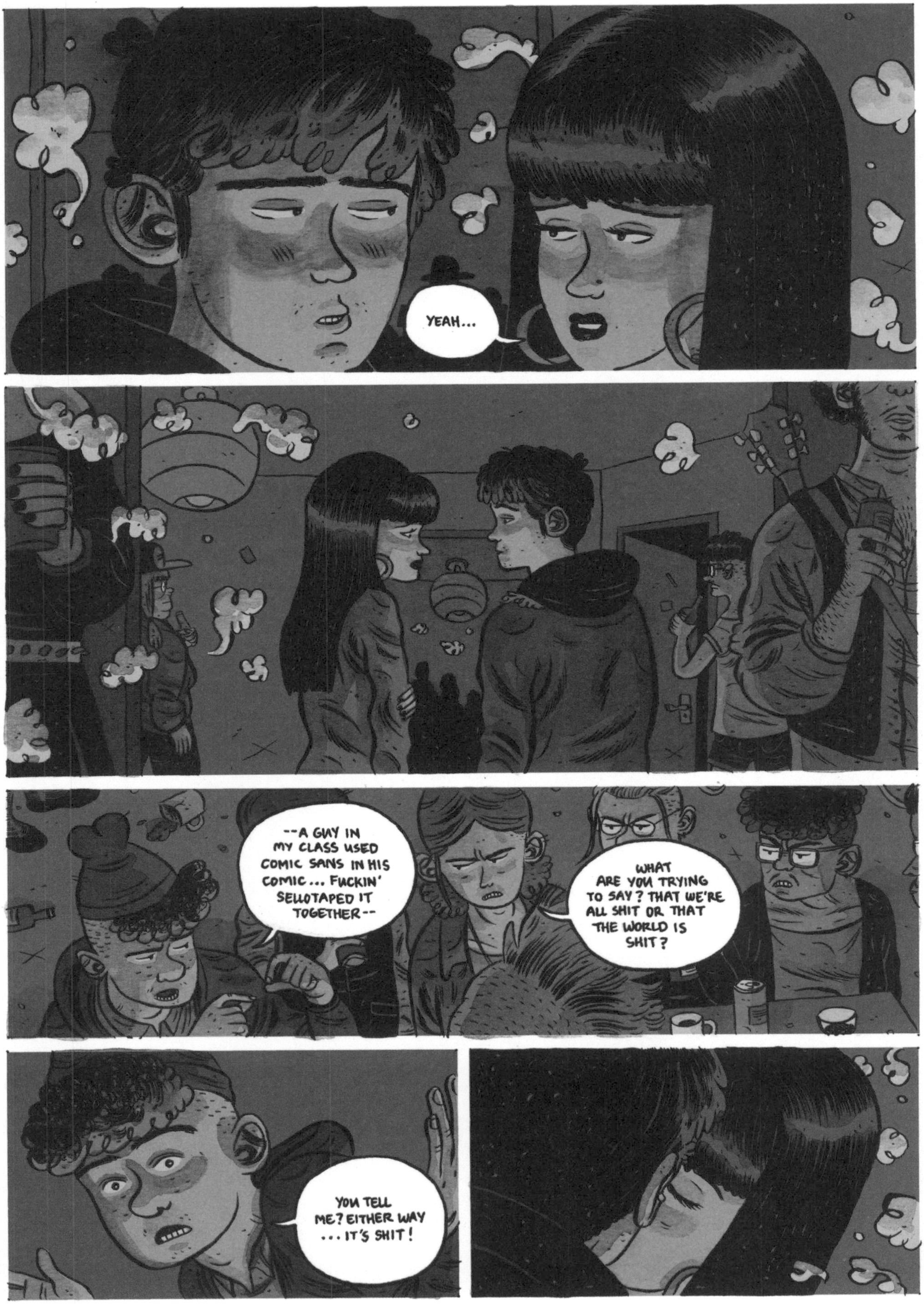
YEAH...
--A GUY IN MY CLASS USED COMIC SANS IN HIS COMIC... FUCKIN' SELLOTAPED IT TOGETHER--
WHAT ARE YOU TRYING TO SAY? THAT WE'RE ALL SHIT OR THAT THE WORLD IS SHIT?
YOU TELL ME? EITHER WAY ...IT'S SHIT!

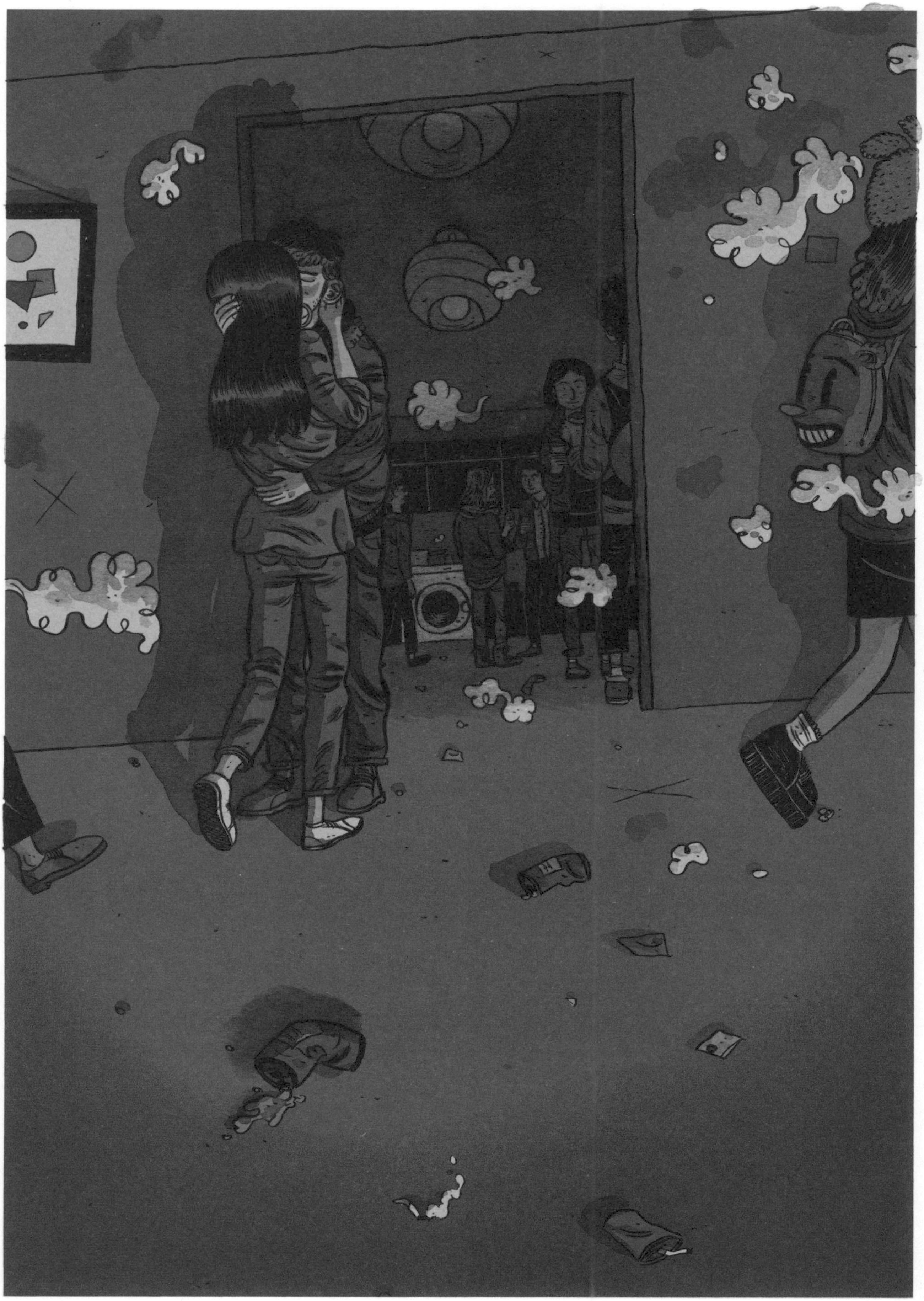

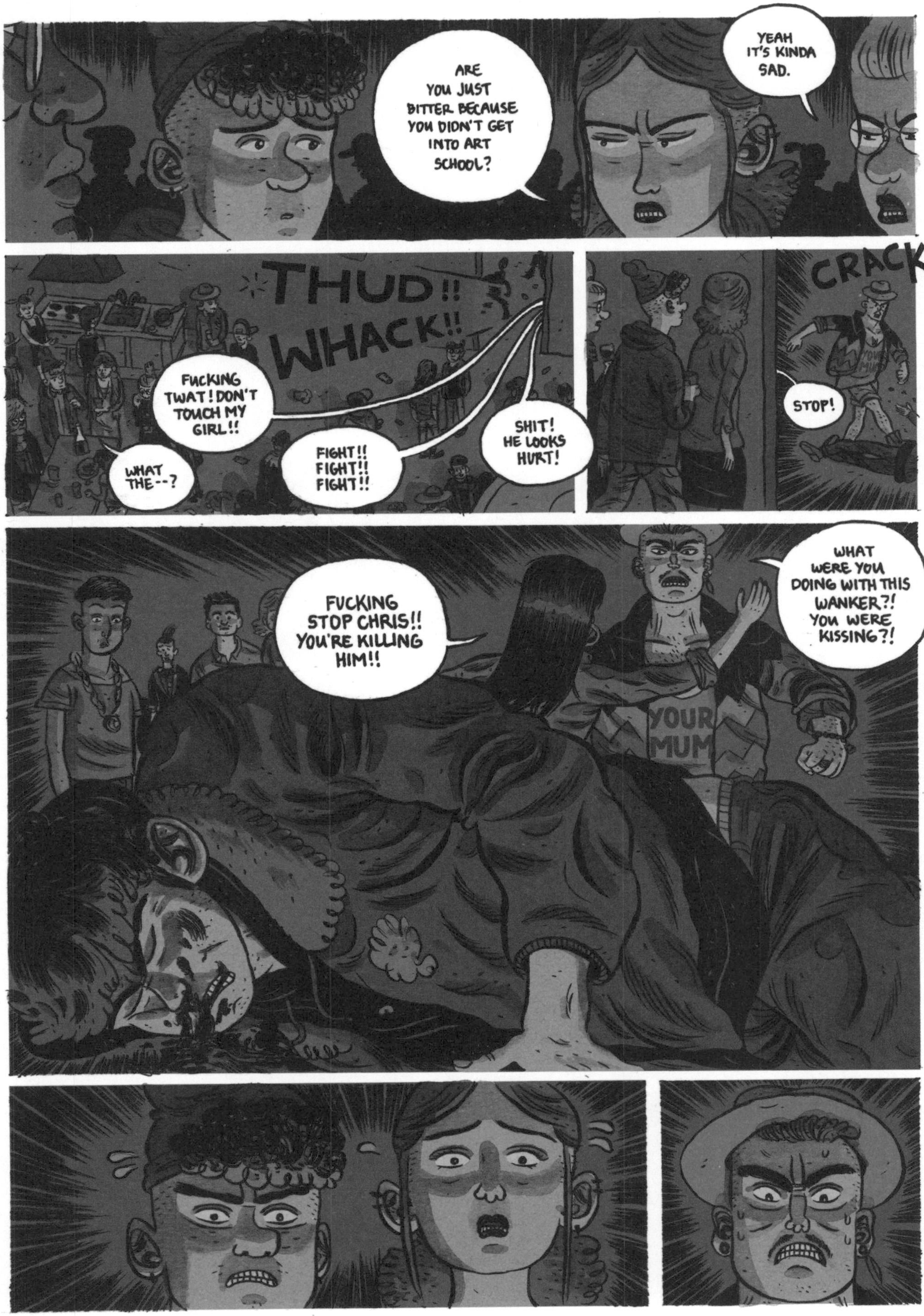
ARE YOU JUST BITTER BECAUSE YOU DIDN'T GET INTO ART SCHOOL?
YEAH IT'S KINDA SAD.
THUD!! WHACK!!
FUCKING TWAT! DON'T TOUCH MY GIRL!!
WHAT THE--?
FIGHT!! FIGHT!! FIGHT!!
SHIT! HE LOOKS HURT!
STOP!
CRACK!
FUCKING STOP CHRIS!! YOU'RE KILLING HIM!!
WHAT WERE YOU DOING WITH THIS WANKER?! YOU WERE KISSING?!
YOUR MUM

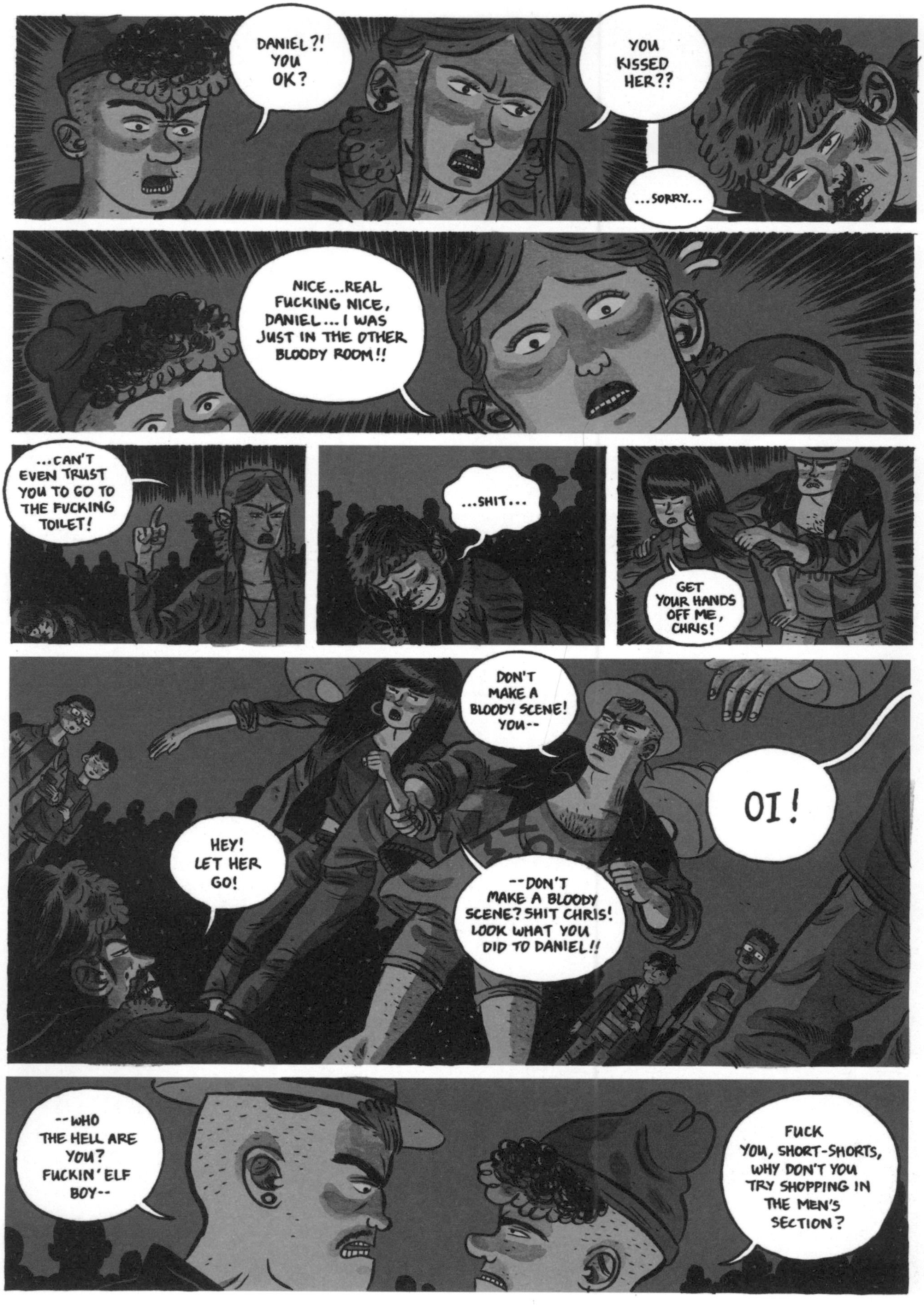
DANIEL?! YOU OK?
YOU KISSED HER??
...SORRY...
NICE...REAL FUCKING NICE, DANIEL...I WAS JUST IN THE OTHER BLOODY ROOM!!
...CAN'T EVEN TRUST YOU TO GO TO THE FUCKING TOILET!
...SHIT...
GET YOUR HANDS OFF ME, CHRIS!
DON'T MAKE A BLOODY SCENE! YOU--
OI!
HEY! LET HER GO!
--DON'T MAKE A BLOODY SCENE? SHIT CHRIS! LOOK WHAT YOU DID TO DANIEL!!
--WHO THE HELL ARE YOU? FUCKIN' ELF BOY--
FUCK YOU, SHORT-SHORTS, WHY DON'T YOU TRY SHOPPING IN THE MEN'S SECTION?

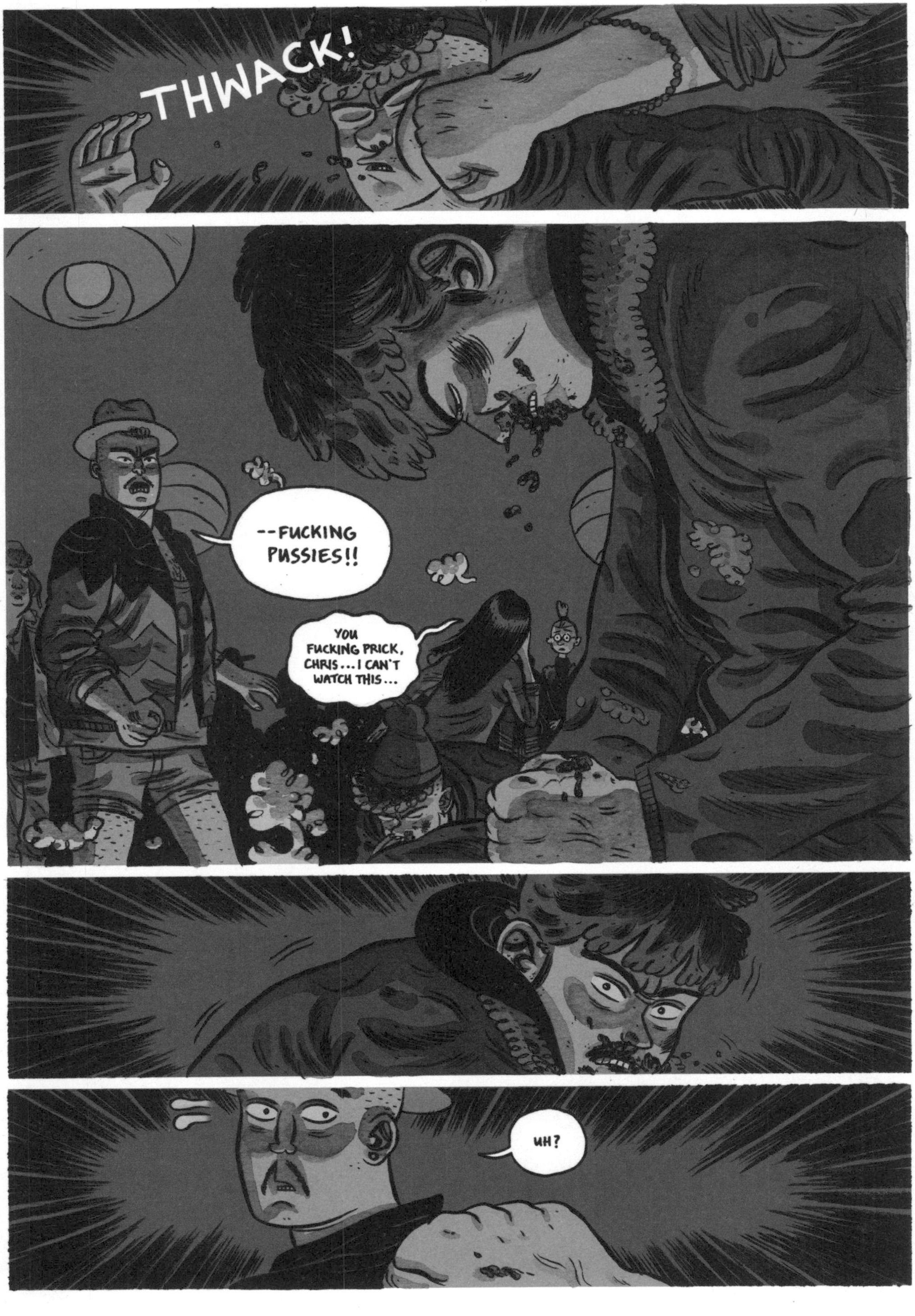
THWACK!
--FUCKING PUSSIES!!
YOU FUCKING PRICK, CHRIS... I CAN'T WATCH THIS...
UH?

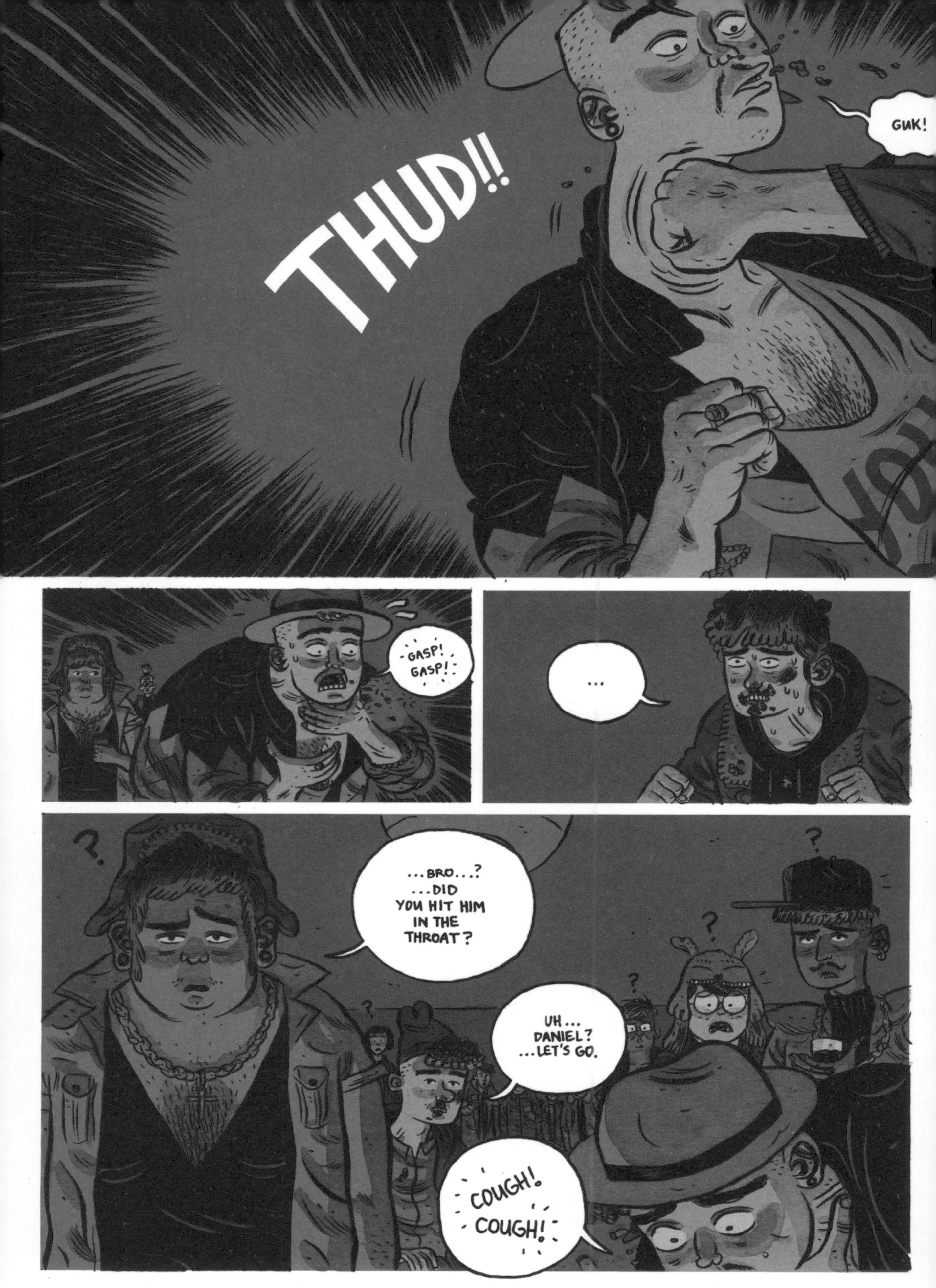
THUD!!
GUK!
GASP! GASP!
...
...BRO...? ...DID YOU HIT HIM IN THE THROAT?
UH... DANIEL? ...LET'S GO.
COUGH! COUGH!

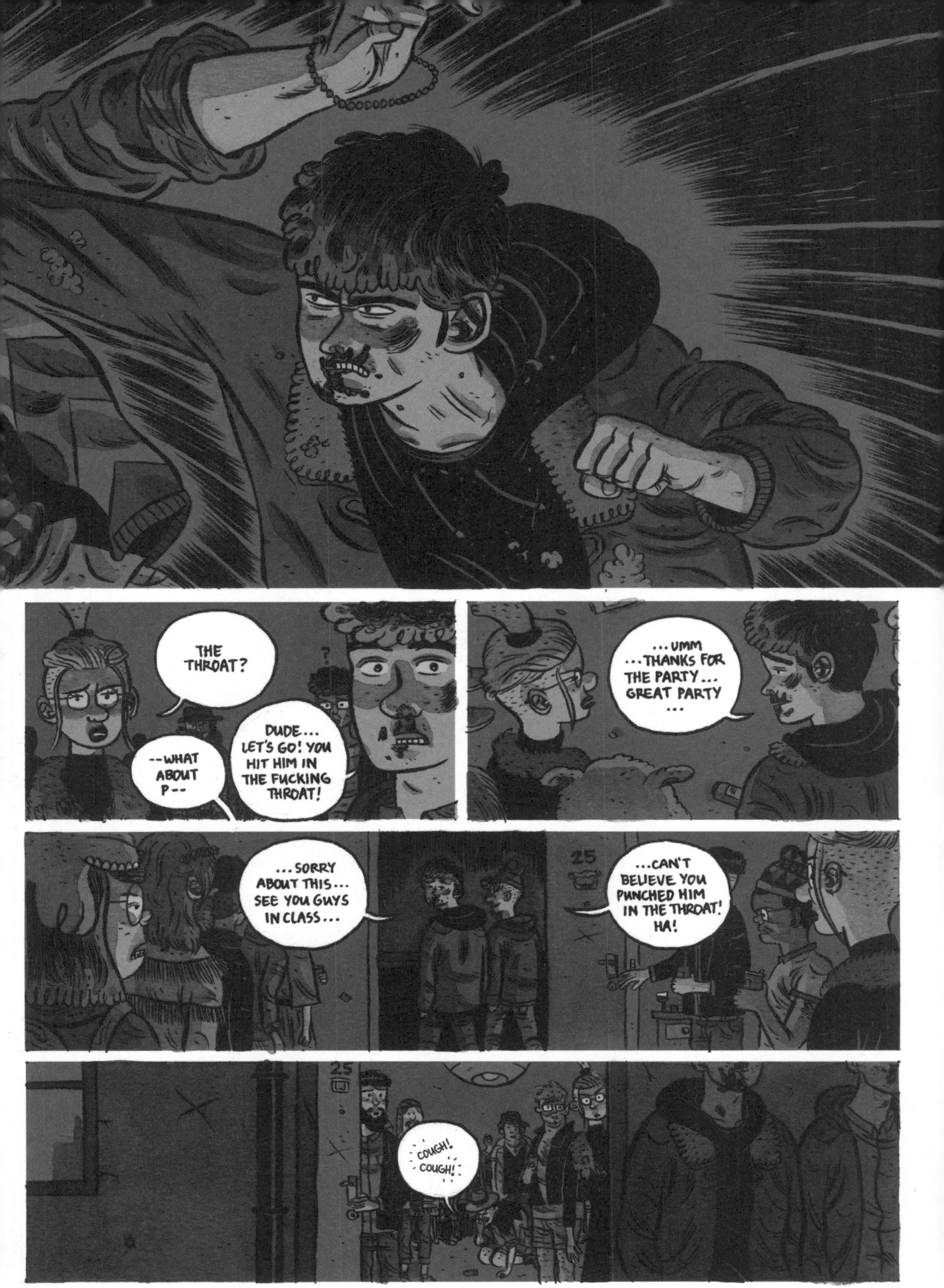
THE THROAT?
DUDE... LET'S GO! YOU HIT HIM IN THE FUCKING THROAT!
--WHAT ABOUT P--
...UMM ...THANKS FOR THE PARTY... GREAT PARTY ...
...SORRY ABOUT THIS... SEE YOU GUYS IN CLASS...
25
...CAN'T BELIEVE YOU PUNCHED HIM IN THE THROAT! HA!
25
COUGH! COUGH!

WHAT DO YOU THINK OF ART SCHOOL IN HINDSIGHT?

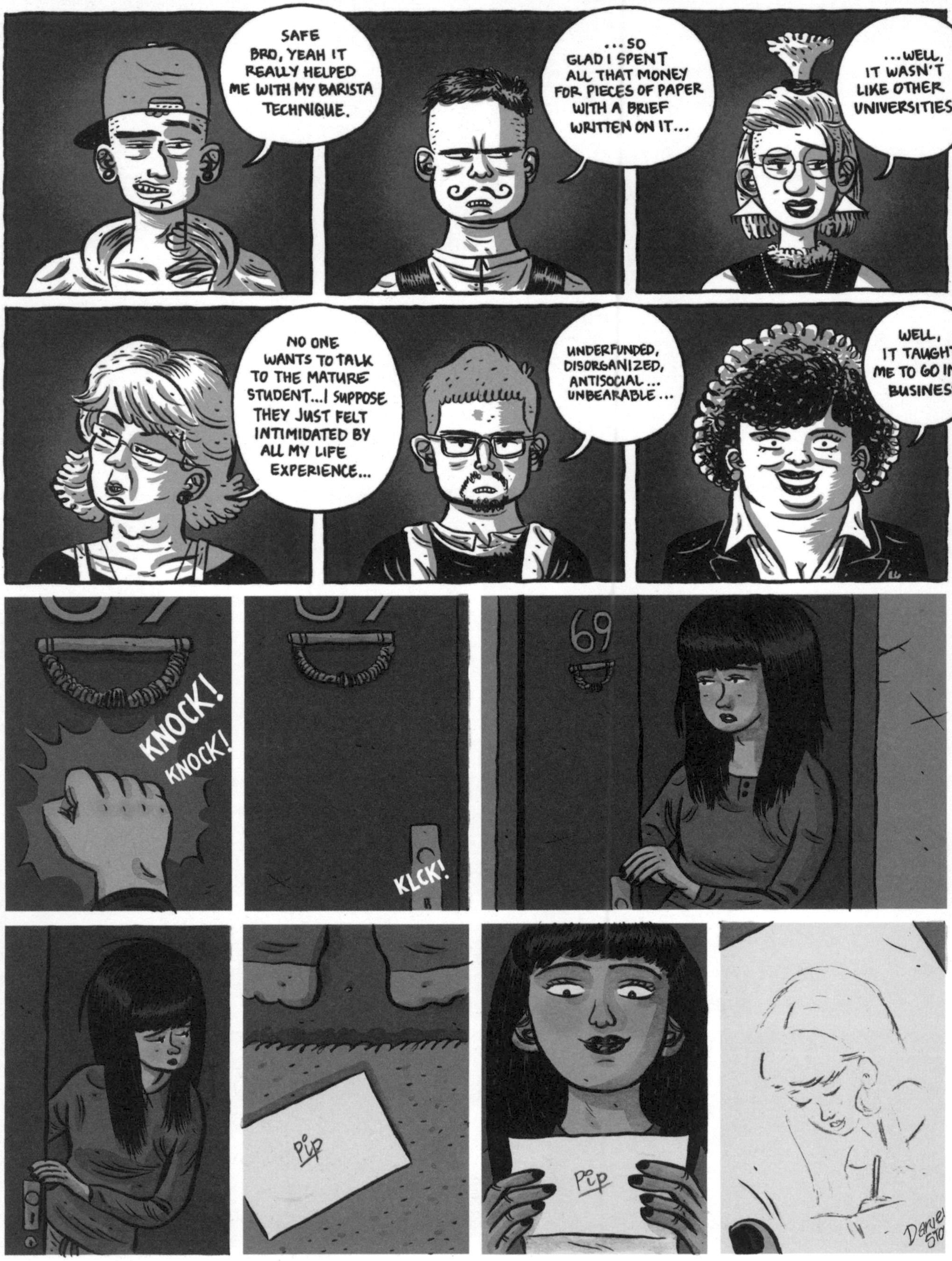
SAFE BRO, YEAH IT REALLY HELPED ME WITH MY BARISTA TECHNIQUE.
...SO GLAD I SPENT ALL THAT MONEY FOR PIECES OF PAPER WITH A BRIEF WRITTEN ON IT...
...WELL, IT WASN'T LIKE OTHER UNIVERSITIES.
NO ONE WANTS TO TALK TO THE MATURE STUDENT...I SUPPOSE THEY JUST FELT INTIMIDATED BY ALL MY LIFE EXPERIENCE...
UNDERFUNDED, DISORGANIZED, ANTISOCIAL... UNBEARABLE...
WELL, IT TAUGHT ME TO GO INTO BUSINESS.
69
KNOCK! KNOCK!
KLCK!
69
Pip
Pip
Daniel

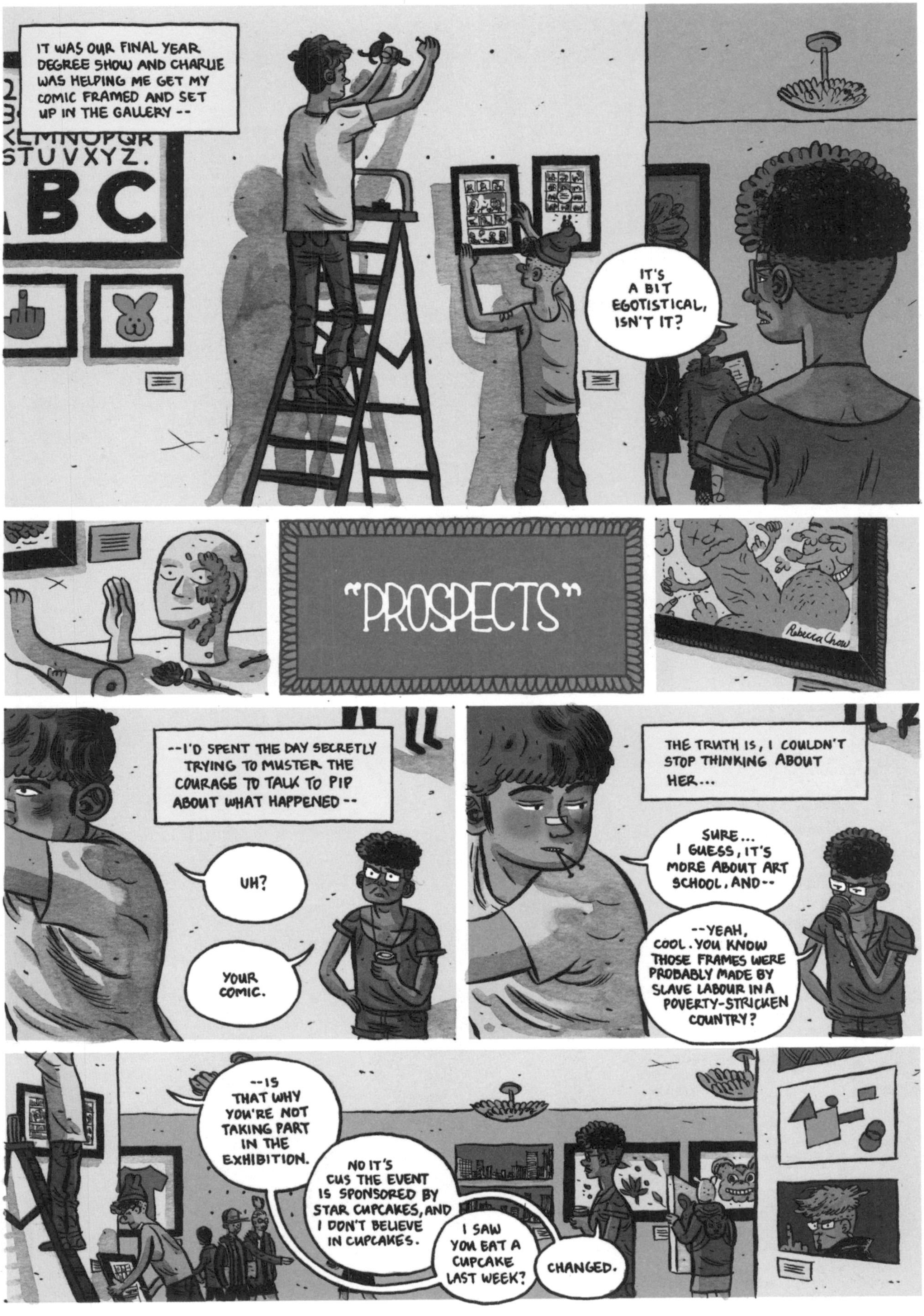
IT WAS OUR FINAL YEAR DEGREE SHOW AND CHARLIE WAS HELPING ME GET MY COMIC FRAMED AND SET UP IN THE GALLERY --
IT'S A BIT EGOTISTICAL, ISN'T IT?
"PROSPECTS"
Rebecca Chow
--I'D SPENT THE DAY SECRETLY TRYING TO MUSTER THE COURAGE TO TALK TO PIP ABOUT WHAT HAPPENED --
UH?
YOUR COMIC.
THE TRUTH IS, I COULDN'T STOP THINKING ABOUT HER...
SURE... I GUESS, IT'S MORE ABOUT ART SCHOOL, AND--
--YEAH, COOL. YOU KNOW THOSE FRAMES WERE PROBABLY MADE BY SLAVE LABOUR IN A POVERTY-STRICKEN COUNTRY?
--IS THAT WHY YOU'RE NOT TAKING PART IN THE EXHIBITION.
NO IT'S CUS THE EVENT IS SPONSORED BY STAR CUPCAKES, AND I DON'T BELIEVE IN CUPCAKES.
I SAW YOU EAT A CUPCAKE LAST WEEK?
CHANGED.

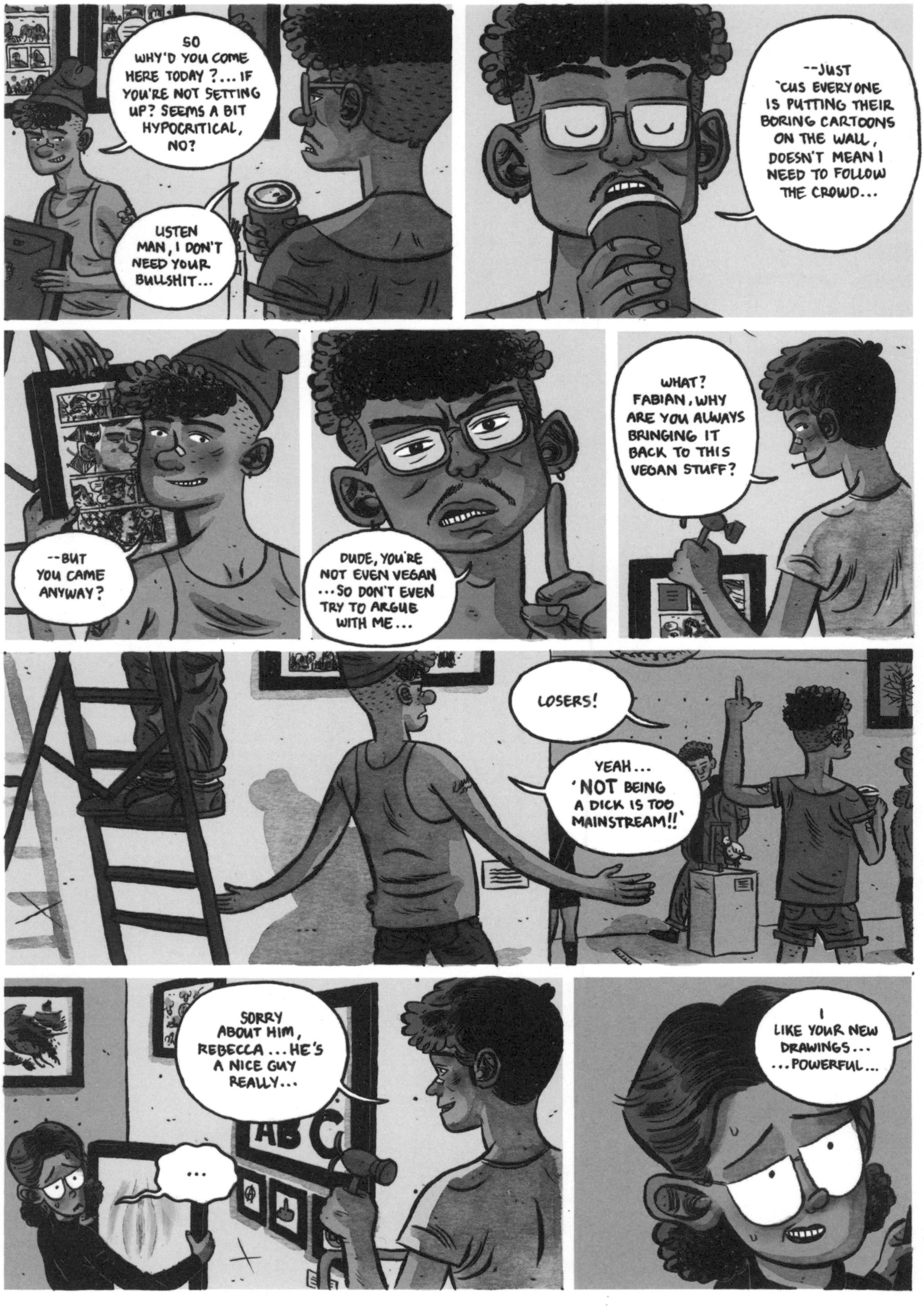
SO WHY'D YOU COME HERE TODAY?... IF YOU'RE NOT SETTING UP? SEEMS A BIT HYPOCRITICAL, NO?
LISTEN MAN, I DON'T NEED YOUR BULLSHIT...
--JUST 'CUS EVERYONE IS PUTTING THEIR BORING CARTOONS ON THE WALL, DOESN'T MEAN I NEED TO FOLLOW THE CROWD...
--BUT YOU CAME ANYWAY?
DUDE, YOU'RE NOT EVEN VEGAN ...SO DON'T EVEN TRY TO ARGUE WITH ME...
WHAT? FABIAN, WHY ARE YOU ALWAYS BRINGING IT BACK TO THIS VEGAN STUFF?
LOSERS!
YEAH... 'NOT BEING A DICK IS TOO MAINSTREAM!!'
SORRY ABOUT HIM, REBECCA... HE'S A NICE GUY REALLY...
...
I LIKE YOUR NEW DRAWINGS... ...POWERFUL...

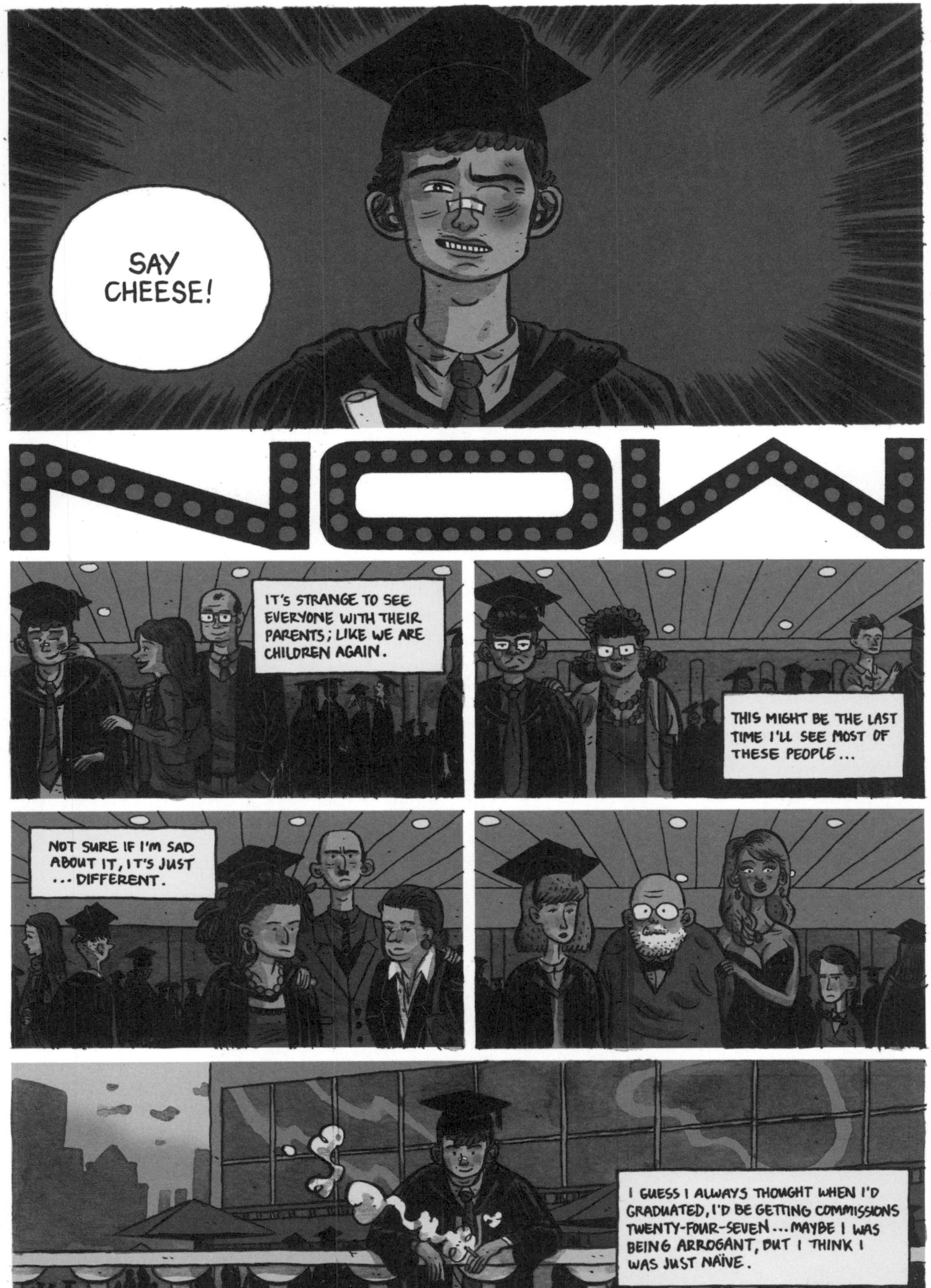
SAY CHEESE!
NOW
IT'S STRANGE TO SEE EVERYONE WITH THEIR PARENTS; LIKE WE ARE CHILDREN AGAIN.
THIS MIGHT BE THE LAST TIME I'LL SEE MOST OF THESE PEOPLE...
NOT SURE IF I'M SAD ABOUT IT, IT'S JUST ...DIFFERENT.
I GUESS I ALWAYS THOUGHT WHEN I'D GRADUATED, I'D BE GETTING COMMISSIONS TWENTY-FOUR-SEVEN... MAYBE I WAS BEING ARROGANT, BUT I THINK I WAS JUST NAÏVE.

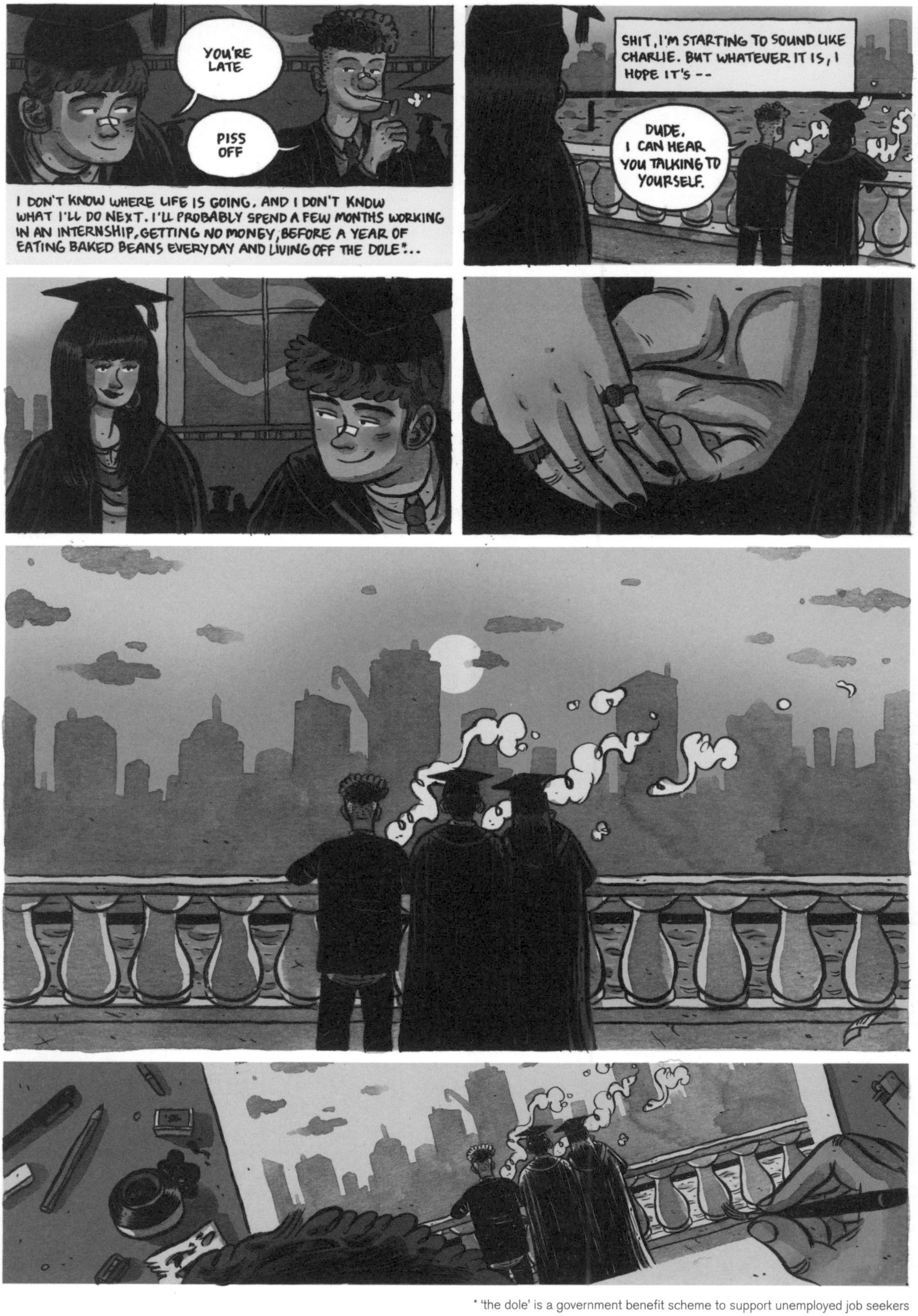
YOU'RE LATE
PISS OFF
I DON'T KNOW WHERE LIFE IS GOING. AND I DON'T KNOW WHAT I'LL DO NEXT. I'LL PROBABLY SPEND A FEW MONTHS WORKING IN AN INTERNSHIP, GETTING NO MONEY, BEFORE A YEAR OF EATING BAKED BEANS EVERYDAY AND LIVING OFF THE DOLE*..
SHIT, I'M STARTING TO SOUND LIKE CHARLIE. BUT WHATEVER IT IS, I HOPE IT'S --
DUDE, I CAN HEAR YOU TALKING TO YOURSELF.

* 'the dole' is a government benefit scheme to support unemployed job seekers

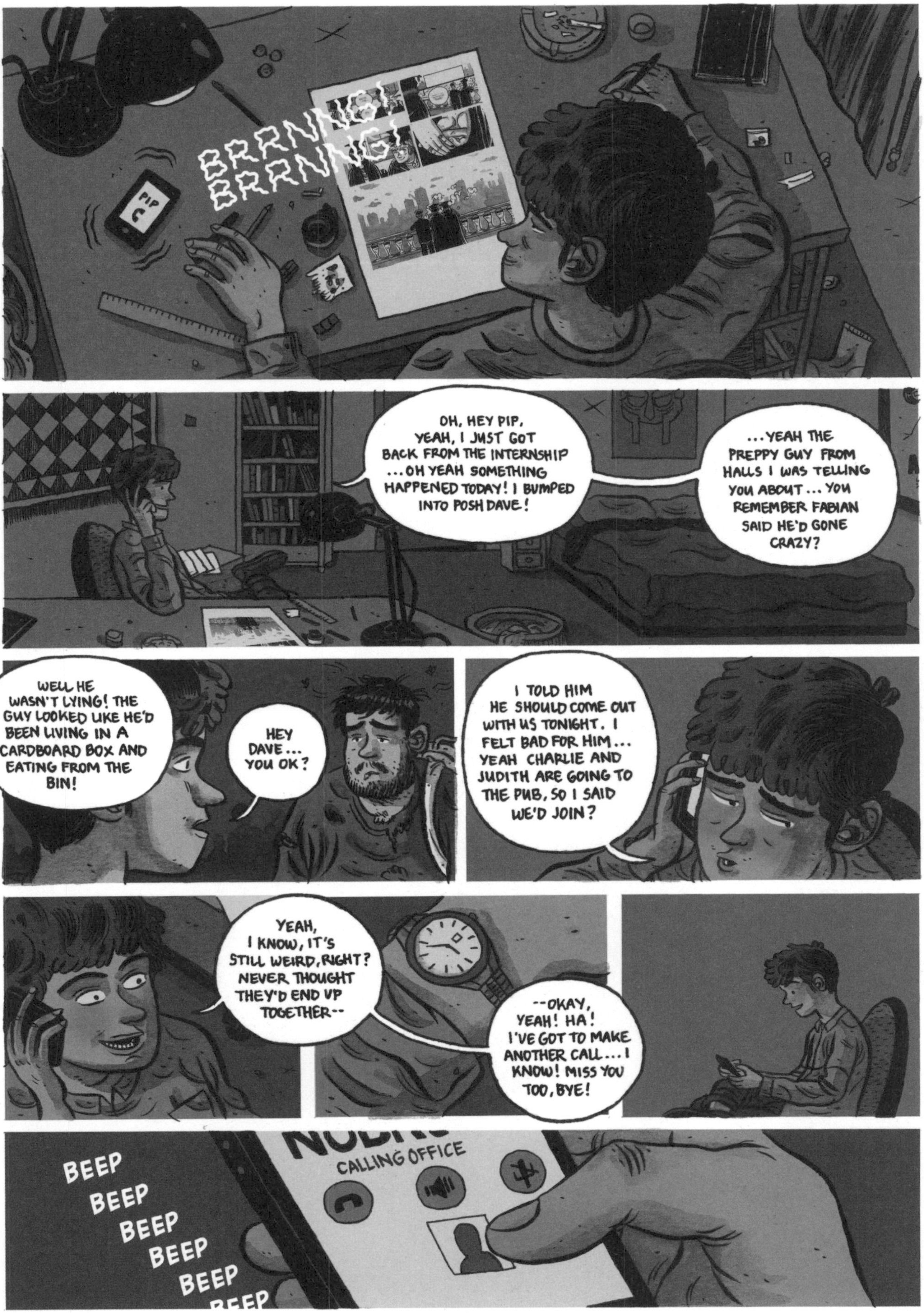
BRRNNG! BRRNNG!
PIP
OH, HEY PIP, YEAH, I JUST GOT BACK FROM THE INTERNSHIP ...OH YEAH SOMETHING HAPPENED TODAY! I BUMPED INTO POSH DAVE!
...YEAH THE PREPPY GUY FROM HALLS I WAS TELLING YOU ABOUT... YOU REMEMBER FABIAN SAID HE'D GONE CRAZY?
WELL HE WASN'T LYING! THE GUY LOOKED LIKE HE'D BEEN LIVING IN A CARDBOARD BOX AND EATING FROM THE BIN!
HEY DAVE... YOU OK?
I TOLD HIM HE SHOULD COME OUT WITH US TONIGHT. I FELT BAD FOR HIM... YEAH CHARLIE AND JUDITH ARE GOING TO THE PUB, SO I SAID WE'D JOIN?
YEAH, I KNOW, IT'S STILL WEIRD, RIGHT? NEVER THOUGHT THEY'D END UP TOGETHER--
--OKAY, YEAH! HA! I'VE GOT TO MAKE ANOTHER CALL... I KNOW! MISS YOU TOO, BYE!
BEEP
BEEP
BEEP
BEEP
BEEP
CALLING OFFICE

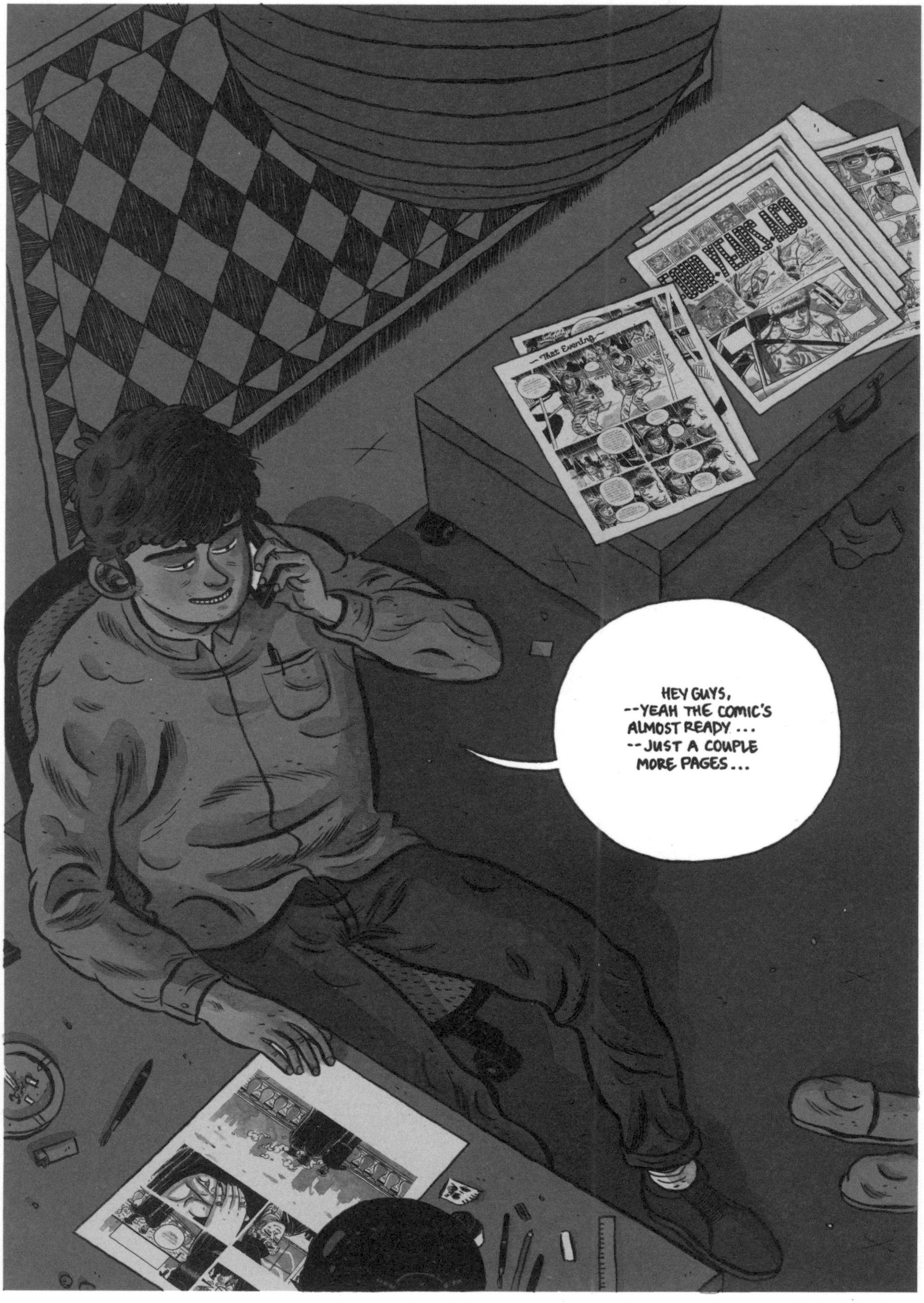
HEY GUYS,
--YEAH THE COMIC'S ALMOST READY...
--JUST A COUPLE MORE PAGES...

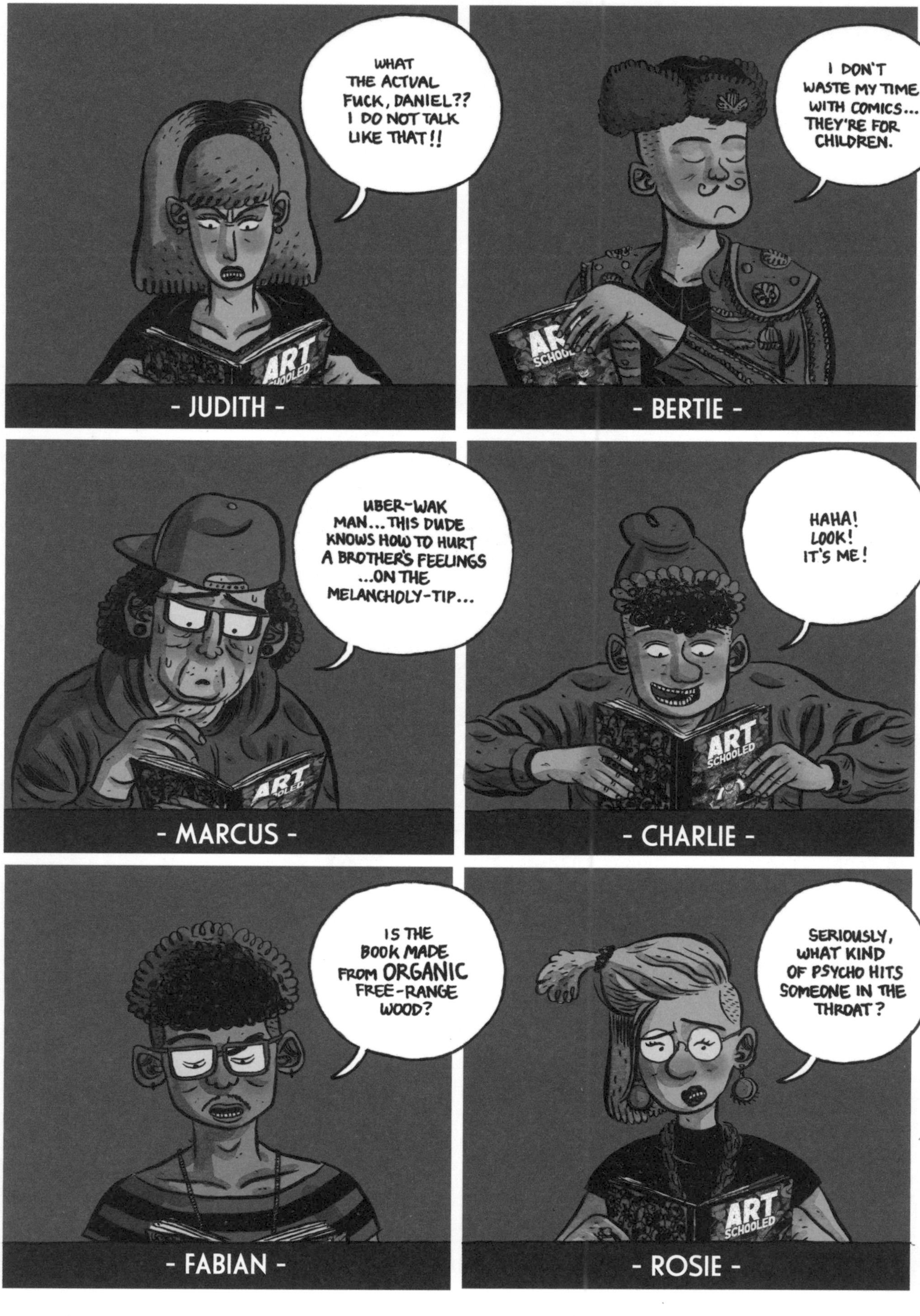
WHAT THE ACTUAL FUCK, DANIEL?? I DO NOT TALK LIKE THAT!!
- JUDITH -
I DON'T WASTE MY TIME WITH COMICS... THEY'RE FOR CHILDREN.
- BERTIE -
UBER-WAK MAN... THIS DUDE KNOWS HOW TO HURT A BROTHER'S FEELINGS ...ON THE MELANCHOLY-TIP...
- MARCUS -
HAHA! LOOK! IT'S ME!
- CHARLIE -
IS THE BOOK MADE FROM ORGANIC FREE-RANGE WOOD?
- FABIAN -
SERIOUSLY, WHAT KIND OF PSYCHO HITS SOMEONE IN THE THROAT?
- ROSIE -

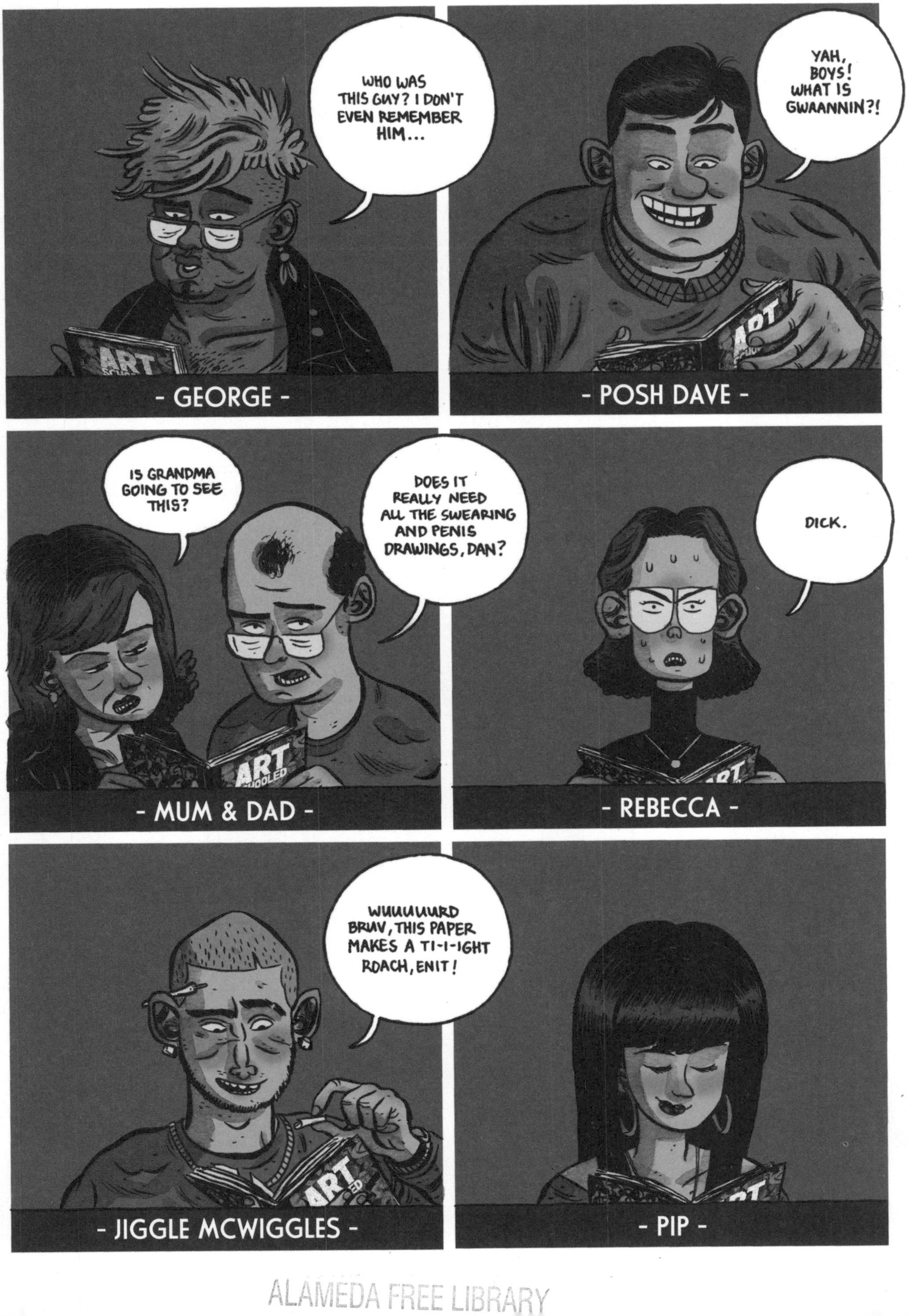
WHO WAS THIS GUY? I DON'T EVEN REMEMBER HIM...
- GEORGE -
YAH, BOYS! WHAT IS GWAANNIN?!
- POSH DAVE -
IS GRANDMA GOING TO SEE THIS?
DOES IT REALLY NEED ALL THE SWEARING AND PENIS DRAWINGS, DAN?
- MUM & DAD -
DICK.
- REBECCA -
WUUUUUURD BRUV, THIS PAPER MAKES A TI-I-IGHT ROACH, ENIT!
- JIGGLE MCWIGGLES -
- PIP -

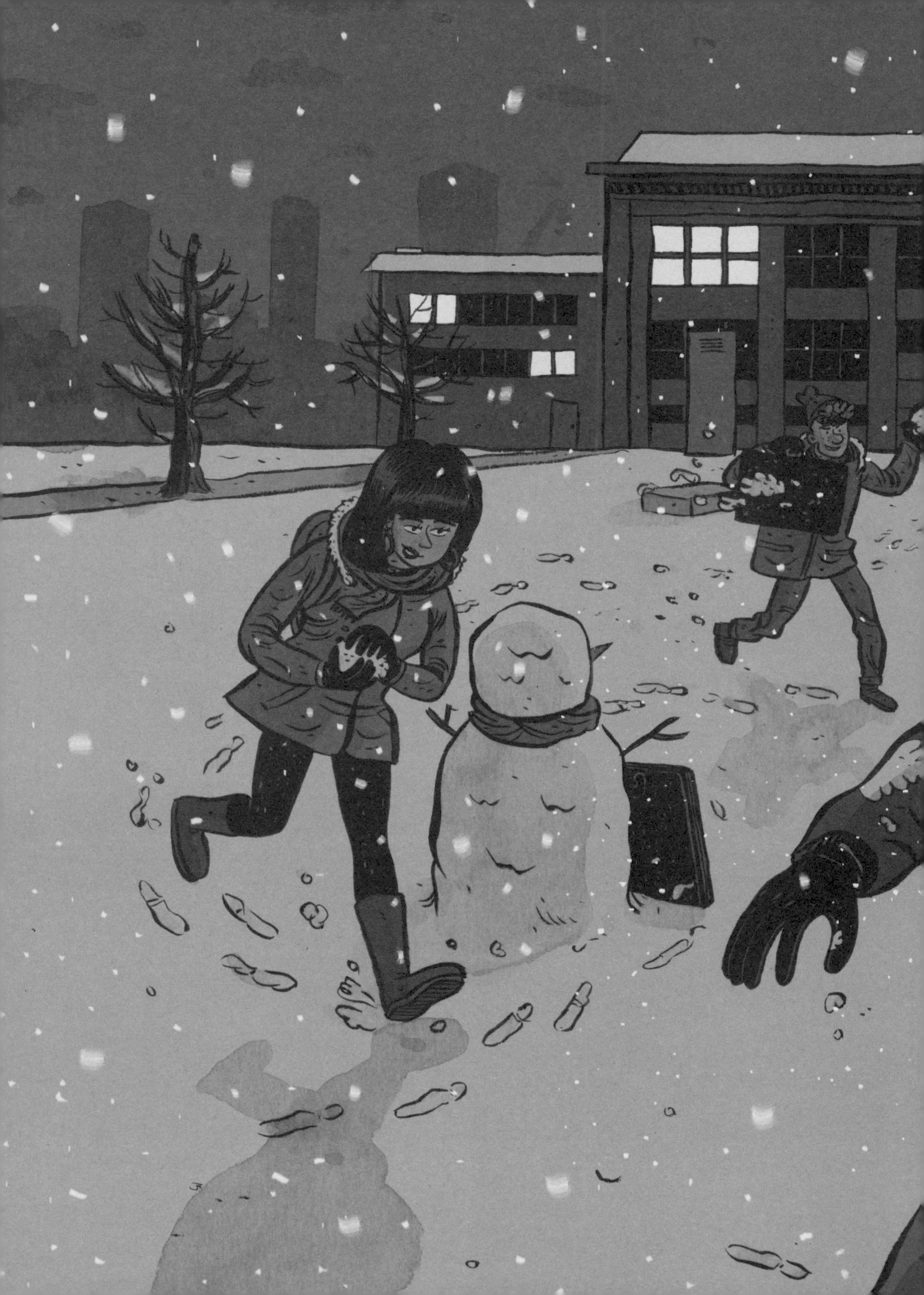

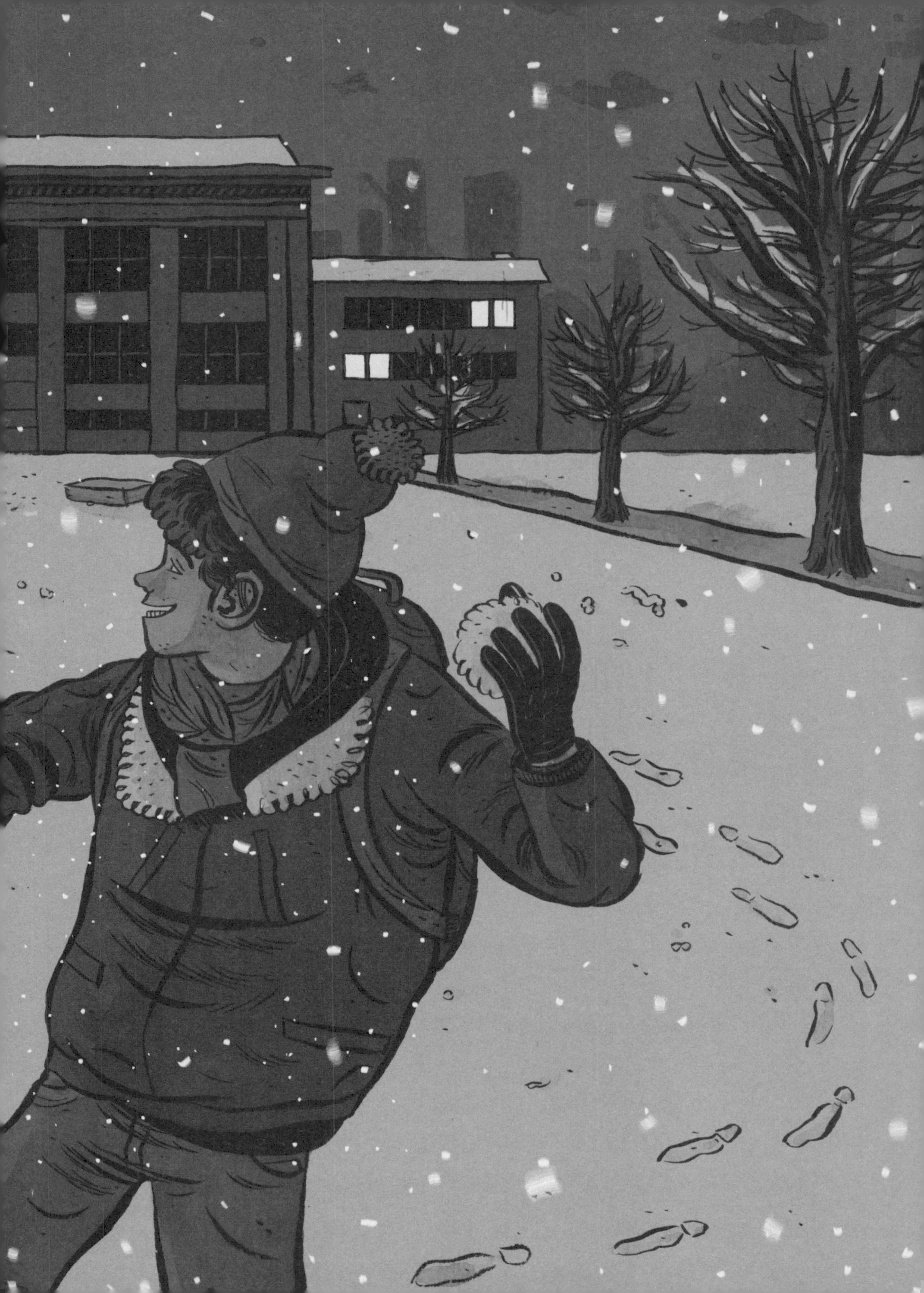

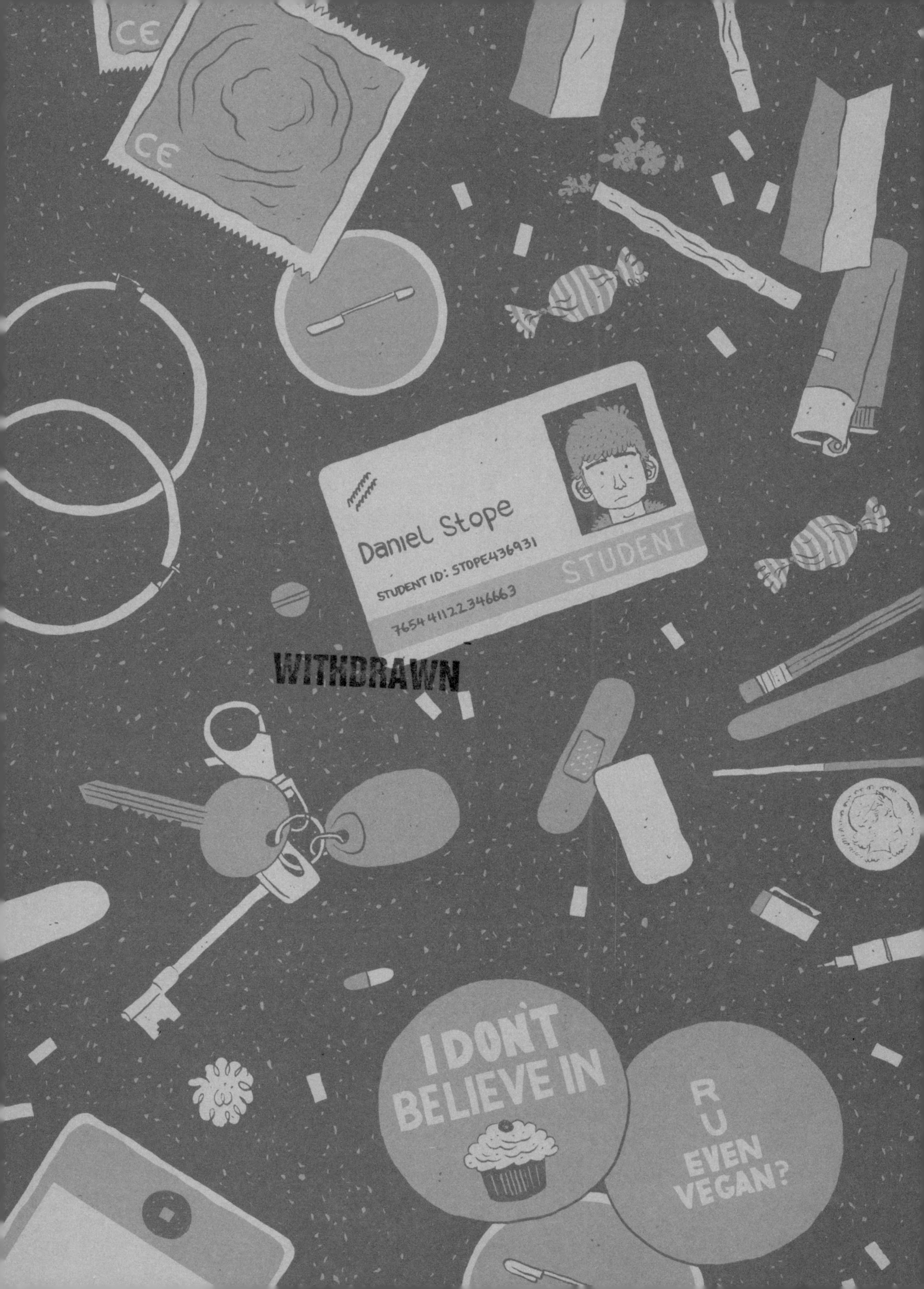
CE
CE
Daniel Stope
STUDENT ID: STOPE436931
STUDENT
7654 41122 346663
I DON'T BELIEVE IN
R U EVEN VEGAN?